CHARIOT
on the
MOUTAIN

CHARIOT
on the
MOUNTAIN

JACK FORD

KENSINGTON BOOKS
http://www.kensingtonbooks.com

KENSINGTON BOOKS are published by

Kensington Publishing Corp.
119 West 40th Street
New York, NY 10018

All Kensington titles, imprints, and distributed lines are available at special quantity discounts for bulk purchases for sales promotion, premiums, fund-raising, educational, or institutional use. Special book excerpts or customized printings can also be created to fit specific needs. For details, write or phone the office of the Kensington Special Sales Manager: Attn. Special Sales Department. Kensington Publishing Corp, 119 West 40th Street, New York, NY 10018. Phone: 1-800-221-2647.

Library of Congress Card Catalogue Number: 2018932847

Kensington and the K logo Reg. U.S. Pat. & TM Off.

ISBN-13: 978-1-4967-1309-4
ISBN-10: 1-4967-1309-5
First Kensington Hardcover Edition: August 2018

eISBN-13: 978-1-4967-1311-7
eISBN-10: 1-4967-1311-7
First Kensington Electronic Edition: August 2018

10 9 8 7 6 5 4 3 2 1

Printed in the United States of America

To the memory of Kitty Payne—
with the hope that her story might inspire us all.

CHARIOT
on the
MOUTAIN

PROLOGUE

Bear Mountain, near Gettysburg, Pennsylvania
July 24, 1845 . . .

THE HORSEMEN THUNDERED ALONG THE NARROW COUNTRY LANE, ironclad hooves flinging up showers of sparks as they pounded the gravel path, all pretense of stealth abandoned. Close behind, a wagon covered with a tarpaulin and drawn by two lathered horses in traces bounced and swayed precariously as it struggled to keep up with the four mounted men.

As they burst into a small clearing, the gauzy midnight moonlight revealed a ramshackle log cabin wedged up against the side of a hill. A sagging masonry chimney claimed one exterior wall, and a lean-to holding stacked firewood the other, while an ancient oak tree stood guard over a stone well in the front yard.

The lead rider yanked his mount to a skidding halt and jumped to the ground. Tall and broad through the chest and shoulders, clad in a flowing canvas duster, with a slouch hat clamped down over his forehead, he snatched a shotgun from the rifle sheath attached to his saddle. The others hastily dismounted and also pulled out shotguns as the wagon surged into the clearing and stopped. The driver clambered down from the wagon seat and gathered up the reins of all the horses.

After fanning out around the cabin, the men took up positions around the building while the leader approached the door. Before he reached it, the door swung open and an old black man stepped outside. He was short and wiry, with tufts of white hair sprouting from the sides of his otherwise bald head, his stooped frame covered only by a long homespun nightshirt. He held a single-shot squirrel rifle, which was pointed shakily at the riders. For a moment no one spoke, and then the leader nodded toward the cabin.

"They in there?" he asked.

"Yup," the old man muttered, looking warily at the other gunmen.

"Where?"

"Back room," the old man answered quietly, taking a step back as the leader and one of the gunmen took up positions on either side of him, shotguns pointed directly at his head.

The leader reached out and jerked the rifle out of the old man's hands, tossing it to the ground.

"You two head round back," he said, nodding to the men stationed on the sides of the cabin. "You come with me," he said to the other gunman.

After barging past the old black man, the two intruders stormed into the house. Inside, they swiftly crossed the small front room and came to a rickety door set in the back wall. The leader rammed his boot into the door, and the wood splintered as it buckled inward. There was a scream as the men rushed inside.

A moment later, the leader exited the back room, dragging a woman behind him. She was a young, light-skinned black woman, dressed only in a cotton nightgown, and she struggled to pull away from him as he yanked her roughly toward the front door. The other man followed, pulling three sleepy and confused small black children with him.

"Leave us be!" the woman screamed hysterically, scrambling to her feet, trying desperately to pull away. "We're free! You can't take us!"

The leader lashed out with a vicious backhand across her face, snapping her head back and knocking her to the floor. "Shut up," he snarled. "You damn well ain't free, and you're comin' back where you belong!"

The young woman glared at him defiantly, blood curling down from the corner of her mouth. "I'm free, and I got papers to prove it. Them too," she cried, looking fearfully toward the three children.

"Throw them into the wagon," the leader ordered, pointing to the children, who were now wailing as they reached for their mother. "Quick!"

"No!" the woman cried. "You can't do this!"

As the leader jerked her to her feet, she thrashed, twisting and flailing, dragging her nails across his face and kicking out at him. He stepped back away from her and then threw a crushing overhand punch, striking her on the side of her head, knocking her again to the floor. Dazed, she stumbled as she fought to stand.

"Tie her up! Good an' tight! Then throw her in the wagon," he yelled as the two other men rushed into the cabin. "And get them damn kids outta here," he ordered. "Now!"

After dashing outside, the leader approached the black man, who was now trembling with fear. He shoved the muzzle of the shotgun under the old man's chin and lifted his head until their eyes met.

"You keep your mouth shut 'bout this, you hear?" the leader said, his eyes narrowed threateningly.

The old man nodded. "Where my money?" he rasped, the gun barrel pushed up against his throat now.

The leader tossed some coins on the ground. "Your damn Judas money," he sneered.

"Ain't what I be promised," the old man said, looking down at the coins. "S'posed be more."

"Lucky you gettin' that much." Digging the barrel of the shotgun deeper into the old man's neck, he leaned close to him. "You go tellin' anybody 'bout this"—he paused menacingly—"next time we be comin' for you!"

The leader turned toward his men, who were dragging the barely conscious and trussed-up woman and her wailing children to the wagon. "Get these damn niggras loaded up, and let's get the hell outta here!" he ordered.

After springing up into the saddle, the leader jerked the reins, wheeling his horse around, and galloped back down the lane, followed closely by the other gunmen and the hurtling wagon with its bound and crying cargo.

CHAPTER 1

Rappahannock County, Virginia
One year earlier . . .

A S THE FIRST LIGHT OF DAWN ETCHED A VELVETY PURPLE RIBBON along the edge of the dark sky, the farm began to awaken. Cook fires flared and frying bacon grease sizzled in the cluster of tar-paper and wood-slatted slave cabins, while the sounds of mules braying echoed from within the stable. Candles flickered to life inside the main house, a rambling collection of rooms that seemed to have been haphazardly grafted, at various times, onto the solid two-story log structure that sat at the center of the homestead. The timbers and walls stretched and sighed, and the floorboards creaked and groaned, as the old farmhouse arose from its slumber.

In the kitchen, a separate log building that was attached to the rear of the main house by a covered walkway, an old slave woman struggled to hang a heavy cast-iron pot on a hook inside the massive fireplace, which took up the entire back wall of the room. The smell of damp wood wafted up from the hissing chunks of firewood as small flames began to lick around the edges. The woman was dark skinned, with a lined, ancient face. A smoke-smudged apron and a threadbare calico housedress draped her short, rotund figure. Despite the chill of the early morning, sweat was trickling in rivulets through the creases in her forehead and dripping down her cheeks as she wrestled with the heavy pot.

A low, narrow door on the side wall of the kitchen creaked open, revealing a cramped, sloping-roofed bedroom, where three small children were still asleep, snuggled together on a single floor pallet. A woman stepped out of the room, wrapping a shawl around her shoulders.

"'Bout time you decided to jine us," the old woman muttered without turning around, still grappling with the pot as water sloshed over the edge. "Princess Kitty done arrived," she sniffed.

The other woman was much younger, in her twenties, and had a pretty oval face with high cheekbones; a delicately angled nose; almond eyes that were dark, with flecks of honey; and light skin the color of soft caramel. Her black, tightly curled hair, splashed with a few rays of red, was pulled back and tied up in a bunch behind her head. She was tall and slim, held herself almost regally erect, and towered over the stooped old woman.

"Don't you go callin' me that," the young woman said, glaring down at her. "I asked you before not to," she added firmly.

The old woman refused to make eye contact with Kitty, talking instead into the fireplace as she bent and poked at the flickering logs piled under the large pot, now swinging from its hook.

"Once old mastuh be dead, you be workin' in the fields, just like the rest of 'em. No more bein' uppity, with your readin' and writin', talkin' like white folk, an' all special treated," the old woman said, straightening up and turning to face Kitty. "That day comin' soon," she added with an evil chuckle.

Leaning down, Kitty pressed her face up close to the woman's. "Don't you go talkin' that way about the master," she snapped.

"You just wait," the old woman cackled, backing away from Kitty. "That ol' man not long for this earth, and then nobody be lookin' out for you, like he done all these years. Then you be just another nigger like the rest of us. Mistress prob'ly go an' sell you off," she said.

Kitty's eyes sparked. She was taking a step toward the woman when she heard her name being called from the front room.

"You best be answerin' when Mistress call," the woman jeered.

"You and me not done," Kitty whispered harshly before she turned and left the kitchen, heading into the main house.

The front room was the largest living space in the original log structure and was dominated by an immense fieldstone fireplace. Rough-hewn furniture was scattered across the bare polished oak-plank floor. Mary Maddox stood before a double-sash window, gazing out into the front yard. She was tall and angular, with thick gray-streaked brown hair tied back in a bun, high sculpted cheekbones, and striking crystalline blue eyes. Decades as a farmwife had taken a toll on her appearance, yet even in her late fifties, she still had a hint of the natural beauty that had made her one of the noted belles of Rappahannock County as a young woman.

"He wants to see you," the mistress said coldly, her back to Kitty. "Please do not agitate him. He's in a great deal of pain."

"No, ma'am. I understand. I'll certainly be very quiet and careful not to disturb him," Kitty answered.

As Kitty turned toward the small hallway leading to the main bedroom, Mary spoke again, this time her voice not as harsh. "He doesn't have much time left," she said softly.

Kitty was unsure if the mistress was speaking to her or to herself. "Yes'm," she mumbled.

Pausing in front of the bedroom, Kitty took a deep breath, then lifted the door latch and slipped into the room, her worn leather shoes sliding quietly along the floorboards. She had not seen the master in more than a week, and she was startled at the frightening decline in his appearance. Before the heart attack, Samuel Maddox had been tall and robust, farm strong after working the fields all his life. Now, four weeks later, she could barely discern the outline of his gaunt, fragile figure buried beneath the down quilts scattered across the bed. His head lay propped up on two pillows, twisted in a strange and awkward angle. The once leonine head of flowing Scottish red hair was now greasy and matted, plastered across his skull, shot through with streaks of pale, watery gray. The room smelled of liniment and whiskey, stale sweat and urine. And of death. She stepped closer.

Maddox struggled to turn his head in her direction. The left side of his face was frozen in a tortured scowl, but he somehow managed to contort the right corner of his mouth into something resembling a faint smile. The fingers on his right hand twitched, beckoning Kitty toward him. She settled herself on the hickory chair next to the bed, reached out and placed her hand in his. Maddox wrapped his long, bony fingers around her hand like a skeletal glove and then sighed deeply. They sat quietly for some time, neither saying a word, until she noticed a single tear escape the corner of his right eye and nestle in the sagging folds of his whiskery cheek. Kitty squeezed his hand gently.

CHAPTER 2

"*L*ORD, PLEASE ACCEPT THE SOUL OF SAMUEL, YOUR SON. LET HIM sit by your side, basking in your grace, through all of eternity. May he come to know your kindness and your blessings. And may he rest in eternal peace."

The minister, a portly figure dressed in an ill-fitting black suit and waistcoat, raised his bowed head, closed his Bible slowly, looked around at the gathering surrounding the open grave in the fenced-in family cemetery, and solemnly intoned, "Amen."

A chorus of amens rippled in response through the ranks of mourners, the voices more pious and pronounced from the dark-clad neighbors surrounding the stoic Mary Maddox, quieter from the platoon of farm and house slaves assembled a few yards back.

Kitty stood off to the side, aligned with neither neighbors nor slaves, her three children fidgeting at her side, their hands entwined in the folds of her drab gray homespun dress. She lingered there, watching silently, as the mourners shuffled solemnly away from the grave site toward the yard between the front porch and the barn, where tables of food and drink awaited.

Mary Maddox remained standing, statue-like, at the edge of the gash in the ground, her gaze locked on the raw pine casket that had been lowered into the grave. After a long moment, she stooped, grabbed a handful of the loose earth piled around the hole, stood, and sprinkled it down onto the top of the casket. After blessing herself with the sign of the cross, she turned and walked toward the mourners, who were now encamped around the serving tables, sipping glasses of lemonade and talking quietly.

As Mary passed Kitty, she offered a slight, icy nod to the slave and then pointed her chin in the direction of the grave. Kitty nodded in return and shepherded her children toward the grave site. She bent and whispered to each of them in turn—five-year-old Eliza Jane, four-year-old Mary, and two-year-old Arthur—and then she and the children knelt in prayer for a moment. As they stood, Kitty dropped a small flower she had been clutching onto the top of the casket. She then ushered the children across the yard and into the main house, her head held high, looking neither right nor left, ignoring the sidelong glances flickering from many of the whispering mourners.

Taking up a position at the head of the main table, Mary accepted condolences and chatted briefly in subdued and somber tones with friends and neighbors. The farm slaves had melted away after the ceremony, absolved from their ordinary labor for the day, while the house slaves were busy tending to the needs of the assembled mourners.

Mary looked up and brightened noticeably as one of the guests approached. Fanny Withers stepped through the circle of neighbors and embraced Mary as the other mourners backed away deferentially, providing a halo of privacy for the two friends.

"Oh, Fanny," Mary whispered, locked in a long embrace. "I just don't know what I'm goin' to do without him."

Fanny pulled away slightly, keeping her hands clasped around Mary's arms, and smiled. She was strikingly attractive, with golden curls framing a long, angular face. Tall, though not as tall as Mary, she carried herself like the local royalty that she was. Although her dress was similar in funereal color to those of the other women gathered in the yard, it was markedly different in style. Silk ribbons and lace adorned the front of the dress, while rows of ruffles cascaded down the back, all in sharp contrast to the stark simplicity of the other mourners' attire.

The people of Rappahannock County were never quite sure

what to make of Fanny Withers. She was, indeed, the belle of the county—beautiful, educated, and charming—yet she had also become one of the shrewdest property investors and toughest negotiators around. She and her sister, Katie, had inherited the largest plantation in the county when their father died, with hundreds of acres of fertile land and dozens of slaves, and under Fanny's direction, their holdings had expanded dramatically. And although she was in her early thirties, she remained steadfastly single, not, however, from a lack of attention showered upon her by nearly every bachelor of good social standing ranging from the farms of Rappahannock County to the salons and drawing rooms of Richmond. For her part, Fanny seemed to enjoy the puzzlement, reveling in her paradoxical roles as both a paragon of Southern culture and a perplexing social renegade.

"You'll manage," Fanny answered, brushing away a tear rolling down Mary's cheek. "You'll find a way."

"Thirty years together," Mary said, drying her face with a small lace handkerchief. "Sometimes hard years, but mostly good years. And now I'm left here all by myself." She forced a smile. "I'm going to miss that cranky old bastard."

"He was a cranky old bastard, wasn't he?" Fanny said, laughing gently.

"Yes, he was," Mary said. Then, after a pause, she added, "But he was my cranky old bastard."

Their private reverie was shattered when two new mourners approached, a man and a woman, walking arm in arm. Fanny released Mary and stepped back.

"I hope we're not intruding," the woman said sweetly. "But Sam and I wanted to offer our condolences before we left."

"Katie. Sam. It was very kind of you to come," Mary said a bit formally.

"Nonsense," Katie Withers said behind a wide smile. She was somewhat shorter than her older sister and very attractive, although with her darker hair and broader features, she was not quite as stunning as Fanny. And her dress, while certainly more fashionable than those of the other guests, did not match the flair and elegance of her sister's ensemble.

"Of course we'd be here," added Sam Maddox. "After all, he was my uncle and me bein' the only blood relative he had left. Certainly ain't gonna miss his funeral 'cause of some occasional disagreements with the ol' man." He was ruggedly handsome, with a thatch of thick brown hair, a sharp nose jutting out of a lean, hawk-like face, and deep-set dark eyes. Even in his late thirties he remained an imposing man, taller than most, with strong, square shoulders. He offered his aunt his most engaging smile, although his eyes remained vacant and cold. "And I surely want you to know, Aunt Mary," he said in his soft, comfortable drawl, "that y'all aren't alone. I'm here to help whenever you might need it."

"Thank you, Sam," Mary answered stiffly. "I'm sure your uncle would appreciate that. And thank you, too, Katie, for your kindness." She nodded to them both and then turned back toward Fanny, who had remained standing silently a few feet away.

Having been fairly unceremoniously dismissed, Katie Withers and Sam Maddox exchanged sullen glances, then turned on their heels and joined a group of younger mourners at the food tables.

"For the life of me," Fanny whispered, shaking her head, "I still can't believe that man was kin to your Samuel. Not just blood kin but carrying the same name, for goodness' sakes."

"I know," Mary answered. "Always felt the same way. Never could figure why my Samuel didn't just shut that boy off. Always trying to bail him out of trouble. And young Sam just never appreciated what all he did for him." She shook her head balefully. "Well, maybe now that Samuel's gone, I won't be bothered by him near as much."

"You can certainly hope," said Fanny. "But I'm afraid that as long as my sister stays sweet on him, and as long as he stays sweet on her money, I'll still be stuck with them both."

Mary smiled ruefully and then took Fanny's arm in hers. "Come. Let's go spend some time with these nice folks." She paused. "Even though when Samuel was alive, he had little time for most of 'em," she said, chuckling.

CHAPTER 3

BY SUNDOWN, THE MOURNERS HAD PAID THEIR LAST CONDOLENCES, offered their last embraces, climbed onto sleek horses and sway-backed mules, rickety wooden-wheeled field wagons and elegant carriages with fine-tooled leather canopies, and left the Maddox farm. Mary and Fanny sat on the porch, in whitewashed wicker rocking chairs, a half-empty bottle of good Virginia bourbon on the table between them and full glasses in their hands.

"Thought they'd never leave," Mary sighed. "Nearly ate and drank me out of everything I got stored up for the winter." She reached out with her free hand and patted Fanny's arm. "Thank you for offerin' to stay with me tonight. Think it's going to be a bit lonely here for a while."

"Nonsense," said Fanny warmly. "No need to thank me. You were the first one to our house when my mother passed away—and the last one to leave. And you've been like a mother to me ever since."

The women rocked in companionable silence for a time.

Fanny nursed a sip of the bourbon and then looked caringly at her friend. "Y'all going to be okay here?" she asked. "By yourself?"

"No, no, I'll be just fine," Mary answered. "I think Samuel had a sense, even before his heart gave out, that the end of his time on earth was drawin' near. He left things in pretty good order. I'll be fine for a while."

"What about the farm?" Fanny asked. "Who all's going to run it?"

"Gonna have to pray on that a bit," said Mary, and then she took a long pull from her whiskey glass. "My guess is there'll be a line of folks knockin' on the door soon enough, lookin' to buy it. I can hear them right now," she said, snickering. She lowered her voice and mimicked the anticipated sales pitch. "'A poor, lonesome widow like you shouldn't have to be botherin' herself about runnin' no farm. I got a right nice price I'm willin' to offer you to take it off your hands.'" She laughed again, louder this time, the bourbon now a cohort in the conversation.

They sat silently for a while, rocking and sipping.

Then Fanny asked in a soft tone, "What about Kitty?"

Mary didn't answer right away. Finally, she said, "What about her?"

"We don't need to talk about this now if you don't think it's the right time," Fanny said, reaching over and grasping Mary's hand in her own. "Just thought you might be needin' to talk a bit, that's all."

Mary stopped rocking and gazed off into the distance. After a time, she looked at Fanny, her brows raised quizzically. "Do people know?"

Fanny nodded. "Some. At least they suspect," Fanny said.

"How?" Mary asked softly, anguish and embarrassment creeping into her voice at the realization that others knew her secret.

"Hard not to," Fanny answered. "Just look at her. Except for her color, she's the spittin' image of a young Samuel. Same hair, same eyes, walks the same." Fanny shrugged. "And he always treated her different, teachin' her to read and write, keepin' her out of the fields." She shrugged again, offering a kind smile. "Hard not to see it if you look close," she repeated.

Mary looked off into the distance again. "I almost left him," she said quietly, as if offering up a confession only to herself. "A few times. Couldn't stand the idea of him sneakin' off to the shacks at night and dippin' it into some slave girl." She waved her hand in the air, as if trying to banish the memory. "Not like I didn't know lotsa men would go take their pleasure with slave girls in the middle of the night, but I just didn't want to believe that my Samuel would be one of 'em. And then, when Kitty was born, he swore on the Bible she wasn't his." She paused, a painful look etched across her face. "So I stayed. Not sure where I could've gone, anyway," she added with a resigned shrug.

Mary grew silent again for a moment and then turned back to Fanny. "But you're right," she said, shaking her head. "And deep down, I always knew. All you had to do was look at her. No question she was Samuel's." She paused, her eyes narrowed. "It was hard for me every time I looked at her. Knowin' that he was her father. Even when she was just a little child—and she was a sweet little thing. Then Samuel sold off her mother to some plantation owner in Louisiana. Guess he thought that might somehow help a bit. And I never tried to stop him . . . ," she added, her voice trailing off.

Neither of the women spoke for a time, Mary seemingly lost in some private musing, and Fanny unsure whether to continue the conversation, aware now of the torment that dwelled in Mary's heart, even after all these years.

Finally, Mary breached the strained silence. "Not very Christian-like, is it?" she said.

Fanny looked at her, puzzled.

"What I mean is, how am I going to explain to God how I've been angry with a young girl for so long—and didn't stop Samuel from sellin' off her mother—when her only sin is bein' the product of my own husband's weakness? Even after we brought her into the house and treated her different from the other slaves, there was still always this barrier between her and me. I tried. I really did. I've always been kind to the slaves—probably kinder'n most white folks thought proper. And I'd go out of my way with Kitty, teachin' her about cookin' and sewin', lettin' Samuel learn her to read and write, despite the law frownin' on it. And Kitty's grown to be a good woman.

"But the notion of her bein' Samuel's was always lurkin' about. I'd catch myself staring at her sometimes, angry at how much she reminded me of Samuel. I knew I shouldn't be holdin' it against her, that he was the one at fault." She shook her head sadly. "Then I started blamin' myself. Maybe 'cause I could never give him any children—and Lord knows we tried—I somehow started feelin' responsible. Like it was someway my fault that he had to go runnin' off to the slave quarters at night." A small sob caught in her throat. "What kind of Christian am I . . . to do those things?"

"Well," Fanny offered, "I don't pretend to be much of a Christian myself. But I'm pretty sure that any forgiving God might just understand how you feel. Fact is, it was Samuel did the strayin' . . . and you were left to live with the consequences. And I'm sure God will balance out your feelings for Kitty with the fact that you've treated her well over the years, a lot better than most wronged wives would've."

The sun had just dipped below the horizon, staining the low sky a slash of brilliant, fiery red. The women remained quiet for some time, gazing unfocused at the florid vista, the bourbon glasses now nearly drained, as they wordlessly grappled with their thoughts.

Finally, Mary broke the spell. "He asked me to free her," she murmured.

Fanny said nothing and simply nodded.

"On his deathbed," Mary continued, "he said he would like to go to his Maker with a clear conscience. He finally apologized to me for what he done. And then he asked me if I would please think on settin' her free."

"Does Kitty know that?" Fanny asked.

"Not sure . . . but I don't think so," Mary answered.

"So? What'll you do?" Fanny said.

Mary took a deep breath and then let out a long, despairing sigh. "Don't rightly know," she answered. "He didn't put it in his will, knowin' how valuable she and her children could be if I needed to sell them off for the money to keep the farm goin'. But it *was* his dyin' wish."

"Well, she'd probably fetch a thousand, maybe fifteen hundred dollars—maybe more—if you needed the money. And her children could bring five hundred or so each. Could sure help if you're havin' problems with the farm," Fanny said. "And," she added pointedly, "you wouldn't be reminded every day of Samuel's infidelity."

Mary answered softly, gazing off into the distance. "Never had any slaves round when I was growin' up. Nobody waitin' on us or doin' our work. Papa couldn't afford none. When I married Samuel, he already had a handful workin' the farm. Understood why we needed 'em. Couldn't run this place without 'em." She paused thoughtfully for a moment. "Never felt real comfortable with the idea, though—the idea that one person could actually own another. Own 'em just like you owned a horse or cattle. And do with 'em whatever you pleased. Always wondered what God really thinks about it—despite what folks say about slavery bein' talked about and accepted in the Bible. Not sayin' I'm some kind of abolitionist. Seems to me folks up north should just stay outta our business. Got no right to tell us how to live our lives."

Mary shook her head. "Like I said, just never been sure about it in my heart. Always tried to treat our slaves well, better than most other folks do. But"—she shrugged in resignation—"don't think this place could survive without 'em." She remained quiet for a moment and then sighed again in frustration. "I just don't know," she said, shaking her head. "Think I'm just gonna have to pray on this awhile before I can figure out what to do," she said softly.

CHAPTER 4

KITTY WAS AWAKE BEFORE SUNRISE. AFTER CHECKING THAT HER CHILdren were still asleep, wrapped in blankets and tangled together like wild vines on their single sleeping pallet, she tossed her shawl around her shoulders, gently closed the door to her room behind her, and snuck out through the back of the chilly and dark kitchen.

The farm was cloaked in silence, all the slaves still locked in the grasp of their last precious moments of much-needed sleep. Kitty picked her way carefully around the farmhouse, across the front yard, and into the slave quarters. Even the soft wash of the false dawn couldn't hide the grimness of the ramshackle single-room structures, each a battered mirror image of the others. She headed directly toward the one shack that showed a small gleam of light through the single paper-covered window, and rapped gently on the rickety front door.

The door cracked open just a fraction, and an arm snaked out and pulled her swiftly through the doorway and into the small room. The inside of the shack belied the shabby exterior. It was neat and clean, with a hard-packed earthen floor. A rough wooden sleeping platform covered by a checkered quilt was in one corner; a cloth-covered table, where a single tallow candle flickered smokily, was in another; and two hand-hewn chairs were perched before the slumbering fire in the mud and brick fireplace. The familiar smell of stale wood smoke and old cooked bacon greeted her as she stepped into the room.

"Thought you might come a-visitin'," said the man who had drawn her inside. He was tall and cornstalk thin, and his face, beneath a nearly bald pate, was deeply furrowed and dark like the bark of an old tree. The slowness of his walk and the hobbled, painful gait betrayed his age as he pulled a chair out from the table and nodded for her to sit. "So," he said, his voice a kindly, syrupy deep baritone, "why you skulkin' round here so early?"

"Uncle Joshua, I be needin' your advice," Kitty said hesitantly, unconsciously sloughing off her white-folks speech pattern and shifting easily into the patois of the slave quarters.

The old man nodded but said nothing, his eyes sad and tired. Ol' Joshua, as he was known—to distinguish him from his son, known as Young Joshua, who worked in the fields—had been the closest thing Kitty had had to a father since the day she was born. When her mother had been sold off, Joshua and his since deceased wife, Sarah, had taken her in and raised her until she was seven years old. That was when she had been moved into the big house by the master and had become a house servant.

"I be afraid," Kitty said, her voice shaking.

" 'Fraid of what, chile?" he asked.

"Now that Mastuh be dead, I be afraid that Mistress be sellin' me. And maybe be sellin' my chillun, too," she said.

"But you bein' a part of that family in the big house fo' years now," he said, leaning toward her and reaching out to clasp her hand. "Master and Mistress be treatin' you kindly all these years. Why you be worryin' now 'bout bein' sold off?"

Kitty dropped her voice. "Mistress know that Mastuh be my daddy. She done know it for years now. She ain't never been evil to me. . . . But sometimes . . . I see somethin' in her eyes when she look at me. Most those times her eyes just be hurtin', like a small chile who had somethin' taken 'way. But every once in a while, they be angry, like it be my fault the master be strayin' from her bed. And at the funeral, she look at me real strange, like somehow he dyin' be my fault and now it be her chance to get rid of me. And rid of them memories."

Ol' Joshua was silent for a moment and then nodded again.

"Mebbe," he said. "Mebbe not. Mebbe it just be you imagin' it, chile."

Kitty's eyes flickered around the room, as if her mind was seeking some escape. Then she turned and looked at him, eyes narrowed. "I got to run," she whispered. "I got to run and take my chillun with me."

The only sound in the cabin was Ol' Joshua's shallow, raspy breathing. After a minute, maybe two, he struggled to take a deep breath, coughed a bit fitfully, and then leaned closer to Kitty.

"You cain't be talkin' like that," he said quietly but firmly. "You know what be happ'nin' to slaves be runnin'. Dem slave catchers and their trackin' dogs be nasty. Dey beat you, then bring you back here, where you get beat again. In front of ever'one. Whipped till you cain't even stand. Make an example of you fo' all to see. Make sure anyone else thinkin' a runnin', they know good an' well what be in store for them, too." He shook his head, his eyes now stern and glinting in the candlelight. "No, chile. You cain't be doin' no runnin'."

Kitty stared directly into Ol' Joshua's eyes, her face hardening in a mixture of fear and anger. "I be leavin' here . . . with your help or without it," she said. "I never known my own mama after she got sold off. I sure as hell ain't gonna let my chillun grow up without they own mama. That for damn sure!"

Pulling her hand away from his, Kitty stood, her voice now defiant. "So, I be goin'. . . . We all be goin'." She paused. "You be helpin' me . . . or not?"

Ol' Joshua sat still as stone, the agony of the decision playing its way across his lined face.

"If we be caught, no one ever know it be you that helpin' us," Kitty said softly, reaching down and placing her hand on his shoulder.

"Ain't me I be worryin' 'bout," he murmured. "I jus' an ol' man gettin' ready fo' the Jubilee an' to meet my Maker. Since my Sarah taken from me, I be lookin' fo' to leave this unhappy earth," he mused. "Lookin' fo' the chariot to take me to the mountaintop, to the Lord, where I finally be free." He shook his head sadly. "No, chile, I ain't worryin' one bit 'bout me. Be you and them little ones I be worryin' 'bout."

The old man reached out, took Kitty's hands in his, and gently coaxed her back into her chair. "Too bad Robert ain't round no more," he said sadly. "Don' know what he woulda thought 'bout this idea."

Robert was Robert Payne, the father of Kitty's children. He had been a free black man, a formerly indentured wagoner who had lived in a small village about five miles away. Kitty had taken up with him when she was a teenager, with Samuel Maddox's permission, and had given birth to their three children since that time. A fourth child, who had been named George, did not survive infancy. They had never lived with each other as husband and wife, but Samuel had allowed them to spend time together on his farm. Robert had died nearly one year ago, after suffering from pneumonia for many months.

"I 'spect he be agreein' with me—to keep the chilluns safe—if he was still alive," Kitty said firmly, her eyes misting at the mention of Robert.

Ol' Joshua was silent for a moment and then leaned his face in close to Kitty.

"You run an' dey catch you—an' chances are dey will—you can be sure dat after the beatin', they be sellin' you off. An' your chillun, too. Good Lord knows dey will. Don' wants no runners round to infect dem others, give dem any ideas 'bout runnin'. An' you know it, too, chile," he said, lightly brushing her cheek for a moment with his leathery, wizened hand.

Kitty let the old man's hand rest on her cheek, salved by the reassuring touch, as she had been so many times as a small child. Her mind was in turmoil, struggling fiercely with the dread of separation from her children and the sense that she had to do something, anything, to protect them—and herself. Audacity and caution both swirled around her brain, each seeking traction and dominance, then joining and unraveling like ink spilled into clear water. But what if Ol' Joshua was right? What if attempting to escape, rather than staying and protecting her family and keeping it intact, actually guaranteed that the fate she most feared would, indeed, become her reality?

She had never seen a slave whipped on the Maddox farm; in fact, the master and mistress had treated their slaves much better than most local slave owners. But then, she didn't remember any of the slaves attempting an escape in her lifetime. But she had certainly heard of whippings and beatings suffered by runaway slaves from other farms and plantations in the area, men and women who had set out on a desperate quest for their freedom, only to be tracked down by the brutal slave catchers and returned in chains, staggering and bloody, to face their punishment. And she knew that many of them had then been sold off, some to the Deep South, others to the hellish plantations in the tropics, disconnected forever from their families. The message was a stark and excruciating one: "Do not try to run. If you do, you will be caught, and you will be punished severely."

Yet Kitty feared that choosing to do nothing—ignoring her trepidation that, as Mistress Mary had once allowed the sale of Kitty's mother so many years ago, she would now sell her off, too, and once and for all purge the stain and the shame of Samuel Maddox's sin from her life—may well condemn her and her children to that same disastrous fate.

She made up her mind. After reaching for Ol' Joshua's hands, she held them to her face and kissed each hand gently.

"Uncle," she said almost prayer-like, "you know I be lovin' you like you be my own papa. An' I know you tryin' yo' best to protect us." She paused. "But I gotta do whatever I can do to protect my li'l ones. I got to run, Uncle. An' I need yo' help."

"Right then, chile," Ol' Joshua said mournfully. "Seems I ain't gonna change yo' mind. Like always. So we be needin' to talk to some folks." He thought for a moment. "Y'all come on back here t'night, after dinner be served. We got some plannin' to do."

CHAPTER 5

THE VILLAGE OF WASHINGTON HAD, ACCORDING TO LOCAL LEGEND, been surveyed and its streets laid out by the then seventeen-year-old George Washington in 1749. An early center for trade and agriculture, Washington had been named the county seat for Virginia's Rappahannock County in 1833. The village consisted of two parallel streets traveling north and south—Main Street and Gay Street—transected by five short cross streets. Nestled within these confines were a church, a post office, two taverns, four stores, an academy, a seminary, and a small collection of tradesmen, including a blacksmith, a tanner, a tailor, a shoemaker, a cabinetmaker, a bricklayer, three attorneys, and a physician.

Most of the stores and tradespeople, along with the post office and taverns, were located on Main Street and the short cross streets. When the village was designated the county seat, a stretch of Gay Street became the site of a number of official structures, most of them erected in 1835, including a courthouse, the clerk's office, the treasurer's office, and the county jail. The courthouse, the most imposing structure in the village, was a redbrick, two-story Greek Revival–style edifice marked by a front-gabled roof that was capped with a square cupola, and fronted by four large white columns framing a central pedimented entry.

Sam Maddox dismounted his horse in front of the courthouse and tethered it to a hitching post. After removing some papers from his saddlebag, he strode across Gay Street to a small, square, weathered two-story wood-frame structure with an elegantly lettered sign on the front door that read ZEPHANIA TURNER, ESQUIRE, ATTORNEY-AT-LAW. Maddox rapped on the door once and then lifted the exterior latch and entered.

The front room was a combination sitting room and office, decorated with fashionable and comfortable wingback chairs encircling a broad stone-faced fireplace. An Oriental-style rug covered most of the oak-planked floor. The walls were painted a soft, elegant eggshell blue, with stylish cream-colored carved moldings along the ceiling.

Zephania Turner sat at a large desk in a corner of the room, surrounded by stacks of books and papers. He looked up and seemed surprised at the obviously unexpected appearance of Sam Maddox.

"Ah, Mr. Maddox," Turner said as he stood, crossed the room in just a few strides, and shook Maddox's hand. "To what do I owe the pleasure?"

Zephania Turner was a slim, graceful man in his early thirties, with a fine aristocratic bearing. He was blessed with handsome, narrow features, highlighted by lively, intelligent, sparkling eyes beneath a broad forehead; and his long light brown hair, plaited and tied up in a silk bow in the back in the old-fashioned colonial style, accentuated his patrician air. He was dressed, even at midday in his own home, in a well-tailored formal jacket and waistcoat. The son of a wealthy plantation owner from the nearby town of Warrenton, he had rejected the life of the landed gentry and had chosen instead to become a lawyer. After studying at the University of Virginia, he had opened his law practice in the village of Washington and had quickly earned a reputation as an honest, intelligent, and diligent—if somewhat eclectic—professional. He was both liked and respected, and consequently his practice had grown, encompassing not just Rappahannock County but the surrounding counties, as well.

"Mr. Turner," Maddox said, "I've come about a business matter."

"Certainly," Turner answered smoothly. "Won't you have a seat?" He gestured toward a wooden-backed chair near the desk.

Once they were both seated, Turner asked, "So, what is this business about?"

"Well," Maddox began, "I think I might be needin' a lawyer, so I thought I might come visit with you first."

"I certainly appreciate that," Turner said in a clipped, formal, almost British tone. He leaned forward and folded his hands on his desktop. "And what is it you think you might need a lawyer for?"

"I been havin' a bit of a rough spell on my farm," Maddox said. "Tried to swap out some wheat fields for tobacco—given the high prices a good batch of tobacco can fetch—but, with the lack of rain and all, it's been a bad year."

Turner nodded knowingly. "I've heard that from a number of other farmers who've been experimenting with tobacco growing. What about your other crops?"

"So, you see, that there's the problem," Maddox said, shifting in his chair. "I was bettin' on the tobacco and used up most of my acreage for it. Got a bit of wheat and some corn planted. But I fear it ain't gonna be enough."

Turner raised a questioning eyebrow.

"Y'see," Maddox continued, "I'm behind with the bank—way behind—and was countin' on a big tobacco crop to get me square. Or at least close to square. But now . . ." Maddox spread his hands and shrugged. "Now it don't look like I'll be able to pay up anytime soon."

"Have you talked to the bank?" the lawyer asked.

"Yep. Not much help. Said I'm too much in arrears—that there's the word they used. Said I got to come up with a big chunk of what I owe . . . or else they got to foreclose. And take the farm."

Turner thought a moment. "Do you have any other source of funds? Or anything of value you could pledge as security?" he asked.

"Well, that's actually why I came a-visitin'. Need some advice— legal advice—'bout just that," Maddox said.

"Perhaps I can help," Turner said solicitously.

"Got a fella over in Warrenton might be willin' to lend me enough to get square with the bank so I can keep the farm." Maddox leaned back, shrugged his broad shoulders, and exhaled a long, frustrated sigh. "But he's wantin' a damn sky-high interest rate—and he's also demandin' some security in addition to the farm."

"Just what kind of security can you offer?" asked Turner.

"Told him I got some farmin' equipment. And two old darkies—field-workers that my papa bought years ago," Maddox said.

"And?" asked Turner.

"And he said that ain't enough," Maddox said. "Said that them two darkies are too old to fetch much if he had to sell 'em to collect. And the farm tools ain't worth enough."

Turner shook his head thoughtfully and spread his hands, puzzled. "I'm not sure, then, how I could be of help."

"So, that's where this comes in," Maddox said, unfolding a document and pushing it across the desktop in front of the lawyer.

"This is your uncle Samuel's will?" Turner asked as he flipped through the two pages of the document.

"Yep," answered Maddox, leaning forward, his eyes now anxious and narrowed. "And I been told by a lawyer in Warrenton that I might just have a claim to his property—farm, livestock, and the darkies he owned."

Turner appeared perplexed. "Why then come to me if you already have a lawyer?"

Maddox's face creased into a malicious grin. "Well, if I got to be fightin' with my aunt Mary—and she never liked me much—over this, I'd want a local fella like you, who's known and respected round these parts, on my side."

Turner leaned back in his chair, his elbows propped on the armrests, his fingers steepled prayer-like in front of his face. After a moment, he folded his arms across his chest.

"Well, Mr. Maddox," he began in a measured tone, "I must admit that I most certainly appreciate the compliment." He paused. "But I also must tell you that I consider your aunt Mary to be a personal friend. As I did your late uncle Samuel. And, in addition, my reading of the will does not comport with that of the lawyer you spoke to," he continued, his voice now more professional and stern. He tapped the will with his index finger. "It seems fairly clear that your uncle meant to deliver to your aunt Mary, on his death, the title and interest to everything—land, livestock, and slaves. With no limitations whatsoever."

Maddox was silent for a long moment, the only sound in the room the soft ticking of a baroque carved grandfather clock in the corner. Then his eyes flared and his face hardened in anger. As he leaned forward, his now steely gaze bored into the lawyer's eyes, and Turner could not help thinking about the man's reputation for violence when he felt crossed. This could be a dangerous man when provoked, thought the lawyer, squirming a bit in his chair as he struggled to suppress a percolating sense of fear, his resolve and professional aplomb under assault.

Then, just as suddenly, the nascent rage disappeared, replaced by a cold, distant countenance.

"Well, then," said Maddox, rising from his chair, "guess I'll just have to find me someone else to take my case. Sorry to have taken up your time."

Turner rose also, walked him to the door, and offered his hand. "I'm very sorry that I can't help you," he said.

Maddox pointedly ignored the outstretched hand and merely grunted, "Good day," before he walked out the door and slammed it emphatically behind him.

A dangerous man, indeed, thought Turner.

CHAPTER 6

"*I*f you be goin', you gotta be goin' soon."

Ol' Joshua's frail figure was perched tensely, like an anxious cat, on the edge of a chair in front of the hearth in his room, the fire hissing and guttering, casting shifting ephemeral shadows on the walls. Kitty sat across from him, her hands folded calmly in her lap, and she nodded at his words. Two days had passed since she first told him of her plan to escape. She had done nothing since, carefully watching Mary Maddox, surveilling her every sound and gesture, hoping for some sign—any sign—that might allay her fear of being sold off. But Mary had said nothing, done nothing, to provide Kitty with any clue to her intentions.

For those two days, Mary had been neither harsh nor kind in her dealings with Kitty. Indeed, she had seemed to be anxious to avoid any contact at all with Kitty or her three children. And, ultimately, it was this sense of avoidance, this enforced distance, that had finally convinced Kitty that she could not risk waiting any longer. It was time for her to act.

"When?" she asked.

"Tomorrow night be best," he answered. "No moon. Feels like some rain'll be passin' through. Shouldn't be many folks out an' about."

Kitty raised her head, her jaw set defiantly. "Then tomorrow night it be."

"You be needin' 'nough food for two days' travel," he said.

"Why just two days?" she asked. "Cain't get far enough away in just two days."

"Two days be what you needin' to get to a place where you be findin' some help," he answered.

"Help? Who be helpin' the likes a me, a runaway slave with three little ones?" she said, puzzled.

Ol' Joshua nodded and gave Kitty a reassuring smile. "There be some folks out there willin' to help runaways. Just got to know who they is and where they at."

Kitty peered at him uncertainly. "So," she asked, "where they at? And how you know they be helpin' me?"

"Once you get 'bout fifteen miles down the road to Warrenton, near Amissville, there be a church jes' off the road. Big steeple painted red. Wait till it dark. Then go round the back door and knock. Preacher and his wife be good folks. You can trust 'em," he said in a soft, comforting tone.

Kitty stared at him. "How you know all this?" she asked.

Ol' Joshua shrugged his worn, sagging shoulders. "I jes' know."

Kitty was silent for a moment, contemplating this surprising plan. "Then what?" she said.

"They be hidin' you for a spell. Got some space down in a root cellar. Then someone be takin' you to 'nother hidin' place. Prob'ly few miles past Warrenton. Then someone be takin' you up north."

"Who all these people be takin' me these places?" Kitty asked, exasperated. "And why they be riskin' themselves to help me?"

Ol' Joshua shrugged again. "Don' know who they be. Don' know why, either. Jes' good Christians, I s'pose. Folks who don' believe God ever meant for one man be ownin' 'nother man. Even a black man."

Kitty gave him a piercing look, her eyes narrowing. "You don' learn all this just listenin'," she said.

"Mebbe not," he answered, a slight knowing smile creeping across the folds of his craggy face.

Kitty stared hard at him for a moment. "You ever try to run?" she asked incredulously. "That how you know all this?"

Ol' Joshua shook his head. "Nope," he said. "Thought about it some, back when I be a lot younger." He paused. "But then I found my Sarah. She tell me no way she be runnin'.'" His smile turned melancholy. "An' since no way I ever be leavin' her, I jes' gave up on the idea."

"But . . . ," she began.

"But jes' 'cause I ain't runnin' don' mean I ain't helpin' some who did. I listen up a lot and then be passin' on what I be learnin' to folks that be needin' help."

Kitty raised a quizzical eyebrow. "So you sure these folks'll be willin' to help?"

"Yep," he said. "They be callin' it a kind of railroad. The Underground Railroad. Not a real railroad with trains an' all, mind you, but jes' folks who hide you an' then help you get from place to place. Till you make it up north. Then other folks'll take you in an' help you find work." He paused, then reached out and grasped her hands. "An' then you be free," he added softly.

The room was quiet; the only sound was the sputtering flame in the hearth.

Finally, Kitty broke the spell. "What happen to us if we be caught?"

Ol' Joshua took a deep, wheezy breath and released it slowly. "They bring you back. Prob'ly in chains. Then Mistress Mary have to decide what she be doin' 'bout you."

Kitty nodded slowly, her jaw set, her eyes hard.

CHAPTER 7

*T*HE NIGHT SKY WAS COAL DARK, WITH ROLLING MASSES OF DENSE, rain-laden clouds pressing downward like the sagging roof of an old tent. The farm had settled into its night rhythms. A few faint dancing glimmers from the last slumbering cook fires were accompanied by the chirping of nocturnal insects and the soft rustling of the animals settling down in the barn.

Shadows flickered along the walls of the slave cabins, not quite full silhouettes, more like the floating of leaves on a gusty day. Kitty, wrapped in a dark shawl, tread silently from the rear of the farmhouse, past the darkening slave quarters, until she arrived at Ol' Joshua's cabin. She carried a sleepy and confused two-year-old Arthur in a sling on her hip and a blanket roll, with some bread, apples, and a goatskin water bag tucked inside, looped around her other shoulder. Eliza Jane and Mary walked on each side of her, their small hands locked inside of hers, their faces mirroring their uncertainty over whether they should be excited or afraid on this adventure.

As she approached the cabin, Ol' Joshua stepped outside and, without a word, took her arm and led her toward the rear of the barn. He knelt and kissed each of the little girls and sleepy Arthur on the forehead. Then he straightened up creakily and embraced Kitty, kissing her once on each cheek.

"Follow the creek down to the old Warrenton Road an' head east toward Amissville," he whispered. "You bes' not be travelin' in daylight, so jes' find some spot to hole up an' let the babies sleep a bit till nighttime."

Kitty nodded as the two girls, now sensing Ol' Joshua's anxiety, stepped closer and clutched their mother's dress tightly.

"Thank you," Kitty said softly, swiping away the tears that slid down her cheeks.

She shifted the sling holding the now sound asleep Arthur and, turning away from Ol' Joshua, grasped the girls' hands once again and moved swiftly down the path toward the creek. Before they disappeared into the woods, she snuck a quick look back over her shoulder, but the stygian darkness was so profound that after just a few strides, she could not see if Ol' Joshua was still standing by the barn.

Kitty and the children kept close to the twisting, shallow creek, which, in the gloom of the dense thickets, provided their only source of navigation. After about fifteen minutes, they emerged from the woods alongside the road. Although it was officially called the Warrenton Turnpike, at this point it was merely a well-trodden, deeply rutted dirt lane, pounded for years by horses' hooves and metal-clad wooden wagon wheels, barely wide enough for two wagons to pass by each other. The road ran generally east to west, cutting a meandering ribbon through the gentle hills of the rolling Virginia farmland.

Kitty was immediately concerned over how little tree or brush cover bordered the road, mindful of Ol' Joshua's admonition about not traveling during daylight and the importance of finding some protective shelter for them to hide and rest. Determined to put as much distance behind them as possible before the first light of dawn, she tightened her grip on the girls' hands, checked briefly that little Arthur, oblivious to the dangers stalking their escape, was still asleep, and began to trudge eastward, toward the church with the red steeple and their first stop on the "railroad."

They had walked silently for nearly an hour when Eliza Jane tugged on Kitty's hand and looked up at her, the silvery relics of drying tears still shining on her cheeks.

"Mama," she whispered, sniffling, "why we walkin' in the night? And where we goin'?"

Sensing that they all needed a rest, Kitty shepherded the girls off the road and sat them down on a small rise. She shifted the sling holding Arthur onto her lap and plopped down next to them. She kissed both of the girls on the cheek, tugged the water bag out of the bedroll, and offered each of them a long swallow.

"Well, then," Kitty said to the two upturned, frightened faces, "remember those books I've read to you about different adventures?"

Eliza Jane and Mary both nodded solemnly.

"Well, this is our adventure," Kitty said, trying to sound as happily excited, yet calm, as possible. "We're traveling to a new place to live."

"But we already have a place to live," said Eliza Jane.

"We live at home," chimed in a terribly confused Mary.

"Yes, but we're going to find a new home. A better home," Kitty said, wrapping her arms around the two girls. "A home where we grow all our own food, and do our own work, and come and go as we please."

"I don't want to come and go," Eliza Jane whimpered. "I just want to be home in my bed. I'm tired, Mama."

Kitty rocked gently, holding the girls close. "I know, darlin'," she said soothingly. "I'm tired, too. We'll stop soon and get some sleep. But for now, we got to keep walkin'."

They all sat for a few minutes, until the girls stopped sniffling. Then Kitty ushered them back on their feet, kissed both of them on the forehead, tucked the water bag back into the bedroll, and slung it over her shoulder.

"So," Kitty said, trying her best to mask her own fear and sound cheerful, "we're off on our adventure."

CHAPTER 8

*I*T WAS SHORTLY AFTER BREAKFAST HAD BEEN SERVED WHEN THE OLD kitchen slave woman came rushing into the dining room, breathless and stammering. Mary Maddox was sitting in her usual seat at the end of the table, savoring the last of her coffee, putting off as long as possible wading into the farm ledger books, a chore she found confusing and depressing. Not for the first time that morning she thought about how much she missed her husband, not just because she now had his farm tasks thrust upon her, although that certainly was a factor, but also because she so missed the simple interaction and conversation of their daily breakfast.

"Mistress! Mistress!" the old woman spluttered, struggling to catch her breath. "Kitty done run 'way! An' her chilluns, too!"

"What?" Mary said, puzzled by the outburst. "Run away? What do you mean?"

The old woman took a deep breath and struggled to calm herself. "Kitty be gone. She ain' be in her room all night. When she din't come out to help fix breakfast, I look in her room and she be gone. An' her chilluns be gone, too. I ask round, and nobody be seein' her since last night. So she musta run off," the old woman added, almost gleefully.

Mary was silent for a moment, then said calmly to the old woman, "Please go find Ol' Joshua and bring him to me immediately."

"Yes'm!" the old woman yelped, then scampered out of the dining room toward the back entrance of the farmhouse.

A few minutes later, Ol' Joshua entered the dining room, bent over, walking painfully and deliberately. He began to speak, but Mary, still seated at the table, interrupted him.

"Joshua," she said sternly, "I'm told that Kitty has run away. Do you know anything about this?"

"No, Mistress," he answered, his tone level and his face inscrutable. "Don' know nuthin' 'bout that."

Mary stared at him. "I know you and Kitty have always been close," she said, not unkindly. "I can't imagine she would do such a thing—and take her children with her—without talking to you about it first."

"No, ma'am," he answered, shaking his head slightly, his dark, creviced face still blank. "She ain' said nuthin' to me. Mebbe she jes' off visitin' with some other folks," he added blandly.

"Joshua," Mary said, leaning toward him, her voice almost pleading, "if she has run off, it can only end badly. For her. Her children. For all of us."

The old man remained silent and stoic.

"Please," Mary said, "if you can help me find her, before it's too late . . . ?" Her voice trailed off.

Ol' Joshua shifted from one foot to the other but said nothing.

Mary sighed deeply, then stood and held herself ramrod straight. "Well, then, if you are not going to help me, then I don't have very much choice, do I?" she said firmly, shaking her head. "Please send Young Joshua to summon the sheriff. Have him tell the sheriff that we have four runaway slaves—a mother and three children—and he should do whatever is necessary to find them and return them."

CHAPTER 9

KITTY AND THE CHILDREN SPENT THE DAMP DAYLIGHT HOURS IN A rickety, weather-beaten hay storage lean-to that was perched on a slope about one hundred yards off the road. They slept fitfully, huddled under the blanket, trying to fight off the blowing wind and the slashing rain that sluiced through the cracks in the ramshackle wooden structure. A few stray cattle approached during the day and nibbled at the hay, gazing curiously at the sleeping interlopers.

Kitty had been dozing restlessly, unable to calm her mind or her nerves. Now, after just a few hours, she was wide awake, her thoughts tumbling about like loose apples in a rolling barrel. During the first part of the journey, as the farm disappeared into the darkness behind them, she had felt a surprising euphoria, not the fear that she had expected, but rather a powerful sense of exhilaration that accompanied this newly seized freedom. But now, as she watched the children shifting sleepily under the blanket, seeking some protection from the stinging, slanting rain, her doubts reappeared and began to overwhelm the earlier joy. A creeping dread started to envelop her, squeezing through her drenched clothes and seeping into her weary bones. *A mistake,* she thought, suddenly panicked by the realization that she was now a fugitive slave and that she and the children would soon be the subjects of a manhunt. *This is a terrible mistake.* She shivered uncontrollably, not from the cold and wet, but from the emerging fear now churning deep within her.

She wrapped her arms around herself, seeking some warmth, and tried to slow her breathing, hoping to dispel the terrifying images of angry men and howling dogs relentlessly pursuing them. Then, suddenly, a strange thing happened. The sodden smell of the wet wool of the blanket, together with the small rustling movements of the sleeping children, combined to somehow calm her. After a few minutes of staring at their inexplicably serene faces, she took a deep breath and exhaled slowly. *I'm doing the right thing,* she thought, striving to convince herself. *This is not a mistake. We'll make it to the safe house, and from there we'll find help. I had to do this,* she concluded, her confidence slowly returning. *It is the only way to keep us together.* She took another deep breath, sighed softly, and snuggled closer to the children to await the nightfall.

The children awoke about an hour before dusk, but despite the darkening skies that had accompanied the storm, Kitty did not feel that it was safe to leave the protection of their shabby shelter until night had descended. They pecked away at small bits of their food—Kitty was reluctant to consume too much of their rations in case Ol' Joshua's estimation of two days' travel time to the safe house turned out to be wrong—and passed the time by telling stories from books that they had read together. The girls seemed to have buried their anxieties a bit and, feeding off Kitty's confidence, now appeared to be more embracing of the idea that they were off on an adventurous journey. However, little Arthur remained uncharacteristically quiet most of the time. After checking his forehead, which felt warm, Kitty was concerned that he might be coming down with something.

As a heavy curtain of darkness finally fell across the turbulent sky, the rain lessened, and Kitty, struggling once again to dampen her lingering sense of dread, felt that it was time to resume their journey. She tucked the remaining provisions away, roused the girls up onto their feet, and wrapped a now wriggling and fidgeting Arthur back into his sling.

Picking their way carefully along the furrowed road in the dense, enveloping blackness was a slow and painful task. The girls stumbled often, scraping knees and ankles, crying out softly when they toppled to the ground, but always helped each other up and soldiered on. Kitty, too, found herself lurching often, struggling to maintain her balance as she clutched the still restless Arthur close to her.

Once, after they had been walking for nearly two hours, Kitty thought she heard the sound of horses up ahead. She grabbed the girls roughly by their shoulders and yanked them off to the side, plunging them all into a nearby thicket. They stayed hidden and silent for perhaps ten minutes, Kitty twitching and swinging her head side to side like a cornered animal, listening desperately for any sounds that might mean hunters on their trail. Finally, satisfied that the sounds, of horses or not, had faded into the night and that they did not seem to be in danger, she gathered up her flock and trudged on.

Kitty was certain that they were on the right road, the one stretching across the county and leading into Warrenton, but she was unsure of any road markers that could tell them how close they were getting to the church with the red steeple. And with the relentless darkness, she worried that they might have missed some sign or structure that would provide a tantalizing hint as to how close they were.

As the first light of the false dawn began to engrave itself across the rolling hills of the horizon, Kitty could tell that the storm had moved past and the wind was freshening and crisp. She knew that the real dawn would be creeping in soon and that they needed to find a place to hide. Scanning the barely visible contours of the countryside, she found that they seemed to be traveling along pastureland that had been cleared of trees and heavy vegetation, land that offered no readily available protection sites. Squinting into the distance, she sensed that the road curved gently off to the right ahead, and she picked up their pace, prompting the tired girls in urgent whispers to go quickly so that they could find a safe place to rest.

As they neared the sweep in the road, Kitty stopped suddenly, startled. Again, she thought she heard the jingling of horse harnesses, but this time the sound was much more pronounced. And definitely coming toward them. She swung her head around, searching desperately for someplace off the road for them to hide. Panicking, seeing nothing that offered any real protection, she seized the two girls and shoved them into a small ditch in the bordering field that she had spotted about five yards from the road. They all tumbled into the shallow trench, and Kitty pressed the girls' heads down into the slick grassy turf.

"Shush!" Kitty whispered harshly. "No talking! Keep your heads down!"

An eerie, spectral luminescence floated around the bend, followed by the hammering of horses' hooves. *Damn! Lanterns!* thought Kitty, realizing that the ghostly light must be coming from lanterns carried by the riders. Instinctively, she reached out and pushed the girls deeper into the sodden ground. She held her breath as four horsemen rounded the curve, riding abreast. Harnesses clinking, the horses reared their heads and snorted, spraying steam from their nostrils, as they picked their way carefully along the dark, uneven lane. The vexatious lanterns swung back and forth, casting long shimmering shadows across the road and into the fields.

Kitty could feel Eliza Jane and Mary shaking next to her, but they never made a sound. She turned her head, barely perceptibly, toward the terrified girls, whose eyes were as wide as a full moon, and nodded to them with what she hoped was a reassuring smile. Peeking up from their sheltering ditch, she saw that the riders had just cantered past their hiding place. She slowly and quietly exhaled.

Then, suddenly, little Arthur began to wail.

CHAPTER 10

THE AFTERNOON SUN HAD BEGUN ITS LEISURELY DOWNWARD TREK across a pristine blue sky, scrubbed clean by the passage of the previous day's storm, as the four horsemen turned off the main road and sauntered up the narrow lane leading to the Maddox farmhouse. Leading the pack was the sheriff, astride a large molasses-colored mare. Attached to the pommel of his saddle was a long rope. At the other end of the rope was Kitty, a noose notched tightly around her neck. She staggered along behind the horse, the hem of her dress ragged and ripped, revealing blood-ied shins and knees, her hands tied together loosely so that she could hold little Arthur in his sling. Eliza Jane and Mary, with nooses around their necks likewise tethered to saddle pommels, stumbled as their little legs, also scratched and bleeding, flailed beneath them, futilely attempting to keep pace with the horses' strides.

The workers in the fields surrounding the farmhouse stopped what they were doing and stared at the bleak, melancholy proces-sion as it wound its way up the lane toward the house. Some shook their heads sadly, others offered empty gazes, while, for a few, tears welled in their eyes and spilled down their grimy cheeks.

On the porch, Mary Maddox waited, having been alerted to the sheriff's approach by one of the field-workers. Her face was impassive, and her features were set, revealing neither anger nor relief. Only her hands, grasping and twisting inside the folds of her apron, gave any evidence of her apprehension about how she should handle Kitty's escape and capture. She knew that all eyes would be on her, judging how she reacted to this challenge to her authority as the new head of the farm.

"Mistress Maddox," Sheriff William Walden said, touching the brim of his slouch hat respectfully, as he reined his horse in a few feet from the porch. "Found 'em 'bout ten miles from here, travelin' along the Warrenton Road. Must've holed up during the day and done their travelin' at night. Caught 'em just before dawn."

"Thank you, Sheriff," Mary said, coldly eyeing Kitty. "I'm very thankful for your efforts."

"Pleasure, ma'am," the sheriff answered. He looked around and, seeing no white man present, only the collection of curious slaves now gathered near the farmhouse, nodded toward Kitty. "Would you like me and my men to handle the whippin'?" he asked. "Need to remind you that the new law requires a whippin' anytime a slave tries to run," he added in a slightly apologetic tone.

Mary was silent for a moment, still staring hard at Kitty. Now no more than ten feet away from the porch as the sheriff reeled in the rope, her face dusty and scored with tear tracks, Kitty stared hard right back at Mary.

Finally, Mary broke off her gaze and turned toward the sheriff. "Thank you for the offer, but I'm capable of tending to the punishment myself," she said coolly. "But I'll be forever grateful to you for your help," she added with a polite smile.

"Y'all need to get back to work now," Mary demanded, turning toward the handful of gathered slaves. Seeing Young Joshua striding up the path from the fields, she beckoned him and nodded in the direction of the captives. "And, Young Joshua, take Kitty and the children to the barn. Shackle her," she ordered, still glaring at Kitty, "and tie up the children. Stay with them until I get there and decide what to do with them."

"Yes'm," he muttered, looking resignedly at Kitty as he removed the nooses, first from her and then from the two girls. Kitty continued to glower at Mary.

"Thank you once again, Sheriff," Mary offered, with a nod of dismissal, before she turned on her heel and strode back into the farmhouse.

An hour later, Mary pulled the barn door open and entered the building. Inside, the large open space was cast in shadows, and it took a moment for her eyes to adjust to the shifting rays of muted light and the darkness. Along the wall opposite the horse stalls sat Kitty and the three children. An iron chain snaked across the barn floor, one end wrapped securely around a thick wooden support post, the other end attached to a single iron shackle clamped tightly around one of Kitty's ankles. The three children were huddled next to their mother, their hands tied together, a rope looped around their waists and secured to a support beam. Young Joshua stood nearby, shuffling his feet and looking completely uncomfortable in his guard role, steadfastly avoiding Kitty's eyes.

Mary nodded at Young Joshua. "You may leave us now," she said firmly.

"Yes'm," he answered, then rushed out the door, happy to be relieved of his jailer's duty.

Mary walked toward the bound slaves and stopped a few feet in front of Kitty. "Well, what do you have to say for yourself?" she asked harshly.

Kitty sat sullenly silent, refusing to even look up at Mary.

"How could you do this to me?" Mary asked angrily. "How could you run off like that? After all Samuel and I have done for you?" Her voice cracked at the mention of Samuel.

Kitty remained silent.

"We treated you like you were family," Mary continued, her angry tone now tinged with the sadness of betrayal. "You and your children. We brought you into the house. We taught you to read and write." She paused and took a deep breath. "How could you do this to me? Embarrass me like this! Now! So soon after Samuel has left us!"

For another moment, Kitty refused to look at Mary. Then she gathered up her torn dress and struggled to her feet, tugging against the restraining shackle and chain. She raised her head boldly and looked directly into Mary's eyes.

"I was not gonna let you sell me off," Kitty said softly but defiantly. "I was not gonna let you separate me from my children. I won't let that happen again." She paused a moment. "You'll have to kill me first."

Mary staggered backward, as if she had been shoved in the chest. She stared at Kitty, a look of complete puzzlement spreading across her face. "Why . . . why would you think I would sell you off?" she asked.

" 'Cause that's exactly what you did to my mama after I was born," Kitty said, nearly spitting the words out. "Didn't want her round to remind you of what the master did, so you just up and got rid of her. Like she somehow never existed. And left me to grow up with no mama, cryin' myself to sleep at night." Her eyes narrowed, hard and angry. "Master's sins ain't my sins. And they certainly ain't my children's sins. And I refuse to let you punish us for what he did to you."

The only sound in the barn was the rhythmic creaking of the open barn door as it swung slowly on its hinges in the breeze. Kitty stood facing Mary, her chest heaving with rage, her bruised and scraped hands clenched into fists. The three children sat huddled together on the ground, wide-eyed, frightened by the confrontation taking place before them.

After a long moment of silence, Mary stepped back again, unsteady on her feet, her composure fleeing as the look on her face changed from puzzlement to dismay. Her gaze darted from Kitty to the children and back to Kitty. Then she swung around and bolted from the barn.

CHAPTER 11

*B*ACK INSIDE THE HOUSE, MARY PACED AGITATEDLY FROM ROOM TO room like a captive animal, lost in the turmoil of her thoughts. Spying the family Bible lying on top of the desk, she snatched it up, deposited herself in a horsehair-stuffed armchair, and flipped the book open, seeking some respite from Kitty's accusations in the wisdom of the ancient passages. Thumbing randomly through the worn and dog-eared pages, she tried desperately to find some message that would soothe the commotion in her heart and mind.

Each time she tried to focus on a page, Kitty's words echoed in her mind, causing the writing to swirl and blur as she struggled to maintain her composure. Was she, in fact, the cruel, uncaring monster that Kitty claimed? she wondered. Had she really considered selling Kitty and her children solely for the financial benefit, to help ease her through hard times, as she had discussed with Fanny? Or was her real motive to erase any vestige of Samuel's infidelity? To again rid herself of the constant reminder of his straying from her bed, as Samuel had tried to do when he sold off Kitty's mother as penance for his sins. Even though Samuel had denied being unfaithful, she had welcomed the woman's departure. She could still remember the stabbing pain of watching the slave woman's stomach swell with the child she believed had been fathered by her own husband, aching constantly with the knowledge that she would never be able to bring a young life into the world. And tormented relentlessly by the fact that Samuel had so casually found another vessel to carry his offspring. It seemed like the right thing to do then, she thought, struggling to convince herself. But what about now?

Angry and confused, she slammed the Bible closed in disgust and tossed it, the pages fluttering as it skittered across the floor. After standing, she walked to the window and gazed across the front yard toward the distant Blue Ridge Mountains, where the sun was beginning to creep below the blue-gray haze of the far-off crest.

She was not sure how long she had remained in front of the window, lost in the churning conflict of her thoughts and memories. It was now dark outside, and she realized that the drama of the day had left her thoroughly exhausted. She turned, found a candle on the desk, lit it with a flaring taper from the nearby fireplace, and walked slowly out of the room and down the hallway.

Inside their bedroom—now just her bedroom, she reminded herself—Mary placed the candle on the bedside table and flung herself onto the bed that she and Samuel had shared for decades. She lay facedown, spread out on the coverlet, her arms wrapped around the pillow that had belonged to Samuel for so many years, his scent still vaguely present. And she began to weep.

CHAPTER 12

SAM MADDOX DISMOUNTED AND FLUNG THE REINS OF HIS HORSE TO A small black boy who was on his knees, picking weeds from the garden near the front porch of the Maddox farmhouse.

"Get her watered and brushed down," he ordered gruffly.

The boy nodded quickly, dropped his handful of weeds, grabbed the reins, and led the large, sweating stallion toward the barn, holding on desperately as the horse jerked and tossed its sleek head.

Maddox mounted the porch steps two at a time and knocked briskly on the heavy oak door. After a moment, one of the kitchen slaves answered the door and invited him in.

"Where's your mistress?" he asked brusquely.

"She be in the kitchen," the slave mumbled.

"Go tell her I'm here," he demanded.

The slave girl scurried off, and a few minutes later, Mary entered the main room, drying her hands on her apron.

"Sam," she said rather coolly. "I wasn't expecting to see you out here."

"Aunt Mary," he said smoothly, taking his slouch hat off and nodding at her, an unctuous smile creasing his handsome, weathered face. "Nice to see you again. Hope all's been goin' well for you since Uncle Samuel's passin'."

"Things have been fine, thank you," Mary said.

Maddox looked around, as if he was expecting to be invited to come in and take a seat, but Mary simply remained standing in the same spot, her hands still wrapped in her apron.

"Well," Maddox said, his smile disappearing, shifting from one booted foot to the other, twisting his sweat-stained hat in his hand. "I was ridin' out this way and figured I'd stop by to check on you."

"That was kind of you," Mary answered dryly.

After an awkward pause, Maddox looked around the house and then turned back toward her. "Heard you had a problem. That some slaves ran off," he said.

"Not really. There was no problem. Just a misunderstanding," Mary said.

"That ain't the way the sheriff told it," Maddox said, cocking his head to one side, his tone somewhat accusing.

"Is that so?" Mary said. "Just how did the sheriff tell it?"

"Sheriff said he was told some niggra slaves ran off and you needed help catchin' 'em. Said he and a posse rode all night, lookin' for 'em, before they tracked 'em down hidin' off the Warrenton Pike."

"Is that so?" Mary repeated.

"Yup, that's sure how he told it," Maddox said.

"Well, I'm afraid the sheriff made it sound a bit more dramatic than it really was," Mary said, offering a tight, polite smile. "Anyway, the slaves are all back, and no harm's been done. But I do thank you for your concern. And now, if there's nothing else, I really need to get back—"

"Actually," Maddox interrupted, "there is something else I need to talk to y'all about." Maddox looked pointedly at a chair in the sitting room, but Mary ignored the hint and refused to budge from her spot in the doorway.

"And what might that be?" Mary asked.

"So," he began haltingly, "you know how close me an' Uncle Samuel were all these years." He paused, apparently looking for some affirmation from Mary, but none was forthcoming, as her face remained impassive. "Well," he continued, "we often talked about what he wanted to do with the farm and all else once he passed on."

"Did you, now?" Mary said.

"Yes'm, we did. And the one thing he was always sayin' was he wanted to be sure you was fine and not havin' to work real hard once he left us."

"That was very considerate of him," Mary said, the irony in her tone lost on Sam.

"Yes'm, it was. Uncle Samuel was like that. But then, you know that better'n most," Maddox added.

Mary simply nodded.

"So then, that's why I'm here. I been lookin' at Uncle Samuel's will." He paused a moment, drawing himself up to his full height before he continued. "And I think you an' me need to talk."

"Talk about what?" Mary demanded, any vestige of hospitality now drained from her voice.

"Well, it seems to me and my lawyer—" he began.

"Your . . . lawyer?" Mary interrupted.

"Yes'm," Maddox continued, his tone hardening. "My lawyer and me think that since Uncle Samuel's will makes mention of me as someone who would be a beneficiary, you and I need to discuss how his estate should be divided up."

Mary glared at him for a moment. "Well," she said icily, "I'm afraid that you—and your lawyer—are sadly mistaken."

Maddox began to speak, but Mary silenced him with a wave of her hand.

"Sadly mistaken," she repeated. "The will is very clear that the entire estate passes to me, and me alone. You are only mentioned as a beneficiary in the event that something of his estate remains when I die. Nothing more."

"I'm afraid that ain't the way we see it," he answered, shaking his head. "The way we see it is, since I have a stake in the estate when you die, you and me need to be discussin' any decisions about the property, and we need to be agreein' about everythin'. Land. Crops. Slaves. Everythin'."

Mary said nothing.

"So," Maddox continued, his tone now steely, any pretense of familial care now abandoned, "I thought we should be talkin' about those runaway slaves and what we should be doin' about 'em. Seems to me we should be sellin' 'em off right away. Can probably get a pretty good price for 'em. Lord knows you could use the cash. And we'd be makin' it clear to the rest of the darkies that there's a steep price to be paid if anyone else is thinkin' of runnin' off."

Mary remained silent, her jaw clenched, her eyes narrowed.

"Well, then," Maddox said, taking her silence for agreement, "once the woman, Kitty, is recovered from her whippin', we should be lookin' to sell the lot of 'em. Should all bring a pretty good price."

Mary spoke, her voice low and calm. "First of all, there have been no whippings. Second, I have absolutely no intention of selling anybody off. And third," she continued, a hard, defiant edge to her voice now, "I don't care what you or your lawyer thinks. You do not—and will not—have any interest in this property. Not while I'm still alive. And I have no intention of seeking your opinions about how I run this farm. Now—or ever."

They stood glaring at each other. Finally, Maddox spoke, barely restraining his wrath.

"I'm real sorry you see it that way. And real sorry that y'all want to turn this into a fight. That surely ain't the way Uncle Samuel would've wanted this all playin' out." He paused, leaned in toward her, and added menacingly, "But if you're lookin' for a fight, you damn sure'll get one."

Mary stepped around him and headed toward the big oak door.

"I'm afraid your trip out here was a complete waste of your time," Mary said curtly. "And of mine. By the way, I'm quite sure that your uncle Samuel had no interest at all in you havin' any say in the runnin' of this farm. And I'm quite sure that I don't, either."

Mary swung the big door open and stepped aside.

"I don't believe we have anything more to talk about," she said tersely, her face a rigid mask of anger.

Sam Maddox shook his head, furious, and then stormed out the door.

CHAPTER 13

"*T*HE NERVE OF THAT MAN!" FANNY EXCLAIMED BETWEEN SIPS FROM a delicate hand-painted teacup.

Fanny and Mary were seated on the veranda of Fanny's home, a sprawling, two-story mansion in the center of the Withers plantation. Built in a curious marriage of the Southern Colonial and Greek Revival styles, with a large, graceful center structure flanked by two slightly smaller wings, and a sweeping veranda guarded by an array of fluted columns, it was acknowledged to be the most grand and impressive home in all of Rappahannock County.

Fanny's father, the late James Withers, fought in the American Revolution when he was a young man. After inheriting a substantial amount of money from his father, who had built a shipping business in Charleston, he decided to abandon the family enterprise and become a gentleman farmer. By settling at the foot of the Blue Ridge Mountains, not only did he achieve his goal of becoming a gentleman farmer, but he actually became quite a successful one, too, regularly expanding his crops and his acreage until he became the largest and most prosperous landowner in two counties, with more than four hundred acres and dozens of slaves.

Since her father's death five years earlier, Fanny had assumed the role of managing the family fields and fortunes. Although the entire estate had been left to both Fanny and her younger sister, Katie had shown no interest in the details of running the farm and was content to simply enjoy the lifestyle that the thriving operation provided her. And that was fine with Fanny.

"I can't believe that he would come out to the farm and talk to you that way," Fanny continued. "And for him to threaten you right there in your own home. And so soon after Samuel's passing." She shook her head. "Just never cared for that man. And never trusted him, either. I cringe every time he comes here callin' on my sister."

"I keep tellin' myself that he's my Samuel's kin and I need to be civil with him, even if he was always takin' advantage of Samuel's good nature. Never paid him back any of the money he was always borrowin'. Never even said thank you. Just could never warm up to him. But this is the last straw. I won't have him tellin' me how to run our farm—my farm now," Mary added wistfully.

"What about him claiming that Samuel's will gives him some say in how the farm's run?" Fanny asked.

Mary shook her head. "The will says no such thing. It simply says that when I die, he's entitled to anything that's left. And I don't intend to have anything left for that man to inherit, not if I can help it," Mary said angrily.

"Maybe you should talk to a lawyer, too. Just to be certain," Fanny said.

"I will, if I have to. For now, I think I'll just wait on him to see what he's plannin' on doin'."

Fanny lifted an ornately engraved silver teapot from the center of the table and filled their cups. They sat quietly, as Mary seemed to be lost in her own thoughts.

"So, what have you decided to do?" Fanny asked. "About Kitty?"

It seemed for a moment that somehow Mary had not heard her, since she simply sat quietly, sipping her tea. Finally, Mary placed her cup down gently on the saucer and looked up.

"You know I've never been fond of the idea of ownin' slaves. Wasn't brought up like that. I don't mean to be judgin' you or anyone else. Just never felt right to me. So I've been prayin' on all this for some time now. Especially since she and her children were caught and brought back." She lifted her head and looked directly at Fanny. "I've decided to set her free. Her children, too."

There was silence on the veranda as Mary sat waiting for Fanny's response.

"Well," said Fanny, obviously surprised by this pronouncement, "are you sure that's the best thing for you to do? Especially after they tried to run away?"

"It's what Samuel wanted me to do," Mary said. "And it's the right thing for me to do," she added, so softly that Fanny barely heard the words.

"What do you mean, 'the right thing'?" Fanny asked.

Mary sighed deeply. "When I asked her why she ran, she told me that she believed I was goin' to sell her and her children. Just like I had allowed Samuel to sell her mother off after she was born." She paused for a moment. "She told me I'd have to kill her before she would leave her children. Before she would let me do to her children what I had done to her. To force them to grow up without their mother. I'd have to kill her first," she repeated somberly.

Fanny said nothing.

"I've been tryin' to remember how I felt when I allowed Samuel to sell her mother. The anger I felt, knowing, despite his denial, that he was the father. The rage inside of me that this woman—this slave—could have provided him with the one thing that I couldn't. A child. And then I realized that that anger should have been aimed at Samuel. He was the one who strayed. Who betrayed me. Who broke our sacred vows." Mary paused. "Not Kitty's mother." Mary looked up, tears filling her eyes. "Do you know that I can't even remember her name? I allowed her to be sent away from her own child—and I can't even remember her name!"

Fanny reached out and covered her friend's hand with her own, then squeezed gently.

"And the worst part," Mary continued after a moment, "is that I actually considered doing it again. That I actually thought about selling Kitty so that I could finally erase that whole episode from my mind. From my life. What must God think of me . . . ?" Her voice trailed off as she bowed her head and shook it sorrowfully from side to side.

"I'm not going to pretend I agree with you about owning slaves and whether it's against God's will. Fact is, I believe it's the natural order of things. That God wants the white folks takin' care of the Negroes, who couldn't take of themselves without us. And I've always tried to be good to my slaves, to make them feel like they're part of our family. But I'll also tell you this about God. He will forgive you if you think you need forgiving," Fanny said reassuringly. "As long as you're truly sorry and ask for His forgiveness, you'll receive it." She squeezed Mary's hand again. "And now that you think you should try to make it up to Kitty—at least in some fashion— you can show her, and God, how sorry you really are. And you can ask for His forgiveness." She paused thoughtfully. "And perhaps you can ask Kitty, too. For her forgiveness."

Mary looked up, wiping the tears from her eyes with her hands. "I thought of that. But what if she refuses? You should have seen the look in her eyes when she was brought back. When she told me I'd have to kill her first. There was such anger." Mary shook her head.

"All you can do is try to make things right by her. Free her and her children. Tell her it's what Samuel wanted. And it's what you want, too," Fanny said. "And then tell her you're truly sorry that you didn't stop Samuel from sending her mother away. And hope that someday she can forgive you. Maybe not right now. But someday."

Mary took a deep breath and exhaled slowly. "That's what I'll do," she said, her tone now resolute. "That's what I have to do. Free her and her children—and hope that it frees my soul, too. And then maybe, just maybe, God can forgive me."

"I'm sure He will," Fanny said, a kind smile flickering across her face. "And perhaps Kitty will, too, in time. But," she added cautiously, "I'm not so sure the folks round here will be so quick to thank you—or forgive you—for freeing a runaway slave."

CHAPTER 14

MARY WALKED INTO THE BARN, FOLLOWED BY YOUNG JOSHUA. IT had been four days since the sheriff had captured Kitty and her children and returned them to the Maddox farm. Mary had spent the past twenty-four hours praying over her decision to free Kitty, hoping for some sign, some Biblical vision that would assure her that she was making the right decision. But none had come to her.

Kitty scrabbled awkwardly up from the ground, clutching and tugging at the chain that kept her tethered to the support post. She had been reading to the children from a tattered, dog-eared tome that Young Joshua had brought her, and they remained seated, eyes wide again with fear, the rope that secured them snaking around their little waists.

Mary noticed that a rag had been wrapped around Kitty's manacled ankle—*probably by Young Joshua*, she thought—to attempt to minimize the chafing of the coarse hammered steel against her flesh. But despite the rag, Mary could see that Kitty's ankle was scraped, bloody, and raw, and she hobbled, favoring the manacled leg, as she struggled to stand straight.

Mary stopped a few feet in front of Kitty. Again, Kitty raised herself up to her full height and glared defiantly at Mary.

"Joshua," Mary said calmly, "please take the shackle off Kitty. And please untie the children."

As Young Joshua stepped forward, Kitty backed away and placed herself protectively in front of the huddling children.

"Joshua, please . . . ," Mary said, nodding toward the blue-steel shackle.

Young Joshua stepped toward Kitty, a large iron key in his hand, his face still cloaked in a mask of puzzlement. He knelt down, inserted the key, twisted until the locking mechanism reluctantly released its hold, and pulled the shackle from her ankle. He tossed the chain to the side and then bent and untied the rope from the children.

"Thank you, Joshua. You may leave us now," Mary said, her eyes still locked on Kitty.

Young Joshua patted the still frightened children on their heads, stood, and gently touched Kitty on her shoulder as he passed her. He left the barn without saying a word, leaving the door open behind him.

"You can't take my children from me. You can't split us up," Kitty said frantically. "I told you—you'll have to kill me first!" Kitty was panicking, her eyes darting desperately around the barn, seeking something that she could seize to use as a weapon.

Mary stepped forward, her hands raised, palms out, trying to calm Kitty down.

"No one is going to separate you from the children," she said reassuringly. "No one is going to sell you—or the children."

Kitty stared at Mary, the fear in her eyes now tinged with uncertainty.

"Kitty," Mary said, taking another step toward her and the children. "No one's going to sell you off," she repeated. "I'm going to free you. And the children."

It seemed at first that Kitty did not hear the words. Or that, somehow, they had not registered.

"I don't . . . understand," Kitty muttered, confused.

"I'm going to free you. And your children," Mary repeated.

"Why would you be freein' us?" Kitty said, her eyes narrowed in suspicion. " 'Specially after we run away?" Kitty shook her head violently. "I don't understand," she repeated, wary and apprehensive, her entire body tense, her hands clenched.

"I don't expect you do," Mary answered. "I'm not even sure

that I do," she added, almost as if to herself. Mary spotted two milking stools nearby and pulled them over. Gesturing toward them, Mary said, "Sit. Please."

Kitty, clearly unsure of what was happening, sat down cumbersomely, then extended her injured ankle in front of her. Mary sat down opposite her, started to reach across to Kitty, who flinched away. Mary pulled her hand back and placed both of her hands in her lap.

"I did a terrible thing to you," Mary began, her voice quiet and hesitant, "those many years ago. When I allowed Samuel to sell off your mother. It was a terrible thing. I know that now."

She searched Kitty's eyes but found nothing, just a cold, empty stare.

"I was very young," Mary continued. "And prideful. And I was jealous, so jealous, because I was a failure at becoming a mother, but your mother . . ." Her voice trailed off as she shook her head sadly. "I know now that it was not her fault. She didn't mean to hurt me. It was Samuel's fault." A note of anger seeped into her voice. "All of it was his fault. Your mother had no choice. I realize that now. But I was just so angry that I couldn't see that then. I needed to blame somebody, somebody other than myself. Even somebody other than Samuel. So . . . I blamed her," Mary said, her tone now somber.

"She had no choice," Kitty said, seething. "She do what Master says, or she's punished. What kind of choice is that?"

"I know. I know. At least, I know that now. And I tried to accept it. To move on with my life—with our life—hoping that someday I'd have my own child, our own child. But each time I looked at your mother and saw the swelling in her belly and then, later, saw you as an infant in her arms, and knew in my heart that you were his, the anger was too much for me to bear," she said, raising her head to look directly into Kitty's eyes. "So, God forgive me, I didn't try to stop him when he decided to sell her. I let him destroy your family. For my own selfish reasons."

There was a long strangled silence in the barn. The children, who sensed the tension in the conversation, had remained quiet, tucked in tightly behind their mother. Finally, Kitty broke the spell.

"Why now? Why tell me this now, after all these years?"

Mary looked pained, almost haunted by the memory, as she shook her head sadly. "It took your threats—that I'd have to kill you before I could separate you from your children—to make me realize how evil my decision had been. That made me understand what I had done to you, to your life, the hurt that I had caused. And I finally came to realize what a terrible thing I had done. Too late, of course, for your mother and you. But, hopefully, not too late for you and your children."

Kitty looked down at her three children, whose wide-eyed gazes were bouncing anxiously between their mother and their mistress. She reached out and placed her palm on each of their tiny faces, one after the other, faint swirling images of her own mother flickering elusively in her mind, the pain of her absence bubbling, unbidden, once again to the surface.

"And it's what Samuel wanted," Mary said.

Kitty's head snapped up, and she looked quizzically at Mary, her head cocked to one side.

"Just before he died. He asked me to free you. And the children." Mary sighed. "You were special to him. Even though he couldn't really show it very often. It's why he brought you into the house and out of the fields. Why he insisted you learn to read and write. And learn to speak like white folks." She shrugged. "So he asked me to free you."

Kitty was still perplexed. "He asked you," she said hesitantly, "but you don't have to?"

"No. I don't have to," Mary agreed. "But I want to. I realize now that it's the right thing to do. It won't bring your mother back. I know that. But it's the right thing to do, for me as a Christian. And for you, as a mother."

Kitty was silent, struggling to understand what was happening and why, torn between a creeping sense of joy at the shocking and unexpected prospect of freedom and the anger that still seethed within her at the loss of her mother.

"But we ran away," Kitty said. "And the sheriff had to find us and bring us back. Isn't there some kind of punishment for that? A whippin'? Or somethin'?"

"There'll be no whippin'. And no punishment."

"But what will the folks round here think about that? About you not punishin' us? And about you settin' us free? They can't be likin' that. Not with all the talkin' it'll set off with all their slaves!"

"That's for me to worry about. It's not your problem," Mary said solemnly, then stood. "Would you and the children come with me now up to the house?" she asked, her tone chastened yet kind. "Y'all need a good meal. And we need to attend to your leg." She extended her hand to Kitty. "And we have much we should talk about. Please?"

After a long moment's hesitation, Kitty stretched her hand toward Mary, who took it and clasped it in both of hers.

CHAPTER 15

"**S**O? DO I HAVE A CASE OR NOT?" SAM MADDOX DEMANDED.

Across the low, stumpy wood-carved table in a dark corner of a tavern, Moffet Strother adjusted his glasses once again as he peered at the document in front of him. He grasped the paper in one hand and shifted it around, trying to capture the flickering, elusive light of a thick tallow candle buried inside a clouded, cracked glass jar. Finally, he placed the paper down on the table-top. After removing his glasses, he wiped the wire-enclosed lenses with a smudged handkerchief that he had pulled from his jacket pocket and looked up at Maddox.

Any observation of Moffet Strother would yield little evidence to suggest that he was actually a lawyer, much less a competent one. Dressed in rough home-spun trousers and a worn canvas jacket, his hair long and unkempt, he looked more like a trades-man—which, in fact, he was, engaged primarily in the business of buying and selling horses and farm animals. But he had studied law for a time in his early years and would occasionally take in some work as a lawyer on the side, mostly writing up simple wills and con-tracts. He shifted his considerable bulk, which was perched precar-iously and uncomfortably on a battered, unsteady stool, and squinted across the table at his newest possible client.

"A case? Yes," Strother answered, contorting his round face in thought. "A winning case? That, I can't be so sure of."

"Why not?" Maddox responded angrily. "Says right here"—he

jammed his forefinger at the bottom of the document—"that I'm entitled to the estate when she dies. Don't it?"

"Yes. That's what it says. But the question—the real issue for a court—is whether you have anything to say about the property in the estate before she dies."

"Well, why the hell would my uncle put that in there if he didn't expect for there to be somethin' left for me to inherit? Seems to me, he's just sayin' that she gets to use everythin' until she passes on. Then it all goes to me!"

Strother nodded slowly. "Possible a court might see it that way. Certainly is possible. And that's what we'd be arguin'. But I'm just tellin' you what she'd be sayin'—that you only get whatever is left, if anything, when she passes. That if your uncle really wanted to leave anything specifically to you now, he woulda done it right then and there in the will. Until then, until she's gone, you got no say in anythin'. That's what she'll be arguin'."

Maddox thought for a moment and then leaned forward, glowering at Strother, his eyes narrowing and fierce. "But you sayin' we got a shot?" Maddox said.

"Yes, yes, we certainly do," Strother answered quickly, anxious not to lose this possible new client. "Yes, we do," he repeated. "And," he added thoughtfully, "there's also the chance that if she knows we're takin' her to court, she might be willin' to settle. Reach some arrangement that gives you control of some of the property right away."

Just as quickly as it had surged, Maddox's anger was now swept away. He sat back, apparently satisfied with the possibilities offered by the lawyer.

"Well, then," Maddox said, "seems to me we should get started. Let her know we're serious 'bout this."

"Yes," Strother agreed. "I think the sooner the better."

"So, what're you suggestin' we do to get started?" Maddox asked.

"Well," Strother began pensively, doing his best to act the role of a lawyer contemplating his best course of legal attack. "I'm thinkin' we should start off by gettin' an injunction against her.

Keep her from sellin' any of the land or sellin' off any property. Until we get a judge to figure out what the will means."

Maddox nodded vigorously as he listened. "That's good," he said. "That sounds real good. So, let's get started on all that right away."

Strother cleared his throat and then continued, somewhat uncomfortably. "There is one other thing. I must inquire about my fees, if we are to commence this case. I'm sure you understand."

"Certainly do. I'm a businessman, too. Understand you need to get paid." Maddox shrugged and raised his hands, palms up. "But problem is, I'm a bit short right now. So, here's what I'm offerin'," said Maddox. He smiled companionably, but his eyes were hard. "I'm needin' to raise some cash. So my plan is, when we win or she settles, to sell off some of the property—some of the land and some of the niggras—and you'd get paid from that. Agreed?"

"But what happens if we don't win? Or she doesn't settle?"

Maddox shrugged again. "Guess that would mean you ain't done much good of a lawyerin' job, then, wouldn't it? No sense payin' you if you lose."

Strother was silent for a moment, weighing the odds in his mind. Finally, he let out an exasperated sigh and extended his hand across the table. "It's a bit unusual, but I believe I can accept that arrangement, Mr. Maddox. I am now your lawyer."

Maddox shook the extended hand and smiled. "Sounds good to me. Guess we can be gettin' started right away, then. But before that, I'm thinkin' we should drink to our success." He beckoned toward the tavern owner, who was stationed behind the bar. "Drinks on you, of course," he added smugly.

CHAPTER 16

"**Y**OU THINKIN' YOU CAN TRUST HER?" ASKED OL' JOSHUA.

"Not sure," Kitty answered.

They were seated at the small table in Ol' Joshua's cabin. Kitty was wearing a new housedress, given to her by Mary Maddox, which had replaced the torn and bloodied one she wore after her capture, and she had a clean bandage wrapped around her injured ankle. Eliza Jane, Mary, and Arthur were tucked away on the floor in a corner, playing with a collection of rag dolls.

"Since she let us out of the barn and back into the house, she been nothin' but kind, takin' care of my leg, makin' sure we have enough to eat and are gettin' enough rest." Kitty shook her head, perplexed. "Don't make no sense," she continued. "Was certain she'd be sellin' us off, and now, all of a sudden, she be treatin' us like real family. Not just like slave family—but like real family. And all this after we tryin' to escape. If I'd known she be reactin' like this," she added, chuckling, "I'd tried to run off long ago."

Ol' Joshua was silent, watching the three children play in the corner. Then a sad smile crept across his face.

"Once you free, you gonna leave here?" he asked.

"Don't know. Ain't never really thought about it," she said.

Ol' Joshua thought a minute and then said, "What about Robert's people? Where they all be?"

At the mention of Robert's name, Kitty's face became clouded, and her eyes hazy.

"Don't know where they be. He never said much 'bout them. Don't know if they be free or slave." After a moment, she added, "But I sure wish Robert still alive. Been nice to move in together, bein' free and all. Maybe even packed up the children and headed west, over the mountains, got our own farm, a whole new life," she said wistfully. "Would've been real nice."

They sat in a comfortable silence for a while, their eyes again on the children playing, but both of their minds elsewhere. Finally, Ol' Joshua spoke.

"Why she be doin' this? Why now?"

"She say it because the master ask her on his deathbed," Kitty said.

"But nobody know that for sure," Ol' Joshua said. "And, even if he did, nobody be forcin' her to go and do that if she don' want to."

Kitty nodded in agreement. "All that be true. Seem to me she don't need to be doin' it if she don't want to. And with Master gone, seems like she havin' a hard time runnin' the farm—"

"So," Ol' Joshua interrupted, "all that bein' true, why she be freein' all you when she could be sellin' you for some good cash money? That just don't make no sense."

"Somethin' inside her changed. Least she say it did. Don't know if it was just Master's dyin'. Or somethin' else. But she changed. Always thought she be hatin' me for all these years. Seemed like it, anyways. And then, when we be caught and brought back, instead of whippin' the hide off me, she start tellin' me she's sorry for sellin' off my mama. And that now she be freein' all of us." She paused a moment. "And you know what be most surprisin'? All this came after I threatened her, tellin' her she gonna have to kill me if she be thinkin' of sellin' me and takin' me away from my babies."

"Just don't figure," Ol' Joshua said, clearly puzzled.

"Nope. Don't figure at all. But I ain't gonna do nothin' that might change her mind. Soon as she be freein' us, I'm away from this place fast as our feet can take us." She reached across the table and placed her hand on top of the old man's. "Not happy 'bout leavin' you, though. Or Young Joshua," she said.

"And we not happy 'bout havin' to say good-bye to you, either," he said. After taking her hand in both of his, he raised it to his cracked, taut lips and kissed it.

"Funny how the Good Lord works," he mused softly. "We took you in after Master Samuel and Mistress Mary had your mama sold off, raised you up like you was our own. Figured you'd be round to take care of us until you placed us both in the ground." He paused and looked off into the distance, a faraway look shrouding his eyes. "Then the Lord decides to take my Sarah from me. And now He be takin' you from me, too. He be guidin' Mistress's soul, tellin' her to set you free. Good Lord give you to us because your mama taken from you. Now Good Lord takin' you away from me, again all 'cause your mama was taken from you."

He turned and looked deep into Kitty's eyes, which were now soft with tears. "Maybe it all do make sense, after all," he said.

CHAPTER 17

"*I* AM, INDEED, SORRY TO IMPOSE ON YOU, MRS. MADDOX. BUT I thought it was important for us to speak as soon as possible," Moffet Strother said.

Strother was standing on the porch of the Maddox farmhouse. Mary was stationed in the doorway, a gracious smile on her face.

"Certainly, Mr. Strother. Always pleased to see you. But I didn't realize that my husband had been involved in any business with you—that is, before he passed away."

"Well," Strother began, discomfort apparent in his voice, "that's not exactly the reason I'm here."

"What, then, can I help you with?" Mary asked, puzzled.

Strother cleared his throat. "I'm actually here in my capacity as a lawyer."

"As a lawyer? For who? About what?" Mary asked guardedly.

Strother straightened himself up to his full height, although Mary Maddox was still half a head taller than him.

"I represent your nephew, Sam. He's asked me to talk to you about your late husband's will—"

"First of all," Mary interrupted coolly, "he is not my nephew! He was Samuel's kin but most definitely not mine. And second, there is nothing to talk about concerning the will. I thought I made that very clear to him."

"I'm afraid that's not the way he—that is, we—see it," said Strother.

"I don't particularly care how you—or he—sees it. I know what the will says, and I know what my husband wanted. And he wanted the entire estate to go to me. The *only* reason that Samuel even mentioned Sam in the will was that neither of us has any other living blood relatives. And he had to list somebody in case something happened to me. That's it. No other reason. And certainly no intention to give that good-for-nothing some share in our hard-earned property. Not while I am still alive," she said. "And," she added, her face now flushed and taut with wrath, "you can advise your *client* that I plan on livin' a long time. And I plan on makin' sure that everything's gone—one way or the other— when I do leave this earth. He'll be gettin' nothin' from me! Not now and not then!"

Strother struggled to maintain his composure, surprised and knocked off balance by the sudden vehemence in Mary's tone and attitude. "I can certainly understand your concern," he began soothingly, "but it seems to me that we might want to discuss this matter civilly before . . ."

"Before what?" Mary snapped.

"Well, we'd be most unhappy if we were forced to bring a court of law into this. Should be a family matter. No sense in lettin' the law make this decision for us. Somebody'd definitely be losin' then."

Mary started to speak again, but Strother held up his hand.

"Please, ma'am. Just let me have my say and I'll be leavin'." He continued hurriedly. "We're most definitely hopin' that it won't come to that. What we're hopin' is that you might be willin' to see our point here and come to some agreement that would be fair for all. Fair for you and fair for my client."

Mary was silent and appeared to be contemplating his offer. Strother began to think that perhaps he had convinced her to take a more reasonable approach to Sam's claim. However, that hope was shattered a moment later.

"Mr. Strother," Mary said, the visible anger dissipated but her voice still stern, "I'm very sorry that you wasted your time travelin' all the way out here to see me. Your client should have made it clear to you—as I made it clear to him—that there is *nothing* for us to discuss. The will leaves everything to me, and that is that."

"I'm very sorry you feel that way," Strother said, reaching into the inside pocket of his coat and pulling out a sheaf of papers. "But since that is your position, I have no choice but to serve you with this," he said, handing the papers to Mary.

Mary was perplexed. "And just what might this be?"

"It's an injunction," Strother answered a bit self-importantly.

"What is that?"

"It is an order signed by the circuit court of this county. It says that you are prevented by law from disposing of any of the property left to you in the will until the case has been resolved in court."

"What?" Mary exclaimed. She scanned the papers. "You can't do that. The will says clearly that the property all belongs to me!"

"Well, we'll see about that. Once we get to court. But in the meantime, you cannot dispose of any of the estate. Anything at all."

Mary glared at the diminutive lawyer and then threw the papers to the ground. "I'll ask you to please leave my property, Mr. Strother. Now!" she said, her voice rising.

"I'm very sorry . . ." Strother began.

"Now!" she repeated. "Or do I have to go get my shotgun to convince you that it's time for you to go?"

"Again, I'm very sorry," Strother stammered, backing away as quickly as he could. "I will be leavin', then." He nodded toward the papers on the ground. "And I'll be leavin' those for you."

"And I would suggest that you do not return. And please tell your client that he is not welcome here, either. And you should both remember that if either of you does show up again"—she paused a moment and offered a sinister smile—"I'm a very good shot!"

Damn that Sam Maddox, Mary thought as she stormed back into the house and slammed the door behind her so viciously that a nearby flower vase trembled and nearly toppled over. *I should have known he'd stoop to something like this. Thinks he can bully me by threatening to take me to court. I wish Samuel had dealt with him while he was still alive. Guess it's up to me now.*

Mary paced around the room, contemplating what she would need to do next.

CHAPTER 18

THE VILLAGE OF WASHINGTON WAS BUSTLING WITH WAGONS, HORSES, and people buzzing about like bees streaming from a broken hive. The circuit court judge was in town, which meant that the one-room redbrick courthouse on Gay Street, in the center of the hamlet, was now also the center of the Rappahannock County universe for that week. The traveling jurist would arrive for a week at a time every few months. Litigants would be lined up outside the courthouse for hours, waiting their turn in their quests for justice. During this week the normally quiet, hard-packed, wagon wheel–rutted dirt streets pulsated with activity, and the atmosphere was more like that of a county fair than a somber judicial period. Farmers would bring their produce into the village and the merchants would display their goods prominently, hoping that the influx of people would lead to a buying bonanza.

As Mary crossed the street in front of the courthouse, amid the meandering pedestrians, horses, and wagons, she was struck, as always, by how many people would descend upon the village when the circuit court judge arrived. She recalled being fascinated as a young girl by the idea that so many people would arrive and pack the few snug blocks, and wondering where they all came from.

Weaving her way through the crowd, wearing her best visiting apparel of a long calico dress, lace-up leather shoes, and a shawl, she approached the law office of Zephania Turner. As she prepared to knock, the front door swung open and the lawyer, his arms wrapped around a bundle of legal folders, nearly barged into her.

"Mrs. Maddox," he exclaimed, struggling to maintain control of his perilously shifting cargo, "I'm so sorry. I didn't see you there."

"My apologies, Mr. Turner," Mary said, reaching out to help restore some balance to his load. "I know how busy you must be this week"—she nodded toward the courthouse across the street—"but I was hoping you might have a few minutes to talk with me about a legal matter. A somewhat pressing legal matter, I'm afraid."

"Certainly, certainly," he said. "I don't need to be in court quite yet. I'm always delighted to see you," he added, with a warm smile, holding the door for her to enter the room.

Once Mary had settled into the chair across from his desk, and Turner had carefully deposited his folders back on a nearby shelf, he dropped down into his chair.

"So, then," he began kindly, "how have you been managing since the death of Samuel?"

"Fairly well. Thank you," Mary answered.

"I'm glad to hear that. Never an easy time when we lose a loved one. Never been married myself, but have to imagine it would be a terrible adjustment," he said, shaking his head sympathetically.

"Yes, it is," Mary said softly.

"Well, then, Mrs. Maddox," Turner said, anxious to change the subject, "what is it I can help you with?"

"I'm having a bit of a problem, and I need some advice," Mary said.

The lawyer simply nodded for her to continue.

"My husband's—late husband's, that is—nephew, Sam, seems to think that Samuel's will gives him some claim on the estate."

Turner grunted. "I suspected this would happen."

Mary looked at him, puzzled. "Why would you have suspected that?"

"Sam came to see me some days ago. He wanted me to look at

a copy of the will and tell him if he had any right to any of the property left by Samuel."

"And?" asked Mary, surprised by this revelation.

Turner shrugged. "I told him that I thought the will made it fairly clear that he had no claim. That the entire estate was intended to go to you. I also told him that given my friendship with Samuel over the years, I would not feel comfortable representing him."

"May I ask what his reaction was?"

"He was not very happy with me, I guess you could say," Turner said, with a rueful smile. "Actually stormed out after I told him that. Not a terribly polite young man, is he?"

"No, indeed. Always had a bit of a short temper," Mary said. "I used to tell Samuel that he'd come to no good. But Samuel, rest his soul, was always tryin' to help him out. Never understood what he saw in that young man."

"So, has he found another lawyer?" asked Turner.

"Moffet Strother," said Mary.

Turner said nothing and simply raised a skeptical eyebrow.

"He came to visit me yesterday—Strother did—threatenin' that he and Sam were goin' to take me to court over the will, unless I agreed to some kind of settlement," Mary said.

"And?"

"I'm afraid I wasn't very polite to him. Told him I had no intention of sharing anything with the likes of Sam. So then he hands this to me," she said, unfolding a set of wrinkled papers and placing them on the desk, in front of Turner.

"An injunction?" he said, scanning the document.

"That's what he called it," Mary continued. "Said it prevents me from selling any of the estate—land or property—until a judge decides if Sam has a claim or not."

Turner read through the papers and then placed them on his desk. "That is correct. An injunction is actually an order to keep everything status quo—meaning no changes—until a judge has a chance to look at the case and make some decisions. So, essentially, this says that you can't do anything to dispose of any of the property until a court says so. So, then, what do you propose to do?" he asked.

"Depends. On a lot of things, actually. First off, I'd like your opinion on his claims about what the will says." She placed a copy of the will in front of him. "I'd pay you for your time and advice, of course," Mary added.

Turner waved his hand in the air, dismissing the offer. "No need for that. As I said, Samuel was a good friend for many years. Happy to take a look at it for you."

He shifted his gaze back to the will in front of him. After a moment of study, he looked up at her. "I can see what they're focusing on. The language is a bit unclear. But," he continued reassuringly, "I don't think a court would see it the way Sam and his lawyer do. Let me read it, and then I can explain it to you."

The lawyer reached for a pair of wire-rimmed glasses, placed them on, picked up the will, and began reading aloud. "'I give and bequeath unto my beloved wife, Mary Maddox, my whole estate, real, personal, and mixed, to do with and use as she may see proper during her natural life.'" He looked up at Mary as he jabbed at the paper with his forefinger. "This is the part they're relying on. 'If there should be anything left at the death of my wife, Mary Maddox, it is then my wish and desire that my nephew, Samuel Maddox, shall have the remainder of my whole estate at the death of my wife, the aforesaid Mary Maddox.'"

"Seems very clear to me. I get the estate, and when I die, if there's anything left, Sam gets it," said Mary. "How in the world can they be sayin' that somehow Sam gets a say in things now?" she asked, both confused and angry.

Turner removed his glasses and deposited them carefully on the desk. "Here's their argument," he began patiently, like a teacher explaining a confounding concept to a frustrated student. "They're going to argue that this language—giving the remainder of the estate at your death to Sam—creates something the law calls a 'life estate.' What a 'life estate' usually means is this. A man dies and, in his will, states that a particular beneficiary gets possession of some property—usually a home—for them to use until they die, at which time the property goes back to the estate and then that portion of the estate is transferred to a final beneficiary. The person who receives the 'life estate' can use the property until they die, but they can't usually dispose of the property. Are you following me?" he asked.

Mary nodded. "I understand. But that's not what Samuel meant to do. And that's not what the will says," she added adamantly.

Turner nodded. "I agree. And I think a court would agree also—"

"You *think* a court would agree?" Mary interrupted. "Does that mean you're not sure?"

"Well, Mrs. Maddox," the lawyer began, leaning back in his chair, "I learned a long time ago that it can be calamitous to try to absolutely predict what a judge or jury might do. Never really know for sure. But that being said," he added quickly and encouragingly, "I don't believe that a court would be quick to alter what appears to be Samuel's clear intention because of a somewhat imprecise phrase."

Mary thought a moment.

"I understand your reluctance to make any promises, Mr. Turner, but I need to know what my chances of winning this case will be," she said.

"Fair question." Turner nodded. "Best I can tell you is that I'd be very confident in your chances."

"Very confident, but not certain?"

"That's correct," Turner said. "But confident enough that I would most certainly be willing to take your case on. If you asked, of course," he added hastily.

Mary let out a deep sigh and then began to gather up the papers from the lawyer's desk. "Thank you, Mr. Turner," she said as she stood. "You have been a great help. And you have given me a great deal to think about. I suspect I'll be back in touch with you soon."

"Good day to you, Mrs. Maddox," Turner said as he escorted her to the door. "Please feel free to call on me anytime."

"Good day, sir. And thank you again," Mary said as she stepped outside.

Instead of turning right toward the fence where her horse and two-seater carriage were tethered, Mary turned left and began to walk in the other direction. After picking her way carefully along the rutted lane and around the piles of horse manure, and threading her way through the crowds, she stopped in front of the courthouse. The sight should have reassured her, she thought. The solid redbrick structure, with the impressive white doorway and the imposing wood and leaded glass steeple standing watch over the small village, had always seemed so powerful, so symbolic of the notions of fairness and justice. And yet, even though she knew completely in her heart that her Samuel would never have left his nephew in control of any part of his estate, Zephania Turner could not provide her with the absolute assurance that she would win her case inside that building. Probably, he had said, but not definitely.

So then, she asked herself as she gazed at the courthouse, *what do I do now?*

CHAPTER 19

"*I*S YOUR MISTRESS AT HOME?" MARY ASKED THE YOUNG SLAVE GIRL.

"Yes'm," the girl answered as she pulled the great carved oak door open and stepped aside to let Mary enter.

"Thank you," Mary said, stepping into the spacious center hall, which ran the length of the house.

The girl gestured toward a set of double doors that opened into the sitting room, but Mary shook her head.

"Thank you, but I'll just wait here for her."

The girl nodded and then scampered up the curved, cascading staircase to fetch her mistress.

Fanny Withers appeared a moment later and glided swiftly down the stairs to greet her.

"Mary," she exclaimed, obviously delighted to see her friend. "I'm so happy you're here. Why didn't you let me know . . . ?" Her voice trailed off as she noticed Mary's somber, worried expression.

"I'm sorry to just barge in like this," Mary said hesitantly.

"Nonsense. Are you all right?" Fanny asked, clasping Mary's hands in hers.

"I'm not sure," Mary answered, her eyes flitting about the hallway. "I'm not sure," she repeated.

"Here, come and sit with me and we can talk," Fanny said solicitously, putting her arm around Mary's shoulders and turning her in the direction of the sitting room.

Mary resisted and turned toward the front door. "Could we talk outside?"

"Certainly," Fanny said, puzzled, as she placed her arm inside Mary's and guided her out the door. They crossed the veranda, descended the sweeping porch steps, and walked toward a nearby stand of trees.

Fanny led them into the small grove, toward a wrought-iron bench. The grove was the Withers family grave site, a manicured lawn set beneath a canopy of gracious elms, dotted with a platoon of headstones, most smudged and worn by time and the elements, marking the final resting places of generations of family members.

"Let's sit here," Fanny said, easing Mary down onto the bench.

They sat silently for a few moments, Fanny waiting patiently for her friend, as Mary was clearly wrestling with her thoughts. Finally, Mary squared her shoulders and spoke.

"I think I have to leave," Mary said.

"But you just got here," Fanny protested, bewildered.

"I mean, I have to leave the farm. Leave Virginia."

"I don't understand," Fanny said, shaking her head. "Why would you have to leave here? Leave your home?"

Mary took a deep breath and looked off into the distance. "I met with Zeph Turner, the lawyer, about Sam's claims that he has some right to Samuel's estate," she began hesitantly.

"And?" Fanny prodded.

Mary turned now to face her friend. "And he said he thought that, push comes to shove, I'd win in court."

"But that's good, isn't it?" Fanny asked.

"Yes . . . but he couldn't guarantee it. Said we'd *probably* win, but he was a little worried by some language that's a bit unclear. And that was the problem."

"What kind of language? And what does it mean?" Fanny asked.

"Language that, if a court agrees with Sam, gives him a say in anything I'd want to do with the estate. With the land. The property. The slaves. Everything. Heard he's already tried to pledge the slaves as collateral for some of his debts."

"But if Mr. Turner thinks that you'll win . . . ," Fanny began, trying her best to sound reassuring.

"*Thinking* I'll win is a whole bunch different from being *certain* that I'll win," Mary said, exasperated. "A whole bunch different. I don't know that I can run the risk—however small—of losing if that means Sam gets his hands on everything."

"Don't see that you've got much of a choice," Fanny answered. "Seems like you've got to trust that the court'll do the right thing. And Zeph Turner's a good lawyer—and a good man. I think you can trust him. Besides," she added, "what other choice do you have?"

"There is another choice," Mary said soberly.

Fanny stared at her quizzically, her eyebrows raised.

"I can leave here. Not for good. But just for now. Before a court gets involved."

"What? Leave here?" Fanny asked. "Why? And go where?"

"I've thought this through very carefully," Mary said. "And I think it's the only answer. I've got to leave here and take Kitty and her children with me. Go someplace where I can set her free. And then I can come back and deal with Sam."

"But how can running away be the answer?" Fanny pleaded. "Sam will surely come looking for you. And what about the court? You'd be violating a court order. How do you ever come back and not go to jail?"

Mary took a deep breath and continued. "You know that I've decided to free Kitty and her children, and you know why. I've tried to make my peace with her over selling off her mother, and I've promised her that I will never let the same thing happen to her and her family. But if Sam got some control over the estate, you can bet that he'd sell her and those children without givin' it a second thought. Especially if he's hard up for cash. And if there's even the remotest chance of a court ruling in his favor, I just can't wait around and let that happen."

Fanny thought for a moment. "Have you told Kitty yet? About planning on setting her free?"

Mary nodded. "I told her. And I told her why, about how sorry

I am that we sent her mother away. And how I will never let that happen to her again."

"And?"

"Don't think she believes me yet," Mary said, shaking her head ruefully. "Why should she? After what I did to her? But that's exactly why I can't run the risk of losing," she added, her jaw clenching. "I can't allow that to happen to her again. And this time, I won't. I'll do whatever I have to do—if it means leaving everything—to free her. Whatever I have to do!"

"Have you talked this over with the lawyer?" Fanny asked.

Mary shook her head. "I don't want anyone else to know about this. Besides, I can't imagine he'd advise me that it's all right for me to ignore a court injunction and just run away," she said.

"So, what will you do about coming back after you've freed Kitty?" Fanny asked.

Mary offered a grim smile. "I've decided I'd rather ask for forgiveness later, when I return, than ask for permission now."

Fanny shook her head. "This just doesn't seem right."

Mary began to speak, but Fanny held her hand up to silence her.

"Wait. Just listen to me a minute," Fanny insisted. "I understand your feelings about Kitty. And what you did to her and her mother. I truly do. But," she added, exasperated, "you can't just throw your whole life away because of what happened years ago."

Again, Mary tried to interrupt, but Fanny stopped her.

"Let me finish. Please! Mary, you can't just go running off and freeing slaves just like that. Not when a court tells you to hold on. Even if you think it's the right thing to do." Fanny paused, struggling with her thoughts, and took Mary's hands in hers. "Maybe it seems like it's the right thing. For you and for Kitty. But you can't just ignore the law and go running off. You do that, makes you no better'n those abolitionists up north, who want to come down here and steal our slaves so they can set them free!"

"But this is different," Mary insisted.

"Maybe to you it is. But to most everyone else round here, it's not going to look that way. Mary," Fanny implored, "this is our way of life. This is who we are. What'll my slaves—and everybody else's slaves—think when they hear that you just up and vanished with Kitty and her children after a court said you need to figure out who owns them? What kind of message will that send? Folks round her are still on edge after that Nat Turner and his slave mob murdered all those people a few years back. And if they hear that someone like you—someone who's lived and worked here all your life, someone they knew and trusted—up and ran away so she could free some of her slaves, spitting in the face of the law and our traditions, what'll they be thinking? Certainly not gonna be welcoming you back with open arms. And the court might just throw you in jail when you come back."

The women were silent for a moment.

"Is all of that worth it?" Fanny finally asked, exasperated. "Leaving your home? Risking jail? Is *that* what Samuel would have wanted?"

Mary chuckled. "Samuel'd probably say I was a damn fool. And maybe I am. Sure as hell everyone else'll think so. But we ruined Kitty's life once before, when Samuel got rid of her mother. And I'll have to reconcile all that when I face my God sometime soon—sooner than later, I expect. Don't think we're given many chances in this life to make up for our sins—to really make up for them, rather than just saying how sorry we are for committing them in the first place. But I believe—I truly believe—that this is God saying to me, 'Let's just see how truly sorry you are for what you did. And now that you got a chance, what're you going to do about it?' And," she added wistfully, "seems like Kitty and her children are really the only family I got left now that Samuel's gone."

"Well, then," Fanny said after a long silence, "damn it all, I just can't agree with you. I think you're wrong. I think it's a terrible idea and you'll live to regret it." She paused and gave an exasperated shrug. "But you're my friend—my very dear friend—and I'm trying to understand. I really am." Fanny straightened her shoulders and took a deep breath. "I'm deathly afraid we'll both regret this . . . but you've always helped me in my time of need. Really the only one I've been able to count on since my mother died. So I guess now it's my turn. You can count on me," she added, now mirroring her friend's determination. "Whatever you need me to do to make this work. And God help us both!"

The two women embraced.

"So then, tell me about this plan," Fanny said as they separated. "And what I can do to help."

CHAPTER 20

"*R*UN AWAY? ALL OF US? AND YOU, TOO?" KITTY ASKED, HER TONE a mix of anxiety and bewilderment.

They were seated around the small table in Ol' Joshua's cabin. Concerned about the possibility of anyone overhearing any discussion about her plan, Mary had insisted that they meet here, where there was less chance of prying eyes and ears, rather than in the farmhouse.

"I can't see any other way," Mary said firmly, looking first at Kitty and then at Ol' Joshua. "If we stay, there's a chance that a court will rule against me. And if that happens, I might not be able to protect you. Or the children. Knowing Sam, first thing he'd do is go sellin' you off to pay down his debts. Probably then try to sell the farm, too." She shook her head. "Can't risk that."

"But where would we go? And how would we get there?" Kitty asked.

"I've worked out a plan, with Miss Fanny's help. She's the only other person—other than us here—who knows what we're doing. And it must stay that way. Nobody else can know!"

Both Kitty and Ol' Joshua nodded solemnly.

"We need to leave within the next few days. We'll all travel together. Fanny's giving us a horse and carriage that should be able to carry us and the children and some belongings. But we can't take much."

"The first few days'll be the mos' dangerous," Ol' Joshua said. "Lotsa folks'll be lookin' for you. Lookin' hard." It was apparent he was still not convinced that all of them running away was a good idea. "Where y'all go first?"

"We've laid out a route. At least for the start of the trip. Fanny has spoken—in confidence, of course—to someone who's familiar with these things and is going to provide us with the names of folks who are willing to help. Provide us with food and shelter."

Kitty and Ol' Joshua shot each other a suspicious glance.

"Why's Miss Fanny so anxious to help us?" Kitty said. "She owns more slaves than anyone round these parts. I know she's your friend and all, but just doesn't make much sense that she'd want to help other slaves to run off. What if word gets out that she's helpin' us? Can't be good for her!"

"Because she is my friend. And because she knows how important this is to me," Mary said, looking directly at Kitty.

"So, then," Kitty asked after a moment, "where we headin'?"

"First stop will be a church outside Warrenton," Mary said. "Eventually, we'll head to Pennsylvania. Once we get there, we'll figure out how to go about settin' you all free."

After Kitty and Ol' Joshua exchanged quick glances, Mary said knowingly, "Suppose that's where you were headin' when you ran off?"

Kitty nodded.

"We'll be told when we get there where we'll go next," Mary continued. "Apparently, there's a number of secret routes— names and places—that're used for these escapes. Whole journey even has a name, I'm told. Called the Underground Railroad. Not a real railroad, mind you, but rather places—mostly churches and homes, especially Quaker homes—where folks'll hide you and look after you before passing you on to the next stop."

Mary shot a curious look at Ol' Joshua. "Do you know about all of this, Joshua? About this Underground Railroad?" she asked.

The old man just shrugged enigmatically, his ancient, sad, rheumy eyes revealing nothing.

"But can all these people be trusted?" asked Kitty. "I've seen the signs posted all over, offerin' money—lots of money—for help capturin' runaway slaves. Why would these folks— strangers who don't know us from Adam—want to help us when they could be

makin' lots of money by turnin' us in?" She paused. "Don't make
no sense."

Mary looked again to Ol' Joshua. "Joshua?" she said.

But the old man simply shrugged once again.

"Fanny's been assured that these folks'll look after us. That we
can trust them. Many of them have been doin' this for years,
helpin' slaves escape to the North. They're not in it for money.
They won't take anything from us for helpin'. Claim they're doin'
God's work," Mary said, with a touch of skepticism seeping into
her voice.

Kitty looked at Mary carefully, her head cocked quizzically.
"And you're all fine workin' with these people? People who are
hopin' to do away with slavery? People who wanna help steal your
'property' and set your slaves free? To end slavery for good? That's
all fine with you?" Kitty asked reproachfully. "And with Miss Fanny?"

Mary said nothing for a time and stared into the fireplace, almost as if she had not heard Kitty's questions. Finally, she spoke,
her eyes still locked on the dancing flames and sparking embers.

"I don't know," she said quietly. "A month ago, I probably
would've said that those people were meddlers and should be arrested and thrown in jail. Whether you believe in slavery or not,
it's the law down here. It's our way of life. Don't know if it's ever
gonna change—even if deep down I think it should. But until it
changes, the law says if you help take someone else's property,
you should be punished. But now . . ." Her voice trailed off. After
a moment, she looked into Kitty's eyes, and a small, almost sad
smile etched itself across her face.

"But now," she continued, "I don't care about slavery or state's
rights or anything else. I don't care about our way of life or what
my neighbors will think of me. I care only about getting you and
the children away to a safe place. Someplace where Sam and the
Virginia courts can't get their hands on you." She sighed. "So, yes,
I'm fine with them helpin' us."

"And what happens if we get caught?" asked Kitty.

"We can't let that happen," said Mary.

CHAPTER 21

*I*T WAS NEARING MIDNIGHT WHEN THE CARRIAGE, DRAWN BY A SINGLE horse, drove up the drive to the Maddox farm. Fanny Withers sat on the front seat, reins in hand, and skillfully guided the horse to a stop at the front porch. The carriage was beautifully crafted, with spring-cushioned wheels meant for comfortable traveling, not for farmwork. A passenger compartment, with facing leather seats that could hold four passengers, sat behind the driver's seat, partially enclosed by a wood-framed, canvas-covered roof and open sides. A saddled horse was tied to the rear of the carriage.

Mary was waiting on the porch. The farm, including the main house and the slave cabins, seemed retired for the night, the buildings dark and silent. Ol' Joshua appeared out of the shifting nighttime shadows and took the reins from Fanny, then wrapped them securely around a porch post. Fanny leapt agilely from the carriage and embraced Mary.

"You're still sure?" Fanny said. "That this is what you want to do?"

Mary nodded decisively. "Want to do. And have to do," she said.

"We should get going quickly, then," Fanny said. "You've got a ways to travel before daybreak."

"Please go get Kitty and the children," Mary said quietly to Ol' Joshua.

The old slave said nothing and disappeared inside the house. A moment later he returned, leading Kitty, who held a sleeping

Arthur in her arms and was followed closely by Eliza Jane and Mary. The girls each carried a small leather satchel, which Ol' Joshua took from them as they stepped onto the porch. Kitty bent down and whispered something to each of them. They both nodded solemnly, eyes wide but determined.

"Come, girls," Fanny said gently as she ushered them down the steps to the carriage and helped them get settled into the back passenger seats. She then took the still sleeping Arthur from Kitty and handed him to the girls.

Mary and Kitty stood on the porch, eyes locked together. Mary appeared anxious and a bit fearful, but Kitty seemed stoic.

"You certain you want to do this?" Kitty asked. "Certain you want to leave all this"—she gestured with her hand toward the farm—"to free us? 'Cause if we leave here tonight, there's no turnin' back. Not for us, anyway," she added ominously, still not absolutely certain that she could trust Mary if they ran into trouble.

"I've told you," Mary said resolutely. "We are going to do this. Together. It's the right thing to do. What I want—what Samuel wanted. And it's best for you. Now, we need to get going."

As Kitty stepped off the porch, Ol' Joshua, who had tucked the satchels under the passenger seats, approached and wrapped Kitty in his arms. They said nothing and simply held each other in a long embrace. Finally, Kitty pulled away, tears streaming down her cheeks.

Ol' Joshua placed her face between his hands and kissed her lightly on the forehead. "We be seein' you again—me and your aunt Sarah—when the Jubilee come. Till then, you take care of yo'self and them chilluns," he said tenderly.

Choked up by her tears, Kitty could say nothing. She simply smiled sadly, nodded, and turned away toward the carriage. Mary, who had climbed into the driver's box, reached down and helped Kitty climb aboard. The girls had settled into the back seats, wrapped in blankets by Fanny, and were holding the sleeping Arthur in their arms.

After grabbing the reins and untying her horse, Fanny hoisted herself into the saddle and came alongside the carriage.

"I'll ride with you till we get to the turnoff for my place," Fanny said. "I'll leave you there. No sense too many of us being out on the road this late. Only attract attention." She nodded toward the carriage horse as Mary took up the reins. "She's good and steady. Won't be spooked by much. Just take her slow and easy and she'll be fine."

"Sounds like you're talkin' about me—not the horse," Mary said, with an awkward grin.

Fanny offered an unconvincing smile in return. "You just be careful and keep in mind everything we planned. Y'all will be fine."

"Fanny," Mary began, her voice cracking. "Thank you . . ."

Fanny raised her hand. "No need to be thankin' me now. Plenty of time for that when you get back. Y'all just be real careful, now." She hesitated a moment and then looked at Kitty. "Kitty, you be careful, too," she said a bit stiffly. "And take good care of your mistress."

Kitty nodded but said nothing.

Fanny clucked softly to her horse, turned, and cantered off into the darkness. Mary slapped the reins of the carriage horse, tugged its head around, and they trotted after Fanny, away from the farmhouse and down the drive.

Ol' Joshua stood transfixed for a few seconds and then disappeared into the night.

As the small procession traveled away from the farmhouse, the door to one of the slave cabins was cracked open a few inches, and a candle inside flickered. Seconds later, the light blinked out as the door closed silently.

CHAPTER 22

THE TWO HORSEMEN GALLOPED UP THE DRIVE TOWARD THE FARM-house, the horses lathered and panting from a hard ride. It was nearly noon, and the farm slaves, who had just been called in from the fields by Young Joshua for their noontime meal, were gathered around the space in front of their cabins.

The horses, their reins yanked hard, came to a skittering halt, and Sam Maddox, along with the sheriff, jumped to the ground. Maddox spied Ol' Joshua seated among the slaves and walked toward him.

"Joshua," Maddox said sternly as he approached. "Lookin' for your mistress."

The old man looked up briefly from his tin plate of food. " 'Pologies, Mr. Sam. Not sure where Mistress Mary bein' right now," he said as he turned back to his food.

Maddox glanced around at the other slaves, who had all stopped eating and were now shifting around uncomfortably, their attention completely focused on this confrontation. He turned back to Ol' Joshua.

"Funny, 'cause I heard that she ain't here," he said, his voice calm but menacing nonetheless. "Heard that she up and left last night. That she took Kitty and her brood with her." He paused. "That right?"

"Don' know nothin' 'bout that," Ol' Joshua said as he continued eating.

Maddox was silent for a moment as he stared down at Ol' Joshua. Suddenly, his boot flashed through the air, sending the old man's plate of food flying. Maddox swiftly bent down, grabbed Ol' Joshua by the front of his shirt, and yanked him to his feet.

"Listen good, ol' man," Maddox snarled. "Ain't nothin' happen here that you don't know 'bout." He shook the old man violently. "So you best be tellin' me where your mistress's headin'." Maddox shook him again so hard that Ol' Joshua's knees buckled and he collapsed to the ground. Maddox stood over him and raised his fist. "You best tell me now, or this'll be your last day on this earth," Maddox shouted.

Before he could deliver the blow, Young Joshua stepped between them. He was as big as Maddox, and his presence and sheer bulk caused Maddox to take a step back. They glared at each other.

"You best be steppin' aside, boy," Maddox hissed. "If you know what's good for you."

Young Joshua did not move and returned Maddox's glare.

"Sheriff," Young Joshua said calmly. "Don' believe Mr. Sam got any right to beat on this man. Don' belong to him. Belong to Mistress Mary. And he ain' done nothin' to harm Mr. Sam." He turned toward the sheriff. "Sheriff?"

A tense moment passed as no one spoke and the two big men continued to glower at each other. Finally, the sheriff took a step toward the men and placed his hand on Maddox's sleeve.

"Let's go, Sam. She clearly ain't here. We need to find 'em. Sooner we get on the road, better chance we have of trackin' 'em." He tugged gently. "Let's go."

Maddox took a reluctant step back and looked around at the slaves. "Got ten dollars here—cash money—for the first one a you who tells me where Mistress Mary gone to," he said, looking at each of them. "Ten dollars!"

The slaves remained silent, shuffling their feet and avoiding any eye contact. The heavyset female kitchen slave looked for a moment like she was about to speak, but then retreated back into the group without saying a word.

"Ten dollars!" he repeated. "Nobody?"

No one spoke. Finally, Maddox shot an angry look at everyone.

"Y'all can be sure I'll remember this," he said stonily. "And you best be sure I'll remember you," he said, pointing at Young Joshua and flashing an unsettling and malevolent grin. "You an' me ain't finished, boy."

Maddox and the sheriff turned, walked to their horses, and mounted up. Before they galloped off, Maddox looked toward both Young Joshua and Ol' Joshua.

"We ain't finished here. You can bet on that!" he yelled over his shoulder as they bolted away down the drive.

CHAPTER 23

*T*HEY HAD BEEN ASLEEP FOR HOURS, HIDDEN IN A CORNER OF A STOR-age room cleaved out of the rocky ground beneath the church. The trip from the Maddox farm had, fortunately, been uneventful. Fanny had ridden with them for the first mile or so and then had parted ways when she neared her home. The moonlight had slithered in and out of the clouds, providing them with just enough light to navigate the road safely, and they had encountered no other travelers as they journeyed the remaining ten miles to the church outside Warrenton.

The girls had swiftly dozed off in the back of the carriage, and this time, little Arthur had remained asleep for the entire trip. Mary and Kitty did not speak at all, each lost in her own thoughts. And doubts.

When they arrived at their destination, it was nearly dawn. The church was a single-story, whitewashed clapboard structure with double doors in the front and a sagging, shabby bright red steeple perched precariously on the roof. Mary drove the carriage around to the back of the building, where it would be hidden from the sight of anyone traveling along the main road.

"Stay here," Mary whispered to Kitty as she climbed down from the carriage.

It took three rounds of knocking gently on the back door before it was opened. Inside stood an older man clad in a nightshirt, his long gray hair falling to his shoulders, his hand holding a sputtering candle. He had a long, narrow face with deep-set, sleepy eyes. Behind him, peering over his shoulder, was his wife, who was heavyset, wore a sleeping bonnet, and was wrapped in a robe, a concerned look in her eyes.

"Yes? Can we help you?" the man asked.

"I hope that you can," said Mary warily. "I'm seeking shelter for myself and"—Mary stepped aside and gestured toward Kitty— "for this woman and her children. We're beginning a long journey, and I'm told that you might be willing to help us."

The man looked at Kitty and then turned back to Mary. "Are you traveling with them?" he asked.

"Yes," said Mary.

The man seemed puzzled. "For their entire journey?" he asked.

"Yes," answered Mary.

The man turned toward his wife, who, after a moment, nodded to him. He stepped back and swung the door open. "Please come in. All of you," he said.

After Kitty roused the sleepy children, they were all seated at the kitchen table in the cramped living space attached to the rear of the church. The man had introduced himself as Reverend Charles Mortimer, the pastor of the church, and his wife, Martha, had prepared breakfast for the group.

"Where, then, are you heading?" Reverend Mortimer asked cautiously.

"To Pennsylvania," said Mary.

"May I ask why?" he said.

"How much of our story do you want to know, Reverend?" asked Mary, unsure herself about how much she should divulge.

"Well," he said thoughtfully, "I suppose you didn't just stop here accidentally. That you were probably given some . . ." He paused, then continued, "Some instructions about coming here?"

Reverend Mortimer looked pointedly first at Mary and then at Kitty. Both women nodded.

"May I ask what you were told? And by who?" he said.

Kitty spoke first. "My uncle Joshua told me we would find friends here, friends who would be willing to help us along. Friends who would help but not tell anyone about us," she added.

Reverend Mortimer pursed his lips, bobbed his head slowly, and then looked toward Mary. "And may I ask why you've come along?" he said.

Mary wrestled with just how much she should tell him and then decided that if they were going to seek his help, he should know their story. She took a deep breath and then spoke.

"My husband—that is, my late husband—and I have a farm outside Washington. Lived there for about thirty years now. Kitty here has been our slave since she was born. And these are her children. After his death, I decided to free her—to free all of them." She gestured toward the children. "But before I could do that, I ran into a problem."

"What sort of problem?" asked the reverend.

"A troublesome nephew. That's the problem," she said, anger seeping into her voice.

The reverend cocked his head and raised his eyebrows quizzically. "How troublesome?" he asked.

"A great deal," Mary said. "Claims he's entitled to some part of my husband's estate. And would try to sell off some, maybe all, of my property, including Kitty and the children—if he gets his hands on it."

"So you've decided to run away—and take Kitty here with you—before he can do that?" he asked.

"Yes," said Mary.

"And you," he said, turning toward Kitty, "is this what you want?"

"Yes, sir," Kitty answered firmly.

Reverend Mortimer mulled this all over for a few moments and then turned back toward Mary. "I must say, this is a bit unusual. What are you planning to do?" he asked.

"Our plan is to work our way to Pennsylvania, where I can set them all free. Legally. Then, after they're settled, I'll return home," Mary said.

"And how are you planning on getting there?" he asked.

"We're hoping that you can help us with that. Give us some directions." Mary paused and looked directly at both the reverend and his wife. "And perhaps the names of some folks who'd be willing to help us along."

"Would you mind if my wife and I have a private word?" he said. He glanced at his wife and gestured with his head toward the front room. They then retreated for a few minutes to that room, from whence their voices could be heard rising and falling, the words unclear.

When they returned, Reverend Mortimer smiled kindly at the group. "We will be happy to help you," he said, his wife nodding as she stood beside him.

"Thank you," said Kitty fervently, her hands clasped in front of her.

"We appreciate your help. Thank you," added Mary.

"Well, then," said the reverend, "first thing we need to do is have y'all get some rest. Must be pretty tired after traveling all night. Martha here will set up a spot down in the storage area below. A bit dark and damp down there but comfortable enough. And I'll take care of your horse and carriage. Then, after you're rested, we can figure out what's next."

"Come, then," Martha said kindly, reaching for the children. "Y'all need some sleep."

As Martha shepherded the children away, Reverend Mortimer pulled Mary aside.

"This nephew," he said, dropping his voice, "should we be worried that he might be coming after you?"

"Likely he will," Mary said quietly. "Soon as he hears we're gone, I'd expect he'd come lookin' for us. Not the type to give up easy. Not when money's involved."

"Well, then," Reverend Mortimer said, giving her a knowing glance, "we need to take some precautions. I'll hide the horse and the carriage. But you'll need to be sure the children stay quiet down there. Especially if we get any visitors," he added ominously.

CHAPTER 24

*T*HE HEAVY THUDDING OF BOOTS ON THE FLOOR OVERHEAD AND THE sound of sharp voices snapped Mary and Kitty awake. The children were all still asleep, exhausted by the nighttime journey and sated by the breakfast feast that Martha Mortimer had provided. The women exchanged anxious glances. One of the voices belonged to Sam Maddox.

It was midday when Reverend Mortimer had responded to pounding on the front doors of the church. Standing outside were Sam Maddox and the county sheriff. Both were armed with shotguns.

The reverend had welcomed them calmly.

"Good afternoon, gentlemen," he said kindly. "Can I be of some assistance?"

The sheriff began to speak, but Maddox interrupted him. "My name's Maddox, and this here's Sheriff Abbott. We're from Rappahannock County. We're chasin' after some runaway slaves, and we think they may've headed this way. We're hopin' you might be able to help us," he said in a pleasant tone, accompanied by a charming smile.

"Well, I'd certainly like to be able to help you gentlemen," Reverend Mortimer said, matching Maddox's friendly demeanor, "but can't say we've seen anyone fitting that description round here. Fact is, you're the first folks we've seen in probably two days." He shrugged. "Sorry we can't be of any assistance."

The sheriff took a step back and looked around the property, while Maddox peered past the reverend into the church.

"Don't s'pose you'd mind us takin' a look around, then," the sheriff stated, more a demand than a question.

Reverend Mortimer shrugged again. "If you'd like."

"Anyone else here with you?" Maddox asked.

"Just my wife. She's round back in the kitchen," the reverend said.

The newcomers nodded to each other and took separate paths around the church building. Reverend Mortimer closed the doors and retreated through the church to the kitchen.

"There're two men outside—sheriff from Rappahannock County and a man named Maddox. Say they're lookin' for some runaway slaves," he said in a slightly louder voice than normal. "Told 'em we haven't seen anyone but they were welcome to take a look around."

A look of alarm shot across Martha Mortimer's face. The reverend patted her reassuringly on the arm.

"They're takin' a look outside now," he added.

The reverend and his wife peeked cautiously out the tiny back window and saw the two men entering the barn behind the church. After a few tense minutes, the men exited the barn and walked toward the house. Hearing the pounding of footsteps on the back porch, Reverend Mortimer opened the door, and Maddox and the sheriff stepped, uninvited, inside.

"As I suggested," Reverend Mortimer began, "been no one around here for a few days." He looked toward his wife. "Might we provide you with something to drink before you leave?"

"Thank you kindly, Reverend, but there's no need to put yourself out," Maddox said, nodding and smiling at Martha. "But we would like to take a look around inside, long as we're here. Sure you wouldn't mind. 'Specially if, like you said, ain't no one been around," he added, a hard edge creeping into his voice.

"Be my guest," the reverend said, gesturing with both hands raised. "Not much here to look at. Bedroom's right there," he said, pointing to a door just off the kitchen. "And that there's the entrance to the church hall," he added, pointing to an open door through which some of the pews of the church could be seen.

The sheriff walked through the door leading to the church hall, while Maddox pushed open the door to the bedroom and stepped inside. A few moments later, both men returned to the kitchen.

"Nothin' in there," muttered the sheriff.

"Nothin' there, either," Maddox said, pointing his chin in the direction of the bedroom.

Maddox was taking one last look around the kitchen when his gaze fell suddenly on a small hinged panel set flush with the floor and located under one of the kitchen chairs. He pointed toward it.

"What's that?" he asked harshly.

Martha spoke up. "Just the entrance to the root cellar," she said casually.

"What's down there?" asked the sheriff.

Martha shrugged. "Just some vegetables we got stored. Some preserves I put up for the winter. And some personal things. Not much."

Maddox shot a look at the sheriff, who shook his head and raised his shotgun. He stepped toward the panel.

"Open it," the sheriff ordered.

The reverend and his wife exchanged glances.

"I said open it," the sheriff demanded.

The reverend hesitated and then stepped toward the floor panel, slid the chair out of the way, grasped the recessed handle, and lifted the small door, exposing a ladder that led down to a darkened area.

Maddox pushed Mortimer aside, raised his own shotgun, and stepped onto the wooden ladder leading down into the cellar, followed closely by the sheriff. Both men took the three steps quickly and landed heavily on the earthen floor. They looked about the small space, shotguns raised, their eyes quickly adjusting to the dark.

The room was empty.

CHAPTER 25

MADDOX AND THE SHERIFF PEERED CLOSELY AROUND THE EMPTY cellar. A slim shaft of daylight shimmered through the open floor panel, and they squinted as their eyes adjusted to the darkness. The back wall, where the ladder was located, and the two side walls were of chiseled and uneven rock. The far wall was made of rough brick and mortar. A number of wooden shelves, which had been hammered into the brick face, held dozens of glass jars containing fruits and jams, together with boxes of vegetables. Scattered across the packed dirt floor were storage boxes and travel valises.

The men peered into the corners of the room, kicking the boxes and valises aside, looking carefully for any signs that someone had been hiding there recently. Finally, Maddox looked at the sheriff, shook his head, and nodded toward the ladder.

As they emerged from the cellar, Reverend Mortimer and his wife were seated at the kitchen table.

"Well?" asked the reverend.

"Well—nothin'," grunted Maddox.

"Not sure why that should surprise you. Told you no one's been here," the reverend said. "And why would you ever think that we might be harboring fugitives?" he added in a hurt tone.

"Just bein' sure," Maddox mumbled, trying to contain his anger. "Thought if someone's lookin' for help, they'd prob'ly look for it in a house of worship."

"I can assure you, gentlemen," Reverend Mortimer added reassuringly, "that we would never do anything that would be deemed wrong in the eyes of God. Never!"

The sheriff looked to the reverend and his wife. "Obliged to you for your time. Hope we didn't put you out none. We'll be leavin' now."

"Not an imposition at all, Sheriff. Please let me see you out," said Reverend Mortimer, standing. He headed through the door and into the church area.

Maddox bowed slightly toward Martha. "Ma'am. Appreciate your hospitality," he said pleasantly as he followed the other men out of the kitchen.

A few moments later, the reverend returned to the kitchen. "They're gone," he said, placing his hands tenderly on his wife's shoulders. She looked up at him, tension still filling her eyes. "Headed off toward Warrenton," he added.

Mortimer took a deep breath and exhaled slowly. He turned and walked out of the kitchen and into the church hall. Martha followed. After reaching the front of the church, he peered out of one of the windows that flanked the double doors. Satisfied that the men were, in fact, gone, he turned and strode to the wooden-planked pulpit that stood in front of the congregation's pews.

After placing both hands on the sides of the pulpit, he pushed. Slowly, the pulpit slid forward, revealing a hinged panel beneath it, similar to the one on the floor in the kitchen. He bent down, grasped the rope handle and pulled. The panel swung back on its hinges, exposing a ladder that led into a darkened space below. Martha lit a candle that sat on the pulpit and handed it to her husband. He took it and began to descend the ladder.

The candle cast a ghostly glimmer around the sepulchre-like space. The room was a mirror image of the one entered into from the kitchen, but smaller and more cramped. Three of its walls were also of carved-out rock, while the wall closest to the ladder was made of brick and mortar. It was actually a false wall, the other side of the brick found in the cellar below the kitchen. Reverend Mortimer had surreptitiously constructed it approximately one year ago, creating a smaller, but safer hiding space. During the following year, it had served its purpose a number of times.

As Reverend Mortimer held the candle above his head, it illuminated two apparitions. Kitty was crouched in one corner, a brick held ready in her hand, while Mary was in another corner, a broken fireplace poker raised above her head. Both were ready to strike.

Reverend Mortimer raised his hand and spoke gently. "Everything's fine," he said. "They're gone. And none the wiser." He nodded toward the makeshift weapons in their hands. "You can put those down now," he added. "Won't be needin' 'em."

Mary straightened and dropped the poker. Kitty stood also but held the brick for a moment longer, panic just starting to fade from her eyes, before she dropped it to the floor.

"Children?" the reverend asked, squinting as he looked around the room.

Kitty pointed to what looked in the semidarkness like a large wrapped bundle. "Still sleeping," she said, sighing. "Never woke up at all."

"Well," said Reverend Mortimer, allowing a smile to creep across his face. "Quite good of them to choose to sleep through that scene. You've trained them well," he said to Kitty.

Kitty offered a wan smile in return.

"Now, then," the reverend said. "Let's get out of this place. Always gives me the chills down here," he added. "We have some planning to do for the next steps in your journey. You'll be needin' to leave tonight, I'm afraid."

CHAPTER 26

*M*ARY SNAPPED THE REINS, AND THE HORSE, WELL RESTED AND FED, stepped from behind the church and trotted out onto the darkened road. Kitty sat beside her, while the children were once again tucked into the back seats, surrounded by blankets and bundles of bread, cheese, ham, and fruit that Martha Mortimer had prepared for them.

Before they left the church, Reverend Mortimer had talked with them about the next leg of their journey. He had insisted that they travel at night whenever possible, to avoid other travelers, who might be curious about the unusual traveling party. If they had to travel during the day, or if they were questioned by anyone they encountered, he advised that it would be best to tell a version of the truth—although not the complete truth, of course. They should simply say, he suggested, that Mary was going to visit friends in Maryland and had decided to bring her personal slave, Kitty, along with her. And Kitty's children had been brought along because Mary was not certain how long she might be staying.

"It's always easier," he said, "to tell a version of the truth than to try to remember the details of a lie that you made up."

They sat at the kitchen table while the reverend drew up a crude map for them to follow.

"Once you leave here, you'll stay on the Warrenton Road for about two miles, till you come to the Old Mail Road, which heads

up north. Follow that for some ten miles or so, till you pass
through a small village. Other side of that village will be a mill. A
mile past that will be a farm—you'll have to look careful 'cause
it's set back a ways from the road. Owned by a Quaker family. Just
tell them I sent you, and they'll take good care of you. Hide you
for the day, then get you on the road again, with new directions."

Kitty looked at him skeptically. "These people just gonna take
us in—in the middle of the night—and hide us?" she asked. "Just
like that? Why do they do that? Risk their own necks? Without
knowin' who we are or anythin' about us?"

Mortimer offered an encouraging smile. "You're not the first
ones they'll be helping," he said. "And, sadly, not the last. Trust
me. We've been doing this for some time now." He reached across
the table and took Kitty's hands in his. "And we wouldn't be
sendin' you there if we weren't sure you'll be safe. They'll look
after you."

"You make it sound like we really are just on a trip to visit
friends," Mary said, sharing some of Kitty's uncertainty.

At that, the reverend's tone and demeanor changed. "Sorry.
You're right. I don't mean to make this sound like you're on a pic-
nic. It *is* dangerous—very dangerous, indeed. Chances are your
nephew's still out there looking for you," he said, inclining his
head toward Mary. He paused and then leaned forward earnestly.
"But I just want you to know that you have friends, friends you've
not met yet, but friends nonetheless, who'll be looking after you.
People who are willing to risk everything"—he looked directly at
Kitty—"to help you find your way to freedom. Because that's what
God wants us to do."

Kitty remained unsure. "Who are these people?" she asked.
"And who're the folks they'll be sendin' us to after them?"

Mortimer shook his head. "Don't know. Don't know them—
only where their farm is—and don't know where you'll be
headin' next. That's the way it all works. You know only about
your leg of the journey—how we move you along. Nothing more.
Safer for everyone that way," he explained.

The reverend looked at both Mary and Kitty and nodded. "Time
to go," he said, standing.

The three of them walked out the back door to where Martha stood. The children were already waiting in the carriage. The reverend shook their hands, while Martha offered a warm embrace to both of the women.

"God bless you," he intoned solemnly as the carriage bounced away, wheels creaking and the horse's harness jangling. "And keep you safe," he added.

Once again, the trip was uneventful. The night was nearly cloudless, allowing the horse to pick its way along the road at a fairly rapid pace. After they had traveled for about thirty minutes, Kitty turned toward Mary.

"Is he?" she asked.

"Is he what?" said Mary, puzzled.

"Is Sam still out there? Lookin' for us?"

Mary thought a moment. "Probably. You and the children are worth a lot of money. And he needs money—badly."

"What happens if he finds us?"

"You heard Reverend Mortimer. The folks along the way will protect us," Mary answered resolutely.

"You're not answering my question," said Kitty adamantly. "What happens if he finds us?"

Mary was silent for a moment and then reached down under their carriage seat. She pulled a small bundle, enclosed in oilskin, out of a cloth haversack and unwrapped it. "Do you know how to use this?" Mary asked, holding up a flintlock pistol.

Kitty took the long-barreled, single-shot handgun from Mary and held it up. The polished walnut stock and blued-steel barrel gleamed in the moonlight. "This Master Samuel's?" Kitty asked, turning the gun over in her hands.

Mary nodded. "He taught me how to shoot this when I was big enough to hold it steady," she said wistfully. "Used to shoot at squirrels. Even hit a few."

She turned toward Kitty. "Good," Mary said. "It's loaded. Need to keep the powder dry." She hesitated and then gave Kitty a steely look. "And we'll use it if we need to."

CHAPTER 27

*R*EVEREND MORTIMER HAD ESTIMATED THAT THE JOURNEY FROM HIS church to the Pennsylvania state line would cover about one hundred or so miles. Traveling mostly by night, he calculated that it should take them approximately seven to ten days, depending on the weather and their luck, to make the trip.

After leaving the Mortimers' church, they had made fairly good time. The Old Mail Road was straight and level, and provided a relatively smooth footing for the horse. They had been able to maintain a good pace, stopping occasionally to let the horse rest and graze in the grass bordering the road. They'd pulled the carriage off the road just once, when Mary thought she saw lights up ahead. After they'd sat quietly in the bordering woods, but no riders had appeared, they continued.

Once they had traveled through a small, darkened village and then passed by the mill that Reverend Mortimer had noted, they began to peer carefully into the darkness, searching for the farm they sought. They were about twenty minutes past the mill when Kitty spoke, concern creeping into her voice.

"Think we missed it?" asked Kitty, squinting into the darkness.

"Don't think so," replied Mary, swinging her head back and forth. "Wish we had asked which side of the road we should be lookin' on. I just hope it's the right place when we go knockin' on the door."

"Uncle Joshua told me the best way to be sure we got the right place is listen to 'em talk. If they're sayin' 'thee' and 'thou,' pretty sure they're Quakers and we should be safe," said Kitty.

Mary nodded thoughtfully. "Ol' Joshua been involved with sendin' Negro folks along this Underground Railroad before?" she asked, her eyes still sweeping the roadside.

Kitty didn't answer.

Mary turned toward her. "Kitty, I'd hope that by now you realize that you can trust me," she said, exasperated. "Good Lord, who knows how many laws I've broken in the past few days? I'm trying to convince you that I'm your friend. That I'll get you safely to someplace where you can be free. If you don't know that by now, and if you still don't trust me . . ." Her voice trailed off, and she shook her head, clearly frustrated.

Finally, after a long quiet moment, Kitty spoke. "I want to trust you. Really do," she said softly. She paused again and then continued. "Yes. Pretty sure he's helped some folks over the years. Wouldn't really talk about it. Think a few times he passed some folks along to Reverend Mortimer."

"Local folks?" asked Mary.

Kitty shook her head. "Don't think so. Not sure, but don't remember any local slaves runnin' off. Least not until I tried," she added with an ironic chuckle.

They rode along in silence, both looking intently for the farm.

"Maybe we did miss it," Mary said.

"Wait," exclaimed Kitty. "There!" She pointed off to their right. "A light. See it?"

Mary squinted, trying to focus in the darkness, looking in the direction indicated by Kitty. At first, she saw nothing. Then there was a fleeting glimmer of light in the distance, like that of a flickering candle.

"I see it," said Mary.

Pulling back on the reins, Mary slowed the carriage as she looked along the road for an entrance to the farm. Finally, just past a grove of trees, she spied a dirt drive and made the turn. As they got closer, the silhouette of a farmhouse emerged from the darkness. The light from a candle dimly illuminated a front window, while the rest of the house still slept, shadowy and silent in the predawn gloom.

Mary tugged on the reins, and the horse came to a halt in the front yard. She clambered to the ground, joints stiff from a night's worth of jolting along in the carriage. Kitty turned to the children, who were fidgeting in the back, anxious to escape after a long night of confinement.

"Please just sit here quietly," she implored. "I'll be right back. Then I'll get you out."

Kitty jumped to the ground and joined Mary, who had knocked on the front door. A minute passed. They heard whispered voices from inside, and then the door was pulled back a few inches. A man holding a candle stared out at them, examining them closely.

"Yes?" he said cautiously.

"We're travelers," Mary began hesitatingly, "looking for some shelter."

The man said nothing.

"We were told," Mary continued, "by a friend that you might be willing to help us."

Finally, the man spoke. "And who might that friend be?" he asked, his voice laced with suspicion.

Mary wavered, fearing now that they might have arrived at the wrong house. She looked at Kitty, who nodded to proceed.

"Reverend Mortimer," Mary said.

The door snapped shut. They could hear voices inside once again, this time louder and more anxious, the words jumbled together and unclear. Then silence.

After a long minute, the door opened again, wide this time, and the man stepped forward, joined by a woman in nightclothes.

"Please come inside," the man said as he glanced nervously past them toward the road.

"Yes, please do come inside," the woman said kindly as she

reached both of her hands out to Mary and Kitty. "We're happy to help thee."

At the sound of the word "thee," Kitty looked at Mary and let a small smile crease her face.

After the children were settled at the kitchen table, with chunks of bread slathered with jam placed in front of them, the man beckoned Mary and Kitty into the front room.

"I'm sorry we didn't come to the door to let thee in sooner," he said apologetically. "But we were fearful, at first, that it was them returning."

"Them?" said Kitty.

"The slave catchers," he said ominously. "Been here earlier in the day. Said they were looking for an escaped slave and her children." He looked pointedly at Kitty. "And that the slaves were traveling with a white woman who was wanted by the law for stealing them away and helping them escape." Now he shifted his gaze to Mary. "Warned us about helping thee and said they'd be back."

Mary and Kitty looked at each other, apprehension in their faces. Mary spoke first.

"How many?" she asked.

"Five," he answered. "Including the man who claimed to be the slave owner."

"Did he use a name?" Mary asked.

The man shook his head. "Didn't offer it, and I didn't ask. A big man—but polite and respectful. Not like the others. Evil, godless men, they were. An aura of the devil about them. Be happy to never see them again."

"Perhaps we should move on," Kitty said. "Don't want to put you in any danger."

Mary nodded her agreement.

The man looked from one to the other and then shook his head vigorously. "No," he said adamantly. "We will take care of thee. It's what God would want us to do," he said, offering a reassuring smile. "Now, let us get thee all fed and then settled in. Thee—and the children—must be exhausted from thy travels."

"But is it safe for us to stay here?" Mary said. "If they might come back?"

The man took a deep breath and exhaled slowly. "There is always danger in life. But the hand of God will guide us," he said reverently. "Thou will be safe. Come, now. We have no time to waste. In case they do return."

CHAPTER 28

KITTY AWOKE FIRST. SHE LISTENED CAREFULLY BUT COULD HEAR NO sounds other than the sleepy, fitful breathing of Mary and the children as they tossed and turned restlessly, struggling to get comfortable in the hollowed-out ground.

Just before dawn, after they had all eaten their fill following their arrival, the man and the woman had escorted them to the barn behind the house.

"Thou will all be safe out here," the woman had said soothingly. "But I'm fearful that your accommodations will be somewhat lacking in comfort," she'd added.

Kitty looked around at the piles of hay and the storage areas. "It looks comfortable enough," she said.

The man shook his head regretfully. "I'm afraid we need to hide thee better than just putting you out here. I'm certain that this is the first place the slave catchers will look if they return."

"So," Mary said, puzzled, "why are we here?"

In response, the man walked to a corner of the barn where a number of bales of hay were stacked. Without saying a word, he took a pitchfork, stabbed it into a bale, and pushed it to one side. He did the same to a second bale and then a third, eventually exposing a hole, cloaked by a heavy sheet of canvas, in the packed earthen floor. After pulling the canvas back, he pointed into the hole.

"In here," he said, with a contrite look. "Warm and dry, with

enough room, and thou will be well hidden—but not very comfortable, I'm afraid."

"We'll bring thee some blankets and pillows, which should help
a bit," the woman added sweetly, looking at the children.

Kitty and Mary climbed into the dugout first. After the children were lowered into the hole, the woman dashed out of the
barn and returned minutes later laden with pillows and blankets,
along with some food and water. As they all settled in below, the
man handed them a storm lantern that contained a lit candle.

"This will last thee awhile," he said and then handed down a
box of matches. "Best to blow it out while sleeping and then re-
light it when thou are awake. We will come get thee at dusk to get
ready for your departure. Get some rest and do not worry. Thou
will be safe," he added.

Mary and Kitty both offered their thanks and then sat down on
the ground as the man pulled the canvas covering across the
opening. They could hear him sliding the bales of hay across the
ground above to conceal the hiding place.

After she awoke, Kitty struck a match and lit the storm lantern.
Startled by the flaring light, Mary sat up quickly, her eyes wide as
she struggled to adapt to the darkness of the dugout. The children, their circadian rhythms having swiftly adjusted to the time
disruptions of their journey, were still asleep, wriggling about in
the warmth of the blankets and pillows, and blessedly unmindful
of the dangers stalking them.

"What time do you think it is?" mumbled Mary, rubbing her
eyes with her palms.

"Not sure," said Kitty. "Feels like nighttime should be comin'
soon."

Mary cocked her head, listening carefully. "Sounds like rain
outside," she said. "Heavy rain."

Kitty listened and then nodded. "Good and bad, I guess," she
said. "Good that the rain'll keep most folks off the road at night.
And bad 'cause we got to be out there on the road, needin' to get
to our next stop by mornin'."

"Wherever that might be," Mary added.

A few minutes later they heard scurrying sounds above them and then the sound of the hay bales being dragged away. When the canvas cover was stripped back, they gently woke the children and handed the still sleepy figures up to their hosts.

"Hope thou were able to rest," said the woman, offering an apologetic half smile.

"And regain thy strength," added the man, glancing out the open barn door at the torrents of rain, punctuated now by cannonades of thunder. "By the looks of this weather, thou will need it traveling tonight."

Mary and Kitty both looked forlornly at the cascading rain. Mary turned to the man and lowered her voice.

"Slave catchers come back?" she asked.

The man shook his head. "Not yet. But I suspect they're still out there. Heard one of them say they'd stay out searching for weeks if need be."

Mary stepped to the door of the barn and looked up at the troubled, dark, and wet sky. "Where will we go from here?" she asked, turning back to the others.

"Be traveling on this road for another twenty miles or so. Probably take roughly two nights to cover it. Tonight thou'll be stopping at another farm about eight miles down the road. Just as well it's not farther away. Won't likely make very good time tonight in this weather."

"How do we find this farm?" asked Kitty, mindful of their struggles the night before.

"Should be easier to spot than we were," the man said. "There's a creek to cross about a mile before the farm. Thou will see the farm then on the right side of the road, behind a long white fence." He thought a moment and then frowned. "Hope the creek's not a problem."

"Why would it be a problem?" Mary asked.

"Sometimes runs over its banks in bad weather. Weather like this," he added. "There's a small stone bridge that should get thou across, though, even if the water's running high."

"So," said Kitty, with a deep sigh and a hint of a sardonic grin, "seems like a perfect night to travel. Torrential rain, overflowing creeks. Not to mention slave catchers lookin' for us at every turn."

The man shot a concerned look at both Mary and Kitty. "Thou will need to be very careful tonight," he warned. "Very careful."

CHAPTER 29

*B*EFORE THEY DEPARTED, THE MAN WHEELED THE CARRIAGE INSIDE the barn, spread a canvas tarpaulin over the top, and tucked it into the sides to provide some additional protection from the torrents of rain. His wife helped the children into the back of the carriage and wrapped them caringly in yet another sheet of canvas. The man then held the horse's reins as Mary and Kitty climbed aboard. They settled into their seats and turned to offer smiles and nods of thanks to their benefactors.

The man and the woman nodded back to them.

"God bless and protect thee on this journey," the man said somberly as Mary flicked the reins and the horse reluctantly stepped out into the downpour.

The rain was worse than they had anticipated, gushing from the sky to pound the carriage, splashing inside to quickly soak all the occupants, despite the protective tarpaulin. The barrage of crescendoing thunder was now accompanied by slashing streaks of lightning, which, combined with the unyielding onslaught of drenching rain, reduced visibility to no more than a few feet.

It took them most of the night to travel the seven miles to the creek and bridge that would place them about one mile from the safety of their next shelter. The rain was relentless. Waves of water assaulted them as the horse gingerly picked its way along the road, mired in ankle-deep sludge. Hoping the fury of the storm would soon abate, they occasionally stopped under a protective canopy of trees, longing for some relief that never came.

As they came around a bend in the road, the rain lessened just a bit, but it was just enough to allow them to see the vague profile of a stone bridge about a hundred yards ahead. Suddenly, Mary jerked hard on the reins, pulling the horse to a sliding stop.

"What's wrong?" asked Kitty.

"Not sure," Mary answered, shielding her eyes with her hand as she leaned forward and stared intently toward the bridge. "Thought I saw something up ahead, near the bridge."

"Slave catchers? Think they'd be out in this? Still lookin' for us?" Kitty asked anxiously.

"Can't tell," answered Mary, still squinting into the watery darkness.

"Best we check it out first," Kitty said. "Pull the carriage off the road . . . there!" she declared abruptly, pointing to a small clearing. "I'll go ahead to see."

Mary looked at Kitty in alarm but followed her directions and guided the horse into the open space.

"But if it is them . . . ," Mary began as she reined the horse to a stop.

"Won't see me. Not in this," Kitty said confidently, gesturing to the sky. "I'll stay off the road, keep to the woods. Can't afford to take the risk and try crossin' that bridge if it might be them waitin' for us."

Mary nodded reluctantly. She placed her hand on Kitty's arm. "Be careful," Mary said.

Kitty nodded back and then turned toward the children in the rear of the carriage. They were completely soaked by the storm, despite the efforts to keep them covered by the tarpaulin.

"Need y'all to be really good and stay very quiet for Mistress Mary. Be back in just a few minutes," she said, forcing a wooden smile as she touched each child on the cheek.

Kitty leaped down from the seat, landed in a sea of mud, and began to cautiously negotiate her way through the trees and bushes along the edge of the road. Within seconds she had disappeared, ghostlike, from the sight of the horse and carriage.

It took her a few minutes to wend her way to a spot in the bordering undergrowth where she had a clear view of the bridge. She squatted down beside a dense cluster of evergreen bushes and peeked around a thick tree. For a moment she could see nothing other than the outline of the stone bridge. She had just let out a quiet sigh of relief when her heart jumped.

A figure stepped out from a larger outcropping of stone at the edge of the bridge, which provided a shallow, protected niche. The figure glanced down the road in both directions and then swiftly retreated back into his rocky shelter.

Kitty withdrew from her hiding place and silently retraced her muddy steps back to where the carriage was hidden. As she stepped out from the heavy foliage, Mary shot her an apprehensive look.

"Someone's up there just waitin'," Kitty said in a hoarse whisper. "Must be lookin' for us. No other reason to be out in this."

"Feared as much," Mary answered. "Guess we need to find another way," she added decisively.

"Think I found one," Kitty answered.

Mary looked at her, eyebrows raised questioningly.

"On the way back, I saw a path just up ahead. Looked like it led down toward the creek. Might be a ford there where we can cross," Kitty said.

Mary thought a minute. "Worth a try," she finally said. "Sure can't stay here. And daylight'll be comin' soon."

Kitty grabbed the horse's bridle and tugged. "I'll lead the way," she said as the horse grudgingly followed her back onto the sodden road.

Fortunately, the opening to the path lay just a few feet up the road from where the carriage emerged. Kitty quickly and firmly guided the horse off the road and onto the path. It took just a few minutes of coaxing the now exhausted and frightened animal through the woods before they burst out of the trees and shrubbery and into a small clearing next to the creek, downstream and out of sight of the bridge.

Kitty yanked the horse to a halt and turned, panic stricken, toward Mary.

The shallow, meandering creek had been transformed by the storm into a roiling, rushing wall of foaming water.

CHAPTER 30

*T*HE TWO WOMEN LOOKED AT EACH OTHER, DREAD IN THEIR EYES. Attempting to cross at the bridge was out of the question. And the protective cloak of darkness would disappear soon, as the leading edge of dawn approached. They had to get across the creek and find the sanctuary of their next destination. And they had to do it quickly.

"We need to cross here," Kitty shouted. "Now! Before it gets any higher."

The roar of the churning water made it difficult to hear.

"What?" yelled Mary.

"Here! We need to try to cross here! Now!" Kitty shouted back, gesturing toward the rising water.

Mary stared at Kitty and then at the water, all the while shaking her head. "Can we get across?" she asked.

"Have to try," Kitty urged. "No other choice."

Mary thought for a second and then set her jaw and nodded forcefully. "Get in!" she shouted.

Kitty bounded back up onto the seat and turned to make sure the children were packed securely in the rear of the carriage. "Both of you," she yelled to Eliza Jane and Mary, "grab on tight to each other and to Arthur."

The girls shook their heads in response, wide-eyed and mute with fright, and wrapped their arms around each other and their little brother.

"Good!" Kitty said. "Now hold on!"

Mary cracked the reins, but the terrified horse balked, digging its rear hooves into the muddy creek bank. Mary flailed away again, trying desperately to get the horse to move out into the rising watery surge, but it refused to budge, now trying to rise up on its hind legs in protest.

Kitty leaped to the ground.

"Throw me your shawl," she shouted to Mary as she grabbed the horse's bridle and harness.

Mary ripped her soaked shawl from her shoulders and tossed it down. Kitty snatched it out of the air and wrapped it around the horse's face, covering its eyes and blinding it completely to the terrifying scene playing out in front of them. Then she began to tug, pulling the horse forward as Mary snapped the reins furiously.

Slowly, the animal began to move, taking small, mincing steps at first as it entered the water, then more powerful strides as it began to battle the tide. The water rose quickly as the carriage lurched forward, first covering the wheel hubs and then creeping up over the rims. Kitty grasped the bridle tightly and heaved frantically, desperate to hang on and to keep the horse moving, trying to keep her footing on the slippery creek bottom as the surging flow of water tore at her.

Midway across the creek the horse balked for a second time, frightened as it lost its purchase and was pushed sideways with the surge before it once again gained its footing. The water level had swelled upward and the water was now just inches away from spilling into the carriage. Mary urged the horse on while Kitty pulled with all her strength.

The churning tide had reached Kitty's shoulders, and she struggled not to swallow any water as it lashed her face. Suddenly, she stepped into a hole in the creek bed and lost her balance. The rushing white water dragged her under, and she thrashed about, fighting to keep a grip on the bridle, which was now her only lifeline.

As she struggled, heaving on the leather straps, the horse raised its head in protest. Its powerful neck muscles hauled Kitty up, and she sputtered and gasped for breath as she strained desperately to regain her balance. Wrapping her arms around the horse's head, she could see Mary perched on the edge of the carriage seat, ready to jump into the water. Kitty waved her away.

The horse had stopped mid-stream, confused by the drag of Kitty's floating body pulling it downstream and terrified by the force of the battering water. Kitty knew that if she didn't get the horse moving again immediately, they would all be swept away. She gripped the bridle tightly, and forced her legs down into the water, hoping to touch the creek bed.

When she stretched her legs downward, her feet barely touched the bottom, but this afforded just enough traction for her to force herself ahead of the horse and begin to pull once again, jerking the frightened animal's head in the direction of the far shore. The horse responded, sensing the mounting peril and the safety just a few feet ahead, and plunged forward, now towing Kitty along with it. After the horse took three powerful strides, Kitty could feel the ground beneath her rising and saw that the water level had dropped below the rails of the carriage. Mary now stood in the carriage seat, whipping the reins and urging the horse onward. After two more strides, the carriage rose out of the water, water cascading from all sides, and bounded up onto the safety of the shore.

Kitty staggered out of the water and collapsed to the ground.

CHAPTER 31

MARY HEAVED BACK ON THE REINS, PULLING THE FRIGHTENED and frenzied horse to an abrupt sliding halt. She scrambled down from the carriage, hastily tied the reins to a nearby tree, and raced to where Kitty lay on the muddy bank.

By the time Mary reached her, Kitty had risen to her hands and knees and was retching violently, coughing up water she had swallowed during her battle in the creek. Mary knelt next to her and cradled her head. After a few nerve-wracking minutes, the retching stopped. Kitty rolled onto her side and then sat upright, struggling to gulp down deep draughts of air.

"Are you all right?' Mary asked, pushing Kitty's dripping hair from her face.

"Think so," Kitty muttered, still spitting out water.

"Can you stand?"

Kitty nodded uncertainly.

Mary wrapped her arms around her and helped her to stand. They stumbled to the carriage, slipping in the mud, Mary supporting and guiding her. The children were all watching anxiously. When they reached the carriage, Kitty stretched her hand up and touched the face of each of the three children to assure them that she was fine and they were all now safe. Mary carefully boosted her up onto the seat, then untied the reins and clambered up herself.

The rain had not diminished at all during their ordeal, still an unrelenting, solid curtain of water that obscured their vision and hid much of the path before them.

"If we can follow this," Mary said, raising her voice to be heard above the tempest and pointing her chin toward the murky path, "it should bring us back to the road. Hopefully far enough away from the bridge," she added.

Kitty nodded her agreement, still too exhausted to talk.

"I thought we'd lost you," Mary said gently, taking Kitty's hand in hers.

Kitty offered a thin, exhausted smile and squeezed Mary's hand.

CHAPTER 32

THE CHILDREN WERE SOUND ASLEEP, WRAPPED IN BLANKETS AND tucked away in a corner of the loft in the barn, surrounded by bales of hay and farm equipment. It was not as secure as the two previous hiding places on their journey, but they hoped that the ferocious rainstorm would help to keep them safe by keeping the slave catchers off the road for a time. And it was dry.

The Quaker couple had responded quickly to their knock on the front door of the farmhouse and had welcomed the spent and sodden travelers warmly. Hot broth and warm bread had restored their energy and their spirits, at least a bit, while their drenched clothes had been dried before the glowing fire in a massive hearth. Once they had all been settled in the concealed alcove, the physically and emotionally exhausted children had fallen asleep instantly.

Mary and Kitty were still awake, sitting in the darkness, propped up against a bundle of hay, the adrenaline rush that had fueled their escape from the near fatal grasp of the swollen creek not yet sufficiently diminished to allow sleep to visit them. They sat quietly, savoring the warmth of their dried clothes and the thick woolen blankets that enveloped them, oddly calmed by the sounds of the moaning wind and the heavy drumming of rain on the barn roof.

Mary was the first to speak and break the comfortable spell.

"Didn't know you could swim," she said softly.

"Can't," answered Kitty.

Mary sat upright. "Can't?" she exclaimed. "Then what were you doing jumping into the water like that? You could've drowned!"

"Somebody had to," Kitty said, shrugging. "You were busy drivin' the wagon, so I figured it had to be me."

They stayed silent for a few more minutes. Then Kitty spoke.

"When I went under and then got dragged back up by the horse, it looked like you were fixin' to jump in after me," she said.

"I was," Mary answered.

Again, silence.

"Didn't know you could swim," Kitty finally said.

"Can't," answered Mary.

In the darkness, the corners of Kitty's mouth turned up in a faint smile. After a few more minutes of quiet, Kitty turned toward Mary, reached out, and touched her sleeve gently.

"Still don't understand why," Kitty said.

"Why what?" asked Mary.

"Why you're doin' all this," said Kitty. "I mean, I understand what you said about feelin' guilty about sendin' my mother away. And I believe you now. I really do." Kitty paused, struggling with her thoughts. "But why you doin' all this?" she continued, waving her hands and gesturing around them. "Hidin' out in barns and cellars. Sneakin' about in the dead of night. Nearly drownin'."

Kitty paused again, shaking her head. "Setting us all free is one thing," she said, again gesturing around them. "But this—runnin' away with us and hidin' out—this is somethin' different altogether. This could get you arrested." She dropped her voice low and continued. "Could even get you killed."

Mary said nothing in response. At first, Kitty thought that she had fallen asleep. Then Mary began to speak, in a hushed tone so soft that Kitty could barely hear her.

"I'm goin' on sixty years old. Got no family, no brothers or sisters. And no children," she added, the pain obvious in her voice. "When Samuel passed, I realized that now I was all alone. An awful feelin', bein' all alone in this world. I mean, I got some friends, of course, but that's different. Not the same as blood relatives, folks who you share some history with, folks who'll feel somethin' missin', some kind of empty hole when you're gone. Realized I didn't have any of that."

Mary sighed deeply and then continued. "Then I started thinkin' about you. About Samuel bein' your daddy. And I realized somethin'. I realized that, just like me, you didn't have any brothers or sisters. No parents left alive. No family, other than your children. And I realized that maybe this was part of God's plan. That maybe he was sayin' to me that if I was truly sorry for the terrible thing I did to you and your mama—and if I could find your forgiveness—that maybe my salvation would be to start a new family. With you and the children." She paused and then continued gently. "So that's why I'm doin' all this. Because that's what you do for your family."

After a moment, Kitty spoke.

"You know, I named her after you," she said.

"What?" said a puzzled Mary.

"My little Mary. I named her after you. Thought it might've made you more willin' to deal with me and where I came from. Be a little more acceptin' of me still bein' around."

"I . . . I didn't realize . . . ," Mary began, but her voice trailed away.

Kitty said nothing more. She simply shifted closer and laid her head on Mary's shoulder. Within a few minutes, they were both fast asleep.

CHAPTER 33

*T*HEY HAD DECIDED TO REMAIN AN EXTRA DAY. ALTHOUGH NOT MOVing on immediately carried with it certain dangers, the fierce storm had not yet subsided, and they all had agreed that after their ordeal, the food, rest, and warmth would do them all good. And perhaps the additional time hiding out in one location might place more distance between them and the relentless slave catchers. The Quaker couple was only too happy to care for them for one more day.

When they ventured out from their refuge the following night, the carriage brimming with new bundles of food to replace the soggy ruins of the provisions that had accompanied them through the storm, the rain had finally come to an end. The night sky was clear, and the air was crisp and blessedly dry. They thanked their new friends warmly for their care and protection and set off again, following the directions they had been given to the next stop on their clandestine journey.

The night passed without incident, and they arrived at the stopover, yet another farm owned by another Quaker couple, just before dawn. After spending the day sleeping in a root cellar dug into the side of a hill about a dozen yards from the farmhouse, they resumed their travels, with directions to a gristmill near the intersection of the road they had been following and the Old Carolina Road, which would eventually carry them into Maryland.

Just after dawn had arrived, they found the gristmill on the banks of a rushing stream that fed into the Potomac River a few miles away. The owners, a Dutch couple who spoke broken English but welcomed them enthusiastically with hugs and hot food, got them settled in a distant storage shed just minutes before the mill workers began to arrive for work. They promised to return at the end of the day with more supplies and their new directions.

As evening arrived, the couple returned, carrying a basket stuffed with cheese, sausages, and bread for their guests to take with them. This time, however, they were not as cheerful as earlier. The husband, in his heavily accented English, told them that two men—rough-looking men who he assumed were slave catchers—had arrived at the mill earlier and had passed around to the workers and customers flyers offering a five-hundred-dollar reward for the capture of four runaway slaves—a woman and her children—and a white woman who had aided them in their escape. With a troubled look on his face, he thrust a sheet of paper into Mary's hands. She took a moment to read it and then showed it to Kitty.

FIVE-HUNDRED-DOLLAR REWARD

Ran away from the farm of S. Maddox, near Washington, Rappahannock County, Virginia, FOUR NEGRO SLAVES—KITTY, a mulatto-skin NEGRO woman aged about 25 yrs old and 5 feet 8 inches tall, and 3 children; ELIZA JANE, aged about 5 yrs old, a light-skin NEGRO girl child; MARY, aged about 4 yrs old, a light-skin NEGRO girl child; and ARTHUR, aged about 2 yrs old, a light-skin NEGRO boy child. They were last seen traveling in a one-horse carriage, accompanied by MARY MADDOX, a WHITE WOMAN aged about 60 yrs old. They are believed to be heading toward the PENNSYLVANIA border.

The above reward will be paid for their arrest or capture.

SAMUEL MADDOX
Washington, Virginia

Kitty handed the paper back to Mary, her eyebrows raised questioningly. "Now what?" Kitty asked.

Mary shrugged, trying to appear unconcerned. "Should've known this would happen," she said. "They're not gonna just let us walk away. Need to be more careful, that's all. And get to where we're goin' faster." She turned back to the mill owner. "So, where're we headin' now?"

The man shook his head, obviously anxious. "Next stage is a little tricky," he said. "You'll take the Old Carolina Road, which is right over yonder"—he pointed to the road—"a few miles to the Potomac river. A covered bridge takes you across the river to Point of Rocks, in Maryland. Once you cross, you'll still be on the Old Carolina Road. That'll take you through Frederick. Your next stopover is a few miles past the town."

"Why is that tricky?" Kitty asked. "Sounds pretty simple."

The man shook his head again, more vigorously this time. "Problem is that you can't make it all the way from here to the next stop during the night. Too far to go before the sun rises."

"So?" said Mary. "What do we do?"

"This is the part that could be difficult," he said. "Not a good idea for you to camp out somewhere before you reach town. Not with those men around looking for you. You'll have to travel through Frederick in daylight. Should be right after dawn, though, if you make good time tonight. So probably not many folks awake and about. Just pass through quick as you can and hope nobody sees you. About five miles out of town, there's a Quaker meetinghouse, a two-story white building. The back door'll be open, and someone will be waiting for you."

Mary and Kitty exchanged a worried glance.

"Remember," Mary said. "Anybody asks, we're just traveling to Emmitsburg to visit friends."

Kitty nodded, her confidence returning.

"You need to be going, then," the man said.

"God bless you all," the woman said, taking a moment to embrace each of them in turn.

"And God speed," the man added gravely.

CHAPTER 34

FROM ACROSS THE POTOMAC RIVER, POINT OF ROCKS LOOKED EXACTLY as it sounded. An enormous outcropping of jagged stone that seemed to have been haphazardly hewn from the surrounding cliffs by some colossal chisel, it presided over one of the narrower spans of the river. A covered bridge provided passage above the coursing white water, conveying travelers from Virginia into Maryland.

Darkness had settled in completely by the time they approached the bridge. There was a half-moon that occasionally ducked behind a tapestry of scudding clouds, providing just enough milky light to guide them along the road. They had seen no other travelers as yet, and as they peered through the dim, shadowy darkness of the covered passageway, there did not seem to be anyone else crossing the river.

The planking of the bridge groaned and clattered as the horse cautiously stepped onto the span, which was nearly thirty feet above the Potomac. Midway across, the horse began to balk as the sound of the rushing water below became louder, echoing off the wooden walls.

As Mary wrestled with the reins, Kitty leaped down from the carriage and, gripping the bridle, began to coax the horse along, offering a chorus of soothing words to accompany the tugging on the leather bridle.

Finally, they reached the other side of the bridge, and the

horse, now calm, trotted onto the Maryland side of the Old Carolina Road. Hours later, as they could see the first purple-pink imprints of dawn along the edge of the eastern horizon, the town of Frederick emerged from the brightening sky ahead of them.

The Old Carolina Road passed directly through the center of town, which was lined with storefronts, stables, warehouses, and a few homes. Frederick, given its location near the Virginia-Maryland border and close to a number of growing towns, had become a crossroads for travelers and a market town for nearby residents. Usually bustling with commerce and voyagers, as dawn arrived, the town was still slumbering, with no one in sight.

"Who are we goin' to visit? In Emmitsburg?" Kitty asked. "In case anyone asks."

"Don't really know anyone there," Mary answered musingly. "Have to make up a name. Say it's a cousin I haven't seen in a long while. Just let me do all the talkin', if we have to."

Kitty nodded as she glanced around the street, trying to appear casual and to suppress her surging anxiety. *Would be just my luck,* she thought, *if we made it through the dangers of rainstorms and raging creek waters, only to be recognized and captured on a sunny morning in this pleasant little town.*

Mary kept the horse cantering along, anxious to exit the town but not wanting to be traveling at such a speed that they would attract any attention. The children were slumped down in the rear seat, covered with blankets, only their heads visible, and Mary kept her gaze focused straight ahead.

As they neared the end of town, the front door of a two-story boardinghouse that faced the road banged open, and a squat, disheveled man dressed in shabby, mismatched trousers and jacket, a battered black derby perched on his head, stepped outside, striking a match and applying the flame to a narrow cigar hanging out of the side of his mouth.

At first, the man paid no attention to the carriage as it approached, but then, after he furrowed his brow in brief thought, he turned and surveyed it carefully as it passed by. After nearly leaping down the two steps of the front porch, he shambled as quickly as his stumpy legs could carry him to the front doors of the saloon across the street and reached for a piece of rough paper that had been nailed to the door frame. The words *five-hundred-dollar reward* were emblazoned across the top of the page.

The man turned and looked in the direction of the carriage, its silhouette now fading in the distance as it left town, traveling north on the Old Carolina Road. At first, he seemed uncertain as to what he wanted to do; then, having apparently made up his mind, he ran toward the rear of the boardinghouse, where his horse was stabled.

Meanwhile, unaware of the unwelcome attention directed at them by the man on the street, both Mary and Kitty audibly exhaled as they left the town, heading toward their next sanctuary location.

"Good thing we got there as early as we did," Kitty commented. "Didn't seem to be any folks around."

Mary nodded. "Now we just need to find the meetinghouse up the road. Hopefully won't bump into any curious souls before we get there," she said.

About a half hour passed before they heard the sound of horse's hooves behind them. Kitty turned to see a man on a sway-backed horse approaching them. He was not traveling at a pace that alarmed them for any reason, nor did he seem to be especially focused on them, so they simply exchanged glances and continued along, Mary sliding the carriage slightly toward the right shoulder of the road to allow room for the follower to pass them.

As the rider drew up even with them, he slowed his horse and tipped his hat in Mary's direction. "Mornin', ma'am," he said pleasantly, addressing Mary and deliberately ignoring Kitty.

"Good morning," Mary responded, offering a nod and a half smile.

"Out awful early, ain't you?" the man said.

"On our way to visit some friends and thought we'd get an early start," Mary answered flatly, keeping her eyes on the road, hoping to discourage any more conversation.

The man now looked pointedly at Kitty and then the children. "Where y'all travelin' from?" he asked.

"From down south a bit," Mary answered vaguely.

"Whereabouts?" he asked, the suspicion now seeping into his voice.

"Don't mean to appear rude, but we're tired and anxious to reach our destination, so . . . good day, sir," Mary said, then flicked the reins to speed up the horse.

The man lagged behind for a few strides, then, with a swiftness that startled them, spurred his ragged horse forward. When he drew alongside the carriage, he reached out, grabbed the horse's bridle and, using his own horse as leverage, savagely jerked the reins and forced the horse and carriage off the road and into a small clearing.

CHAPTER 35

MARY STRUGGLED WITH THE REINS, TRYING VAINLY TO CONTROL the veering carriage, but the force of the stranger's lunging horse drove the carriage off the road, where it careened to a halt in a clearing. The man jumped to the ground and grabbed the reins, yanking them from Mary's grip.

Kitty leaped from the carriage to the ground. She had taken two steps toward the man when a small single-shot pistol appeared in his hand, pointed directly at her. She stopped and raised her hands.

Mary spoke first. "We have nothing of value," she said calmly, also raising her hands in the air. "We're just traveling to visit friends." She gestured toward the small bags at her feet. "Nothing but some clothes for us and the children." She gestured toward the children, who were cowering behind her in the carriage.

"Shut yer mouth!" the man barked. "I know who y'all are." He gestured toward Kitty with the pistol. "This one is a slave. Them kids, too." He shifted his aim toward Mary. "And you, yer the one helpin' 'em escape." He chuckled malevolently. "And me, I'm the one gonna make five hundred dollars by turnin' you in."

"You are mistaken, sir," Mary said imperiously. "And unless you release us immediately, I intend to file criminal charges against you for assaulting me and my maid."

The man looked from Mary to Kitty and back again, confused by Mary's haughty and indignant attitude, and now not entirely sure that these were, in fact, the people described on the reward flyer.

Mary spoke again, more angry and insistent now. "I demand that you hand me the reins and put that gun away so we may resume our journey!"

Finally, the man made up his mind, the allure of five- hundred dollars overwhelming his doubt. He pointed the gun directly at Mary.

"Think we'll all just head back to Frederick and check out yer story there. But I'm pretty sure I'm gonna be collectin' myself some money soon's I turn y'all over back there," he said, an evil grin spreading across his scruffy face.

Mary looked toward Kitty, who had furtively stepped closer to the man. Kitty nodded, barely perceptibly, in the direction of the bag at Mary's feet. Mary took a deep breath and nodded back.

The man, nervous now, swung his pistol back and forth from Mary to Kitty. "Don't y'all go doin' somethin' stupid now," he growled.

"We have no intention of doing anything until we return to Frederick," Mary said. "Where we then intend to have you arrested. Now, if you'll toss me my reins, we can get going. The sooner we get there, the sooner you'll be in jail, and the sooner we can resume our journey."

"Aw right, then," the man said, a gleam of greed in his eyes. "Let's git goin'. Here," he said, stepping forward and flinging the reins in Mary's direction.

As he tossed the reins, his gun hand dropped to his side. At that moment, Kitty leaped at him, one hand smacking his face, the other slapping down on the gun, which fell out of his grasp. The two of them rolled to the ground, Kitty struggling ferociously, flailing her arms and legs, trying to get control of him. Although the man was short and fat, he was still able to roll to the side and briefly escape Kitty's clutches. He kicked out with his legs, knocking her away from him, and scrambled to his feet, lunging toward the gun.

Mary appeared suddenly at his side and kicked the gun away. He looked up to see her holding Samuel's big pistol in both of her hands. She cocked the hammer ominously and pointed the pistol unswervingly in his face.

"Now," she said stonily, "I think it's time for us to be movin' on. Without you."

Although his eyes were fearful, the man attempted to bluff his way out of this dilemma by trying to infuse his voice with a confidence he didn't really feel. "Don't think you really want to pull that trigger, ma'am," he scoffed. "Ain't like shootin' at targets when yer blowin' a man's head off. Don't see you as the murderin' kind."

Mary looked at him, her gaze level and hard. "Don't think I'd be losin' much sleep over killin' the likes of you," she answered calmly.

He looked from Mary to Kitty, who had clambered up from the ground and was now standing next to Mary. "Prob'ly not even primed to fire," he added, gesturing with his head toward Mary's gun. "Been out in the weather, so powder's prob'ly wet." He shook his head, exhibiting a false bravado that was belied by the fear now creeping into his voice. "So why don't you just put that big ol' gun down and we'll all just go our separate ways. No harm done."

Mary spoke, her eyes narrowed as she stared hard at the man. "Way I see it, two things can possibly happen here. First thing is, I pull the trigger, and you're right—powder's wet and all we get is a flash in the pan." She shrugged and then continued. "Second possibility is, I pull the trigger, and your brains end up splattered all over that tree behind you." She smiled. "I'm kinda likin' the second possibility myself."

The only sound in the clearing was the cheerful chirping of the morning birds welcoming the new day as the now terrified man looked first at Mary and then at Kitty, unsure whether this woman would really shoot and unsure whether he was willing to risk his life for the now less enticing five hundred dollars.

Kitty chimed in with a crooked smile. "I wouldn't wait much longer if I was you," she said. "She might shoot you just for practice."

The man slowly raised his hands.

CHAPTER 36

*T*HEY TIED THE PROTESTING MAN TO A TREE, COILING A LENGTH OF rope they had found in his saddlebag—which he had apparently intended to use on them—around him multiple times, leaving it loose enough that he would eventually be able to wriggle free.

"This ain't right, leavin' me out here like this," he spluttered. "Ain't right. Man could die out here, tied up like this. Who knows what kinda animals about," he added, wide-eyed with dread.

"Just shut up," Kitty said as she stuffed a rag in his mouth. "Tired of listenin' to you cryin' like a baby."

Mary took a dirty handkerchief from his coat pocket and tied it around his eyes, blindfolding him. Then she gestured to Kitty and pointed to their mouths and then to the man, signaling that they should let him hear what they said next. Kitty nodded that she understood.

"Now what do we do?" Mary asked in a whispered voice that was just loud enough for the man to hear. He stopped squirming about and cocked his head to one side, attempting to surreptitiously listen to the women.

"Not sure," answered Kitty, shooting Mary a questioning look.

"Don't think we can keep goin' where we were headed," Mary said. "Maybe we should head back to the river and then up toward Harpers Ferry. Might find some help up that way."

Kitty shook her head, understanding what Mary was trying to do. "Think so. Heard some folks up that way will help runaways," Kitty said.

"Probably our only choice now," added Mary.

"Should get goin' right away, then, before the sun's up much higher and the folks in town are up and about," said Kitty.

Mary grinned at Kitty and then pointed toward the man. She stepped closer and spoke to him.

"We're leavin' you here. Somebody'll be comin' along before too long, and they'll free you up. You hear?" she said, cuffing him lightly on the cheek.

The man shook his head up and down and mumbled something they could not understand.

The women climbed aboard the carriage, both smiling reassuringly at the three children, who had remained seated in the rear. The children offered wan smiles in return, seemingly now somewhat inured to the excitement of the adventures they had all encountered since they began their journey days ago.

Mary flicked the reins and guided the horse gingerly out of the clearing and back onto the road in the direction of the Quaker meeting house, their original destination. After they had traveled a few hundred yards and were out of hearing range of their trussed-up would-be captor, Kitty turned to Mary.

"Think he heard us?" she asked.

"Seemed so," answered Mary.

"Think he believed us?" asked Kitty. "That we changed our plans and are headin' to Harpers Ferry?"

"Not sure," said Mary. "Makes sense that we'd head off in a different direction now that he's spotted us. And gotta believe that he's still lookin' for a piece of that reward money. So maybe he takes the bait, finds Sam, and leads them off after us." She shrugged. "On a wild-goose chase. But one that gives us a better chance of gettin' out of Maryland and into Pennsylvania."

Kitty seemed lost in thought for a moment, then turned toward Mary and spoke. "Maybe meetin' up with him and nearly gettin' caught might be the best thing that could've happened to us if it sends them all off down the wrong trail, followin' the wrong scent," she mused.

"Could be," Mary agreed. "As long as we sold him on the story that we're now off to Harpers Ferry."

"If not?" said Kitty.

"Then we gotta hope that no one finds him back there soon. And that he doesn't find Sam," said Mary.

It was not long before they came upon the Quaker meeting-house that was to be their next stop. They had discussed the idea of bypassing it and continuing on their journey but had finally decided that the risks of traveling many more hours in daylight out-weighed the possibility that someone might be following their trail soon, a trail that could lead to a search of the meetinghouse. And they trusted that the Quakers who would be helping them would also have a secure place to hide them.

They were correct. Welcomed warmly by two Quaker women, who seemed somehow to be expecting them, they were all given a quick meal and then hidden in a small chamber behind a false wall in the rear of the meeting room. The entrance to the hidden space was constructed so skillfully that the clandestine guests could not discern the outlines of the secret door until it miracu-lously popped open before their surprised eyes. The children were asleep before the women had finished tucking them into the feather-stuffed mattresses on the floor, and they were fol-lowed swiftly by Mary and Kitty, who were mentally and physically drained from the ordeal of the past few hours.

CHAPTER 37

*T*HIS TIME, THEIR LUCK HAD HELD. THERE HAD BEEN NO POUNDING on the entrance to the meetinghouse, no shouted demands by rough men to search the premises, no bullying threats of harm for harboring fugitive slaves. They had slept soundly and uninterrupted through the daylight hours and into the early evening, before their hosts knocked softly on the hidden door.

After another round of hot soup, bread, cheese, warm embraces, and good wishes, the travelers embarked again into the night, ladened with more food and directions to the next destination on the "railroad," a home facing the main road on the outskirts of the small village of Emmitsburg, very close to the promised land of the Pennsylvania border.

The night's journey passed without event. The children engaged in whispered games to occupy themselves, while Mary and Kitty spent most of the time in a comfortable silence, focusing on the road ahead.

They arrived at the terminus of this leg of the journey just before dawn. Almost immediately, a man answered their cautious rapping on the back door of an expansive redbrick and white-columned home and hastily ushered them into the house. He was the first of their so-called "conductors" along the Underground Railroad to actually identify himself by name.

Introducing himself as William Steere, he informed them that he was a prosperous merchant—he owned a nearby lumber mill that had been started by his grandfather after the American Revolution—and a prominent member of the local community. Both he and his wife, Louisa, who joined him after just a few minutes, were older—probably in their late sixties—and rather frail looking. He was tall and stooped, with thinning gray hair crowning a long, narrow, pinched face, one marked by wire-rimmed glasses perched upon the edge of his nose. Louisa Steere was in some ways a mirror image of her husband. She was nearly his height; had pale, sickly, almost translucent skin, and strands of white hair pulled back harshly into a tight bun; and was so severely skeletal looking that she listed unsteadily to one side when she walked.

They appeared rather proper and quite reserved. Certainly not the more robust antislavery crusaders the women had met over the past few nights, thought Kitty. William, who reminded her of a schoolmaster in both demeanor and manner of speech, told them that he and his wife had successfully helped a number of fleeing slaves to reach the Pennsylvania line over the past few years. He also told them, after Mary inquired, that he had, in fact, heard that a gang of slave catchers had traveled through the town a few days ago but that they had not come knocking on the door of his residence.

Louisa fed them the first full meal they had enjoyed since they left Mary's farm—freshly prepared oatcakes smothered in molasses and accompanied by chunks of ham and a pitcher of cold buttermilk. While Mary and Kitty heartily devoured the meal, the girls taught a delighted Arthur how to lick the leftover molasses from his fingers.

The Steeres were polite and considerate, if not as warm and embracing as the group's prior hosts. The conversation during the meal was limited and a bit stilted, focusing on the next steps in the trip. It seemed that the older couple approached the presence of the band of fugitives as more of a business problem requiring a practical solution than their playing a passion-driven role in a holy crusade.

After breakfast, William escorted Mary and Kitty into his study in the front of the house, while Louisa took the children to the kitchen for a warm bath. The plan, he explained, was for them to rest at his home, in a hidden alcove above the second floor of the spacious structure. The following day they would cross the border line into Pennsylvania, less than two miles away. As he spoke, he pointed to a large framed map of Maryland that hung from the wall. They would then travel about three miles from the state line to the tiny hamlet of Fairplay, he said, his finger tracing the short path on the map. There they would be met by several Quakers, who would escort them as they journeyed to an area near Gettysburg, where arrangements had been made for Kitty and the children to reside temporarily with a family of free Negroes.

Once again, as she listened and peered at the map, Kitty marveled at the efficiency of the "railroad" and its nearly magical system of rapid communication. In the span of a mere eight days, word of their escape and trek had been spread nearly one hundred miles through the network, and an array of "conductors" had sprung to their aid. Now, as they neared the end of their perilous journey, it appeared that their safety—and their freedom—lay a meager five miles away.

The plan, William assured them, was very simple and secure.

"You'll stay here today and tonight," he said in his schoolmaster's voice. "Get some rest and restore your spirits. Then tomorrow, around noon, we'll set out for the border."

"*We?*" asked a surprised Mary.

"Yes," he answered. "I'll be traveling with you."

"Why? Isn't that dangerous for you?" asked Kitty.

"Not at all," he said, scoffing at the idea. "Done it that way dozens of times."

"And we'll be traveling in daylight?" asked a clearly puzzled Mary. "Won't people in town notice us?"

"Actually safer traveling through the village in daylight. Not as suspicious. Just some travelers passing through. Nothing to arouse concern." He paused. "Truth is," he said conspiratorially, "even though Maryland is still a slave state, lots of folks up this end of the state feel very strongly about the evils of the institution. And are willing to help. Or at least look the other way. And with me accompanying you, given my position here, men would think twice about accosting us in broad daylight," he added self-assuredly.

Mary and Kitty exchanged concerned glances. Traveling in daylight, they were both thinking, given the size of the reward that was shadowing them, did not seem particularly safe. And they also had their own doubts that Sam Maddox would ever let frail old William Steere stand in his way and prevent him from seizing Kitty and the children, given their value to him as slaves on the open market.

"Well, then," William said, oblivious to their concerns, "it's time for all of you to get some rest, especially the children. We'll awaken you before dinner. Then you'll get a good night's sleep and be prepared for these last steps in your journey to freedom," he intoned solemnly.

CHAPTER 38

THE NEXT DAY DAWNED BRIGHT AND CLEAR, WITH A BRISK WIND AND a chill in the air. Mary and Kitty had awakened before the sun rose. They sat with their backs to the slanting attic wall, still wrapped in their blankets, waiting for the Steeres to beckon them for breakfast before they launched what was hopefully the last leg of their journey. The children were still asleep, tucked into a corner of the cramped space and wrapped in the bundles of soft coverlets that Louisa Steere had provided.

The women had been silent since they awoke, each lost in her own thoughts. Finally, Kitty turned to Mary and spoke quietly.

"This really a good idea?" she asked. "Travelin' in broad daylight? Old Mr. Steere comin' along with us?"

Mary shook her head, exasperated. "Not the way I'd do it, if the choice was ours. But he seems pretty confident we'll be all right. It's worked before doin' it this same way, so should work now, too," she said.

"But he ain't had Sam Maddox chasin' after folks before," Kitty said.

"True," Mary answered after a moment.

"We all've done pretty good so far by ourselves," said Kitty. "Don't see any reason why things should change now."

Mary nodded slowly in agreement. "I know. But maybe we'll just have to trust him that he knows what he's doin'. After all, it's worked fine before," she said, sounding more confident than she really felt.

"Works fine . . . until it don't," Kitty said skeptically. "And if don't work fine this time, old Mr. Steere's still comin' home to this house. But we ain't goin' home," she added bitterly. "Maybe you included."

There was a soft knocking on the door, and Louisa stepped into the room. "Time to rise," she said pleasantly. "Big day ahead of you."

Mary and Kitty exchanged resigned glances as they struggled to their feet, careful not to bump their heads against the sloped ceiling.

After yet another hearty breakfast, they packed their few small bags into the carriage and all climbed aboard. The children seemed puzzled by the fact that they were traveling in the daytime, but said nothing, sensing the tension felt by Mary and Kitty.

William Steere exited the barn, leading a horse by the reins. When he came alongside, he tied his horse to the rear of the carriage and began to climb into the driver's box, next to Mary.

"That won't be necessary," said Mary, her tone a bit defensive. "I can handle the carriage. Been drivin' it since we left days ago."

"I'm sure you can, my dear," he proclaimed in a patronizing tone, which annoyed both Mary and Kitty. "But I think it's better that I handle the remaining portion of the trip."

Mary reluctantly slid over closer to Kitty as Steere struggled to pull himself up into the carriage. Once he wriggled into the seat, he took the reins from Mary and, after nodding imperially to Louisa, guided the horse around the house and onto the main road.

It took less than ten minutes to travel through Emmitsburg. It was more a village than a town. The main street consisted of a few storefronts, several homes, and a wood-frame building that served as both the town hall and the post office. They passed a few people going about their early morning business, but no one seemed to pay much attention to the travelers. Mary turned toward Kitty as they passed the last structure in the village, and they shared a look that said, "Maybe this will be fine, after all."

When they had traveled another mile or so, William abruptly pulled back on the reins and the horse came to a juddering halt.

Mary and Kitty looked around frantically, searching for whatever danger had caused him to stop suddenly. When they spied nothing, they both turned toward William.

"What's wrong?" demanded Mary.

"Nothing," William answered, an odd smile creasing his lined face. "Thought you might want to embrace the moment."

Both women stared at him quizzically.

"See that stone?" he said, gesturing to a large granite block about two feet square, with intricate figures etched into each side, that was securely planted in the ground a few yards off the road. "It's a boundary marker. A crown stone, they call it."

The women continued to stare at him, and he seemed to be enjoying their puzzlement.

"Let me explain. Back in seventeen sixty-three," William began, now cloaking himself in his professorial role, "the colonies of Maryland, Pennsylvania, and Delaware were locked in a dispute over boundaries, a dispute that had been going on for years. Finally, after years of disagreement, they settled on a solution. Two respected Englishmen—Charles Mason and Jeremiah Dixon, both of whom were surveyors and astronomers—were commissioned to survey the boundary lines between the three colonies. The quarreling parties agreed to abide by the calculations and determinations of Mason and Dixon."

He went on. "And after nearly four years of work, this"—he tilted his head toward the stone—"is the result. The boundaries were surveyed and marked using these boundary stones. Find one of them located every five miles or so. Carved into the surface of each side, as you can see, is a coat of arms. The one facing us is from the Calvert family, the founders of Maryland. On the other side, right there"—he pointed—"is the coat of arms of William Penn."

William Steere paused dramatically.

"Ladies, welcome to Pennsylvania," he said. He then looked directly at Kitty. "And welcome to your freedom!"

CHAPTER 39

BOTH WOMEN WERE STILL, STARING, TRANSFIXED, AT THE CROWN stone. The fact that they were now in Pennsylvania seemed almost anticlimactic after the dangers and uncertainties of the past few days. Although they knew that passing to the other side of this crown stone meant freedom, strangely, nothing yet felt different. Indeed, both Mary and Kitty continued to scan the road before and behind them, their eyes flickering nervously, fearful that their pursuers were hiding somewhere nearby, waiting, even at this moment, to pounce and steal this elusive and ethereal liberty from them.

Mary turned toward Kitty and gently touched her arm. "So?" she said.

"So . . . what?" said a puzzled Kitty.

"You're safe," Mary exclaimed. "Aren't you happy?"

Kitty hesitated for a moment, unsure of her feelings. "Not yet, I guess," she answered. "Know I should be. But God's honest truth, I don't feel any different from what I felt yesterday. Still thinkin' that Sam's out there lookin' for us and ain't gonna give up till he finds us. And if he does, ain't so sure that just bein' on the other side of this rock"—she inclined her head in the direction of the crown stone—"gonna save us."

Mary sighed deeply and nodded. "Guess I feel the same way right now. But, hopefully, we'll be better once we get to where we're headin'. Wherever that is," Mary said.

William, who had been listening intently to the conversation, chimed in. "Not at all unusual," he said, still sounding like a school-master lecturing a class. "Most of those we've escorted across the border feel the same way. After so many years of living in bondage, the taste of real freedom may take some time for you to acquire." He gazed at the crown stone. "But make no mistake," he added pontifically, "you are now free."

"Thank you, Mr. Steere," Kitty said, offering a weak smile. "Don't mean to sound ungrateful. We truly appreciate what y'all have done for us. And all the others who helped us. We truly do. It's just that . . ." Kitty hesitated, looking reflectively off into the distance for a moment.

"Just that," she continued, "if you've been a slave all your life, just 'cause you pass over a border line with some fancy engraved rock doesn't make everythin' go away, like it all never happened. Like you said, just gonna take some gettin' used to, I guess." Kitty looked at Mary and placed her hand gently on Mary's arm. "But we're forever grateful. Truly."

Mary smiled and patted Kitty's hand. "Well, the sooner we get to where we're goin', the sooner y'all will start bein' free and then feelin' free. So," Mary said, turning to William eagerly, "perhaps we should get goin'. Folks are waitin' for us up the road ahead."

William nodded and flicked the reins. As the carriage rolled past the crown stone, Kitty twisted in her seat and stared back at it. Two small tears seeped from the corners of her eyes and trick-led down her cheeks as a faint smile crept across her face.

It took less than an hour for them to reach Fairplay. If Emmits-burg, Maryland, was just a village, then Fairplay, Pennsylvania, was a mere hamlet, with the main road—if it could be called that—sparsely dotted with a handful of houses, two business es-tablishments, and one stable. Tethered to a rail in front of the sta-ble was a farm wagon pulled by two bulky gray draft horses. Seated in the driver's box in the front were two men. Although both were heavily bearded, one appeared to be significantly older than the other. They were dressed in farm clothes, and each wore a dark, wide-brimmed hat.

As the carriage neared, each man tipped the rim of his hat in their direction. William Steere spoke first.

"Gentlemen," he intoned, "it is good to see you again."

"Mr. Steere," the older man said, inclining his head respectfully. "It is good to see thee, also." He then shifted his gaze directly to Kitty and offered a kind smile. "And it is especially good to see thee. And the children," he added.

Mary and Kitty offered polite smiles and nods in return.

"We are happy to see you, also," Mary said, a note of relief in her voice.

"Quite happy," added Kitty.

"Ladies, I'd like to introduce you to Aaron Wright," William said, inclining his head in the direction of the older man, "and his son, John. Both Aaron and John have been very helpful to us and our cause in the past. They will be accompanying you to your next destination."

William turned toward Mary and Kitty. "They are good men, and you can trust them," he said soothingly.

"I'm sure we can," Kitty answered confidently, turning toward the two men. "My children and I are grateful for your help."

"And now," William announced, "I must leave you, I'm afraid." He reached across and solemnly shook first Kitty's hand and then Mary's.

Kitty spoke first. "Thank you. And Mrs. Steere, also," she said sincerely, "for everything you've done for us. The Bible talks of welcoming strangers, but you did more than just welcome us. You helped save us. All of you along the way did. We'll not forget you."

"You are a brave man to aid us like this," Mary added. "You have our deepest gratitude. God will bless you."

William stood and awkwardly maneuvered his spare frame down from the carriage, struggling to keep his balance as he landed on the ground. Reaching out to the children, he touched each one on the forehead, without a word, as if he was offering some type of benediction as they parted ways.

"You are in good hands now," he said, tilting his head toward Aaron and John Wright. "Theirs—and God's."

William walked to the rear of the carriage. He untied his horse, mounted it and, with a brief wave of the hand, trotted off down the road toward the border line and Maryland.

"Well, then," said Aaron. "We should all be leaving, also."

"Where are we going now?" asked Mary.

"Thee will all be staying the night at our home, some five miles or so from here, outside Gettysburg. We own a gristmill there and have hosted many like yourselves. Those who are enjoying their first taste of freedom," Aaron said, smiling warmly at Kitty.

"And then?" Kitty asked.

"After that, we will take thee to a home on Bear Mountain, a few miles away. Arrangements have been made for thee and the children to reside there," he said reassuringly. "Until thou might be ready to move on."

"Who will they be staying with?" asked Mary.

"A free black man named Amon Jones has a small farm there. He and his wife, Rachel, have agreed to take thou in as boarders in return for thy labor in the home," Aaron said.

"Will they be safe there?" Mary asked.

Aaron offered an encouraging smile. "Amon Jones is a God-fearing man. Thou will be safe in his care," he said to Kitty.

CHAPTER 40

A LTHOUGH THEY KNEW THAT THEY SHOULD NOW FEEL SAFE—OR AT least safer—Mary and Kitty were still apprehensive. Arriving at the mill owned by Aaron Wright, they were welcomed by his wife, Elizabeth, who escorted them to their lodgings for the night, a spacious and comfortable room in the rear of the mill office, with stuffed horsehair mattresses covering several sleeping pallets and a wood-burning stove in a corner for heat.

At first, they were bewildered by the openness of the space, since they had become used to sleeping in dark and secretive places during their journey. But Aaron's son, John, who had carried their bags to the room, assured them that there was no need for concern. Even though slave catchers had been seen on occasion traveling north from Maryland, he told them, none had ever stopped at their home or attempted to question them or their neighbors.

"Thou are safe here," John said. "Such men would not be welcome. Several of them have been arrested and jailed after they've entered Pennsylvania. Thou are protected by us and the laws."

Later that night, as Kitty struggled to fall asleep, grappling with relentless flashing images of manacles and nooses, whips, dark cellars, rushing floodwaters, and shadowy figures carrying guns, she wondered if the peace and security of real freedom would ever come her way. The sleep that she eventually found was brief, troubled, and sporadic, and she awoke with a deep-seated feeling of dread, which could not be erased by the glorious sunshine and promise of the new day.

They left the Wright home shortly after breakfast, accompanied again by Aaron and John in their creaking, ponderous wagon. The trip to the farm of Amon Jones on Bear Mountain should take about one hour, they were told, although the last mile up the mountain would take up a good portion of that time, since the road was steep, winding, and narrow.

On the way, they stopped to water the horses at a roadside tavern near the village of Bendersville. The owner, a hulking, bearded, genial man who introduced himself as Charley Myers, exchanged friendly banter with Aaron and John, and after the Wrights explained the presence of Mary, Kitty, and the children, he extended his hand to the women and offered what seemed like a heartfelt welcome to the area.

The group arrived at the top of Bear Mountain at mid-afternoon, after a slow, arduous trek up the twisting gravelly lane. Kitty was anxious as they approached the Jones farm, not at all sure what was in store for her now that they had finally arrived at this new place. Mary had decided that she would remain nearby for a few weeks, while Kitty settled in, just in case there were any problems. While there, Mary also intended to execute a document, in a Pennsylvania court, making it clear that Kitty and the children had been manumitted and were, indeed, free.

As the wagon and carriage came upon a small clearing, the dappled sunlight peeking through the canopy of trees overhead revealed a ramshackle log cabin wedged up against the side of a hill. A sagging masonry chimney claimed one exterior wall, and a lean-to holding stacked firewood the other, while an ancient oak tree stood guard over a stone well in the front yard.

Kitty quickly surveyed the small homestead. Although the Maddox farmhouse, where she had spent her entire life, would never have been considered a plantation mansion, it had been spacious, well built, and comfortable. The Jones farmhouse appeared to be none of those things. But, she quickly reminded herself, it was just the beginning of her new life, a place to stay until she, and she alone, decided to leave. It might not have been pretty, but it represented the fact that she was now free.

As they reined the horses in, the front door swung open and an old black man stepped outside. He was short and wiry, with tufts of white hair sprouting from the sides of his otherwise bald head. Dark overalls and a homespun cotton shirt hung loosely from his stooped frame.

Aaron Wright jumped from his wagon to the ground and approached the old man, extending his hand in greeting. "I am Aaron Wright, from outside Gettysburg. This is my son, John," he said, nodding in John's direction. "And these are our friends who we are delivering to thy care," he added, pointing toward Kitty and the children.

"Amon Jones," the old man said, shaking Aaron's hand. "Wife, Rachel's, out back but should be round soon."

Jones shifted his glance toward Kitty and Mary, who had dismounted and were walking in his direction. He stepped toward Kitty. "You be the one stayin' here, I s'pose?" he asked somewhat dourly.

"Y'sir," Kitty said, extending her hand. "Name's Kitty. And these are my children—Eliza Jane, Mary, and the little one's Arthur."

The children, who were now standing in the back of the carriage and were extremely curious about this new place, each smiled shyly and nodded politely at Jones. When he saw the children, his mood seemed to improve and the corner of his mouth turned up in a slight smile.

"Well, then," he said, shaking Kitty's hand, "y'all be welcome here. Wife'll be thankful for the help. And sure be happy to see these chilluns. Long time since any little ones been round here."

Jones then looked quizzically at Mary, who was standing slightly behind Kitty. Mary stepped forward.

"Mary Maddox," she said, offering her hand in greeting, as well. "I'm Kitty's . . ." She hesitated, uncertain what to say next.

"Mary is our friend," Kitty interjected quickly. "She was our mistress but has decided to free us—me and the children. She's traveled all this way to look after us and be sure that we got here safely. She's our friend," Kitty repeated, smiling warmly at Mary.

Jones seemed slightly surprised but simply nodded respectfully at Mary. "Well, then, you be welcome here, too," he said. "Not much room, 'specially with these here chilluns now, but we be happy to find you some space somewhere."

"That's quite kind of you, Mr. Jones," Mary said, "but Mr. Wright here has helped me make some boarding arrangements for a time at a home down the mountain."

Aaron Wright clapped his hands happily and stepped forward. "Now that the introductions have been made, let us help thee with thy bags and to get settled in," he said, directing John toward the carriage.

The children climbed down, scrambled over to Kitty, and clustered anxiously around her, their little hands clutching at her skirt. Kitty bent to speak to them.

"We'll be stayin' here for a while," she said soothingly, "with Mr. Amon and Miss Rachel. They're nice folks who'll take good care of us."

"No more ridin' in the carriage at night?" Eliza Jane asked in a small, trembling voice.

"No more ridin' at night," Kitty assured her, gently touching the upturned face of each child. "No more runnin' away."

CHAPTER 41

*T*HREE WEEKS PASSED WITH NO SIGN OF SAM MADDOX OR THE SLAVE catchers. Kitty and the children had settled in at the Jones farm, quickly and seamlessly becoming a part of the rhythms and patterns of daily life. Kitty helped Rachel with the cooking, the laundry, and general work around the cramped four-room cabin, while Eliza Jane and Mary pitched in, as well. Little Arthur, after a fitful first night, seemed to have recovered nicely from the anxieties of their harrowing journey and now toddled happily around the cabin and property.

Mary, meanwhile, had taken a room in a home at the bottom of the mountain, outside Bendersville. She visited Kitty and the children almost daily and actually helped out with some of the chores on those visits. Rachel Jones, who was in her sixties and was struggling with a variety of physical infirmities, appeared pleased to have the help and also seemed to enjoy the company of both Kitty and Mary. Amon Jones, however, was more taciturn and distant, rarely speaking with Kitty or the children as he went about his business, struggling to manage the meager farm and also working part-time as a butcher in Bendersville.

After the first few days, Mary had traveled to the Adams County Courthouse in a neighboring village, where the local justice of the peace had helped her prepare and execute a deed of manumission, officially declaring that Kitty, Eliza Jane, Mary, and Arthur were, in fact, legally free. He had assured her that the document, together with the fact that Pennsylvania had passed a law outlawing slavery and declaring that any slaves brought into the state would be deemed to be free, would protect Kitty and the children from any attempt by Sam Maddox to seize them and bring them back to Virginia.

Satisfied that Sam Maddox had apparently abandoned the chase, and that Kitty and the children were safe and happy living with Amon and Rachel Jones, Mary decided that it was time for her to return home to Virginia. One afternoon she rode up Bear Mountain to tell Kitty of her plans. When she arrived, Kitty was folding laundry in the front yard, near the stone well, while the children played nearby. As she climbed out of the carriage, the children rushed to her side, squealing in delight. Mary bent and hugged each of them, patting the girls on the head and tickling little Arthur. Kitty grinned at the scene from her laundry post at the well.

"Well," said Kitty as the children ran off to continue their games, "they're certainly glad to see you today."

"As I am to see them," Mary said, a broad smile lighting up her face.

"They're going to miss you," Kitty said after a moment.

Mary looked surprised. "How did you know? That I was leaving," she asked.

Kitty shrugged. "Figured you had to be leavin' sometime soon," said Kitty. "We're all settled here. Kids are happy. Miss Rachel's nice to us. And Mr. Amon . . ." She shrugged again. "Well, Mr. Amon could be a lot worse, I guess."

"Is he unkind to you?" Mary snapped, a look of concern whisking away her smile. "Or to the children?"

Kitty shook her head. "No, no," she said quickly. "Just don't think he's very kindly to anyone. 'Specially to Miss Rachel."

"If you think we should find you another home . . . ," Mary began anxiously.

Kitty shook her head again. "We're fine. No need to be worryin' 'bout us," she said calmly. "Only plan on stayin' here for a while, anyway. Then we'll go lookin' for some work and our own place." She shot Mary a big grin. "Free now. Can come and go as I please."

"If you're sure," Mary said uncertainly.

"We're fine," Kitty said. "Now, let's talk about your plans."

"Thought I'd be headin' back to Virginia in the next day or two," Mary said. "Need to get back and decide what I'm goin' to do with the farm. Figured it'd be a bit easier travelin' during daylight this time—hopefully, without a band of ruffians chasin' after me."

They shared a knowing smile. After a moment, Kitty spoke.

"They'll be very sad when you leave," Kitty said.

Mary cocked her head, her eyebrows raised questioningly.

"The children," Kitty responded. "You've become their grandma, you know. That's how they think of you. Never had one before, but they do now."

Mary said nothing, only gnawed at the corner of her lip to hold back the tears welling up in her eyes.

"We'll all miss you," said Kitty.

CHAPTER 42

AMON JONES TETHERED HIS MULE TO A HITCHING POST ALONG THE main street of Bendersville. He unstrapped a bent and twisted cast-iron plow blade from the mule's back and wrestled it onto his shoulder. Earlier that day he had been plowing a patch behind his cabin, hoping to prepare the ground for planting, when he struck a large rock buried beneath the surface. The impact bent the plow blade, and he had been unable to straighten it. Now he was hoping the town blacksmith could repair the damage. And that the few coins in his pocket would be enough money to pay for that repair.

As he walked toward the blacksmith's forge, stumbling slightly under the bulky weight of the iron blade, he noticed a small group gathered in front of the feed and grain store. As he passed by, he saw two men standing in the center of the assembly, vigorously gesturing with their hands, voices rising and falling as they addressed the cluster around them. Both of the speakers were large, rough-looking men, and one of them held a sheet of paper in his hand, which he intermittently waved before the listeners.

As Jones wended his way around the gathering, one of the listeners broke away from the pack and strode toward him.

"What all that 'bout?" asked Jones as the man neared him.

"Couple of slave catchers," the man answered.

"Who they lookin' for?" asked Jones.

"Nigger woman and some children. Said they ran away from

Virginia. Been chasin' after 'em for a couple weeks now," the man
said. "Offerin' a lot a money to anybody helps catch 'em."

"How much?" asked Jones.

"Hundred dollars," said the man, obviously impressed by the
amount. "Cash money," he added before he hurried away.

Jones stood in the street for a moment, gazing in the direction
of the assembled men. Finally, he turned, crossed the street, and
entered the open front of the blacksmith's forge area. Grasping a
heavy hammer, a man was pounding a red-hot horseshoe back
into shape, a slow, steady, rhythmic drumbeat as sparks flew from
the glowing iron. The blacksmith, an immense, heavily sweating
man wearing a thick leather apron over his clothes, his sleeves
rolled up to reveal massive forearms, looked up when Jones entered, and stepped back from the scarred broad anvil that held
the horseshoe.

"Help you?" the blacksmith asked.

Amon Jones pointed to the disfigured plow blade. "Hit a rock,"
Jones grumbled. "You fix it?"

The blacksmith grabbed the blade from Jones, then spun it
around effortlessly in his big hands as if it were a child's toy. "Think
so," the big man said. "Can't get to it right away, though. Prob'ly in
a day or so."

"How much?" asked Jones uncertainly.

The blacksmith shrugged. "Mebbe two dollars," he said. "Depends."

"On what?" asked Jones.

The blacksmith shrugged again. "How workable the iron is.
How bad the damage is. But," he said, examining the damaged
blade once more, "prob'ly not more'n two dollars."

Jones jingled the handful of coins in his pocket, knowing that
he didn't have that much. "Can I leave it with you?" he asked.

"Sure thing," the blacksmith said, shrugging again. "Get to it
when I can."

Jones nodded his thanks and left the forge. As he looked across
the street, he saw that the group was breaking up, the men wan-
dering off in different directions. The two slave catchers, how-

ever, remained. Jones gazed intently at the two men for a minute, then looked back toward the blacksmith and finally back at the slave catchers. He took a deep breath, exhaled—and walked toward the two men.

"Heard you be lookin' for someone," Jones said.

"Sure are," said one of the men, a tall, broad, ruggedly good-looking fellow. He offered Jones an engaging smile. "And we're willin' to pay good money for information helps us catch 'em."

"How much?" asked Jones.

"Well, that sorta depends on what you got to tell us," answered the man, still smiling, but his hard eyes narrowing as he scrutinized Jones. "There's information that ain't especially helpful . . . and then there's information that helps us find who we're lookin' for." He paused a moment. "Which kind of information you got?"

Jones considered the question and then shook his head slowly. "Have to do some thinkin' 'bout that," he said as he turned to walk away.

"Hold on a second," the man said agreeably, reaching out and grabbing Jones's arm. "Don't go leavin' just yet. Let's talk a bit. Name's Sam Maddox. From Virginia. This here's Tom Finnegan," he added, gesturing toward the man standing next to him. "From Maryland. Best damn slave catcher in the South."

Finnegan gave Jones a hard stare and a barely perceptible dip of his head in acknowledgment.

When Jones said nothing in response, Maddox continued.

"Your name?" Maddox asked.

"Jones," muttered Amon Jones.

"You a free man?" asked Maddox, his tone amiable on the surface but a subtle threat laced through his words.

Jones simply nodded.

"For now," said Finnegan in a low, menacing voice.

Maddox raised his hand in a conciliatory gesture. "Pay no attention to my friend here," he said, inclining his head toward Finnegan. "Gets a bit carried away sometimes. So, let's get back to that information you got for us. And how much money we got for you."

"Not sure," Jones responded. "Like I said . . . got to think on it."

As Jones turned and began to walk away, Maddox reached out and grabbed his arm once again, this time more forcefully.

"Afraid we ain't got time for you to be doin' any thinkin'," Maddox said, all pretense of friendliness now gone, replaced by a steely tone of intimidation. "You know somethin' 'bout who we lookin' for, you best be tellin' us now. We're 'bout outta patience, searchin' round these parts. And we damn sure ain't leavin' here empty handed. Can't find the people we're lookin' for, might as well just grab somebody else to take back with us and sell. One niggra's just as good as the next on the auction block." He paused and then added ominously, "If you know what I mean."

For a long minute no one spoke, Maddox's threat hanging heavily in the air. Then Jones turned and faced the two men.

"Hunerd dollars," Jones said.

Maddox shook his head. "Twenty now . . . the rest when we get our hands on who we lookin' for," Maddox answered.

Jones stared hard at the two men, his eyes flickering back and forth between them, as he considered the offer. The men stepped closer, towering over him, their aura of malevolence enveloping him as he grappled with his dilemma. Finally, he took a deep breath and exhaled slowly, resigned to his fate.

"Deal," Jones said.

CHAPTER 43

KITTY HAD DISCOVERED VERY SOON AFTER THEIR ARRIVAL THAT THE Amon Jones homestead was not a happy place. The farm was struggling to produce enough to sustain all the mouths it had to feed. The land at the top of the mountain was harsh and rocky, and attempting to discover fertile patches for food cultivation through primitive plowing was like trying to find deeply hidden underground water with a divining rod made of a withered tree limb. In addition to the poor soil quality, the region had been engulfed in a period of severe drought for more than a year, further exacerbating the agricultural predicament.

Amon Jones had never been a happy man in the best of times, Kitty suspected. And these were most certainly not the best of times. He rarely spoke—not to Kitty and the children, not even to his wife, Rachel. When he did speak, he was brusque and demanding. He spent most of the daylight hours either working on the farm or offering his meager butcher skills in the surrounding villages. At night, he ate dinner silently and most often by himself, slumped stoop-shouldered over his food, and then retreated to bed, usually without uttering a word to anyone.

Early on, the children had instinctively learned to avoid Amon Jones and his dark moods whenever possible. Kitty also tried to circumvent him as much as their crowded confines would allow.

Kitty was fairly certain that Jones had received a sum of money from those helping them on the Underground Railroad as an inducement to take them in. Since their arrival, Kitty and the children had been helping with all the chores, but she wondered how long it would be before Amon decided that, despite the payment he had received, he could no longer provide for them and it was then time for them to leave. Although, she had to admit to herself that she was looking forward to locating enough work so that they could afford to find their own living space sometime soon.

Rachel, however, was a different story. She seemed to revel in their presence, especially the children's. Childless herself, she embraced the opportunity to mother them, cooking and baking, sewing new clothes, even volunteering to put them to bed at night in the cramped, windowless back room where Kitty and the children all slept.

In addition to the tensions and uncertainty of the Amon Jones household, Kitty found, somewhat to her surprise, that she missed Mary, who had been gone a month now, more than she would ever have imagined. Mary had stayed for two more days after their discussion about returning home. When it had come time for her to begin the journey, the departure was very emotional, especially for the children. They had, indeed, taken to viewing her as the grandmother they never knew, and when she had come to the farm to bid them all farewell, the three children were beside themselves with sadness over her leaving. Eliza Jane and Mary had wrapped themselves around Mary's legs, refusing to release their grip, while little Arthur had simply sat on the ground and wept uncontrollably, his nose running as tears spilled down his cheeks.

After Kitty had pried the girls away and they had collapsed into a sobbing puddle next to Arthur, she walked with Mary to the waiting carriage. They stood facing each other, uncomfortable, unsure, and silent. Finally, Mary spoke.

"I'll be sure to visit again soon. And you be sure to let me know if y'all need anything," she said softly, a catch in her voice.

Kitty shook her head twice, gnawing at the corner of her lower lip.

"And make sure the girls keep up with their reading and writing," Mary added. "Maybe they could send me some letters. . . ." Her voice trailed off.

"Thank you," Kitty managed to say, her voice strangled with emotion. "For everything. Me and the children," she continued, "we'll never forget what you did to help us. Never."

After a long, awkward moment Mary proffered a small, sad smile and then turned and climbed up into the carriage. As Mary seized the reins, Kitty reached up and touched the hem of Mary's dress, smiling as a single tear coursed down her face. And then Mary was gone.

Now, as Kitty thought back on their farewells, she wished that Mary had stayed on longer. After all that they had experienced on their escape north, she now found that there was a void in her life, an absence of someone whom she could talk with, someone with whom she could share her uncertainties and fears. Despite their troubled history together, and against all odds, that someone had surprisingly become Mary.

The day had been exhausting, and Kitty looked forward to crawling under her quilt and finding some refuge from the day's labors in sleep. She and Rachel had spent the afternoon attempting to clear a carpet of large stones from a postage stamp–sized clearing near the edge of the mountain, hoping that the virgin land there, despite the rockiness, might provide a more fertile growing area. They had struggled with the task until dusk, loading an old, rickety wheelbarrow, which they then wrangled to the edge of the field and dumped, creating a mound of debris that looked like some ancient stone monument. The girls had helped also, making a game of who could carry more rocks from the field, while little Arthur had amused himself by tossing smaller stones onto the growing pile.

That night, Kitty, Rachel, and the children had dinner together, a surprisingly tasty stew that Rachel had miraculously cobbled together from the scraggly vegetables remaining in the garden. Amon Jones had not yet returned from a visit to town, and Rachel had begun to worry. Finally, as Kitty and Rachel were cleaning the last of the dinner dishes, the front door swung open on its creaking hinges and Jones entered, head down, shoulders slouched, and quite clearly unhappy. When Rachel tried to engage him in a conversation about his day, he merely grunted, deposited himself in his chair, and pointed to the table, wordlessly demanding his food.

Sensing that Amon Jones was in an even murkier mood than usual, Kitty offered a kindly good night to Rachel, gathered up the children, and shepherded them toward their room. As they passed Jones, Kitty mumbled a good night to him, as well. Jones raised his head slightly and peered at her, an odd look in his eyes. It seemed, for an instant, as if he was about to say something to her, but then a dark, painful expression settled on his face and he dropped his gaze away from her.

Once in their own room, Kitty quickly prepared the children and herself for bed. Eliza Jane and Mary slept together on one pallet, and Kitty slept on another. Little Arthur, depending upon his mood and inclination, shuttled between the two pallets, always finding room to snuggle in next to his sisters or his mother. Tonight he chose to climb in with the girls. Kitty tucked them under their down quilts and kissed them each good night. Then she blew out the single candle and rolled underneath her own quilt.

Despite her fatigue, sleep eluded her. She couldn't get comfortable, tossing and turning, her thoughts tumbling, troubled by Jones's demeanor lately and the strange look in his eyes that night. Finally, she made a decision.

"Time for us to leave here," she whispered to herself.

And, after reaching that verdict, she wrapped her quilt tightly around her shoulders and promptly fell asleep.

CHAPTER 44

*I*T WAS AFTER MIDNIGHT WHEN THE HORSEMEN ARRIVED AT THE ROAD-side tavern outside Bendersville. A sleepy Charley Myers, awakened by the pounding on his front door, pulled on his trousers and boots, lit a candle, and shuffled from the living quarters in the rear of the tavern to the front of the building. After lifting the locking bar and swinging the heavy wooden door open, he found four horsemen outside, the mounts tossing their heads, snorting, and breathing heavily, together with a wagon and four extra, unsaddled horses.

One of the horsemen had dismounted and was standing in the doorway. Myers's gaze quickly took in each member of the group, and his assessment did not make him particularly comfortable, especially at this time of night. The men all appeared to be hard and rough, with hats pulled down low on their foreheads and shading heavily bearded faces, and saddle holsters bristling with guns. And the man standing before him appeared particularly villainous, with deep-set, dark, cold eyes, a scowl on his face, and a gun strapped to each hip. *Certainly not just tired travelers looking for a warm place to sleep,* he thought.

"Help you, gentlemen?" Myers asked, trying to mask the suspicion he felt.

"Sorry to wake you," the man said in a deep, gruff voice, not really sounding sorry at all. "Name's Finnegan. From 'cross the border in Maryland. Hopin' we could water our horses and leave the extras here a few hours, till we return."

"Sure thing," Myers answered, relief in his voice. "Happy to help. Where y'all headin' this time of night?"

The man didn't answer at first, shooting Myers a steely look that suggested it was none of his business where they were heading. Then he relented, not wanting to arouse any more suspicion in the taverner than necessary.

"My friend here," he said, gesturing toward the big, good-looking man on the lead horse, "is lookin' for his woman and children. Run off a few weeks ago. Heard they might be stayin' round here." Finnegan paused and shook his head. When he spoke again, he dropped his voice conspiratorially. "Was me, I'd just as soon say good riddance. But he wants her back." He shrugged. "So, we're lookin' to go get her."

Finnegan removed some coins from his pocket and handed them to Myers.

"This enough?" Finnegan asked.

Myers nodded, pocketing the coins.

"More for you when we get back," Finnegan said.

Myers led the group around to the back of the tavern. The men took turns wordlessly watering the horses and then tethered the extras inside the barn. The whole process took less than twenty minutes.

When they had finished, Finnegan gathered the men together a few feet away from Myers, and outside his hearing, and engaged in a hushed but animated discussion. After a few minutes, Finnegan looked at each man, nodded once, and they all mounted up.

Finnegan looked down at Myers from astride his horse. "Back in a few hours, maybe sooner," he said. "Leavin' right quick once we get back, so be ready for us," he added, a command, not a request.

The men all put spurs to their mounts and, followed by the wagon, charged out of the rear of the tavern and raced off down the road toward Bear Mountain.

CHAPTER 45

KITTY WAS LOST IN A SHALLOW, FRETFUL SLEEP, MARKED BY SHADOWY images of Mary standing on the far side of a wooden bridge, beckoning, her hand outstretched. But no matter how hard Kitty tried, she could not reach her. With each laborious, slow-motion step that Kitty took toward her, Mary seemed to recede, floating backward like a fleeting apparition, a look of anguish spreading across her face, shouting words that Kitty could not comprehend. And then she was gone, disappearing into a swirling, misty darkness.

Suddenly, the door to their bedroom exploded inward, shattered by some devastating force, the wood splintering as the door was ripped from its hinges. Kitty sat bolt upright, her sleep-sodden mind at first unsure if this was real or another segment of her troubled dreams. But as shouting men came storming into her room, the excruciating realization struck immediately that this was no dream—this was real. And she and the children were in great danger.

Before she could react, the first man into the room grabbed her roughly by the arms and hurled her off the sleeping pallet and onto the floor. She landed awkwardly on her hands and knees and tried to swiftly scramble away from him toward the children, who had been startled awake by the crashing noise. Before she could reach the children, who were now crying fearfully, the man grabbed her by her hair and one arm and viciously dragged her through the smashed doorway and out into the main room.

Driven now by the anger that had overtaken her fear, Kitty tried desperately to wrench herself free of the man's grip. As she twisted away from him, she saw his face—it was Sam Maddox, his eyes stormy and filled with hatred.

"Leave us be!" Kitty screamed at him, now furious with rage. "We're free! You can't take us!"

Maddox lashed out with a brutal backhand across her face, snapping her head back and knocking her to the floor. "Shut up," Maddox snarled. "You damn well ain't free, and you're comin' back where you belong!"

Kitty glared at him defiantly, blood curling down from the corner of her mouth. "I'm free, and I got papers to prove it. Them too," she cried angrily, looking fearfully now toward the three children.

"Throw them into the wagon," Maddox ordered, pointing to the children, who were now wailing as they reached frantically for their mother. "Quick!"

"No!" Kitty screamed. "You can't do this!"

As Maddox jerked Kitty to her feet, she thrashed, twisting and flailing, dragging her nails across his face and kicking out at him. He stepped back away from her, and then threw a crushing overhand punch, striking her flush on the side of her head, knocking her again to the floor. Dazed, she stumbled as she fought to stand.

"Tie her up! Good an' tight! Then throw her in the wagon," Maddox yelled as two other men rushed into the cabin. "And get them damn kids outta here," he ordered. "Now!"

Kitty, lapsing in and out of consciousness from the force of the blow, felt herself being lifted and carried out of the cabin. Once outside, she was thrown to the ground and bound up, hands and feet together, by a length of coarse rope. A wad of cloth was stuffed into her mouth.

As two sets of strong hands heaved her upright and her legs buckled under her, she glimpsed Amon Jones near the front door to the cabin. Sam Maddox loomed over him, holding a shotgun to his face. Then she saw Maddox throw a number of coins on the ground in front of Jones. And even through the haze of her grogginess and throbbing pain, she understood. Amon Jones, a free black man whom she had trusted, had sold them out to Sam Maddox.

"Get these damn niggras loaded up," Maddox ordered, turning away from Amon Jones, "and let's get the hell outta here!"

The men dragged Kitty to the wagon, trussed up, barely conscious, but still feebly struggling. They lifted her and flung her into the rear, where she landed painfully on her head and shoulder. The children, their hands bound, were tossed in after her and quickly scrabbled to her side. They cried uncontrollably as they tried to wrap themselves around her.

The driver cracked the reins, and the wagon lurched forward, then hurtled down the mountain road, carrying the bound and crying cargo back to captivity.

CHAPTER 46

*T*HE ORANGE GLOW THAT PRECEDED THE SUNRISE WAS JUST BEGINNING to slither above the horizon when Charley Myers heard the clattering of hoofbeats and then a hammering on the front door of the tavern. He had been dozing in a chair in the front room, awaiting the return of the night visitors. After straining to raise his bulk from the chair and trying to shake off the cobwebs of his fitful dozing, he shuffled across the room and unlocked the door.

Finnegan stood in the doorway, while the other three horsemen waited on restless and lathered mounts. The wagon arrived moments later, one man in the driver's seat heaving on the reins as it braked to a stop.

"Welcome back," Myers said pleasantly.

"Need to swap out the horses," Finnegan said gruffly. "And get these watered, right quick," he added, gesturing toward the tired animals.

"Sure thing," said Myers, stepping outside to help. "Horses are ready round back, watered and brushed down. What about the wagon?" he asked, peering over his shoulder at the wagon, which was not following the others as they headed to the rear of the tavern.

"Wagon horses're fine," Finnegan answered brusquely.

"Any luck findin' the feller's woman and children?" Myers asked, his head still turned and his gaze fixed on the wagon and the shadowy shapes that seemed to be moving about inside.

"Yup," Finnegan answered.

Myers waited for more details, but none were forthcoming, as Finnegan strode over and joined the others, who were swapping out the tired mounts and saddling up the fresh ones. Myers casually sidled over closer to the wagon, trying to get a better look inside. The large, handsome man he had seen earlier astride a horse was now driving the wagon. He was fidgeting with the reins, jerking the horses' bits to keep them steady, and seemed especially anxious for the riders to finish their work and get back on the road.

Suddenly, a head appeared in the rear of the tarpaulin-covered wagon. Although he could not see clearly, the figure seemed to be struggling to rise up. Peering through the dawn shadows, he made brief eye contact with the figure. It appeared to be a woman—a colored woman—and although he could not be certain, she seemed to be bound in rope, with a cloth stuffed in her mouth. She stared at him, her eyes wide, a muddle of terror and anger.

Myers was about to take a step toward the wagon when the driver turned, reached into the rear, and roughly thrust the woman back down onto the floor. At that moment, Myers thought he heard children's voices in the back of the wagon, although he could not clearly see anyone else.

The driver turned toward Myers and shot him a fierce and threatening glare, warning him to get away from the wagon without actually uttering a single word. Myers swiftly averted his gaze and drifted back toward the other horsemen. The riders had finished watering the worn-out horses, had hitched their saddles onto the waiting spares, and were just remounting when Finnegan approached him, holding the reins to his fresh horse. He handed Myers a handful of bills.

"This should do it," Finnegan said.

Myers looked down at the wad and shook his head. "More here'n I need," he said.

"Keep it," Finnegan said. "Appreciate your help, 'specially in the middle of the night." He took a step toward Myers and leaned in close. "Anybody come askin'," he added, his tone now low and menacing, "you didn't see nothin' tonight. No riders. No wagon. No nothin'. Understand?"

For a moment there was a strained silence between the two men. Then Myers nodded his head slowly. Finnegan clapped him once on the shoulder.

"Good man," Finnegan said, a grim, crooked grin turning up one corner of his mouth.

Finnegan leaped into the saddle of his horse and joined the others as they took off at a gallop down the road toward the Maryland border. As the wagon rumbled past, Myers was jolted by a terrible thought. He recognized the face! He now realized who the bound and gagged woman in the wagon was. And he realized that he had to get help—before it was too late.

After rushing to the barn, he swiftly saddled his own horse, struggled into the saddle, and took off at a fast trot down the road in the direction of Bendersville. As the sun rose on what promised to be a bright and clear day, he could see the blooming silhouettes of dust stirred up by the horsemen and the wagon in the distance ahead of him. He knew now where they were going. And he knew that he had to get to the Wrights' gristmill as soon as possible to tell them what had happened—that the young Negro woman they had aided and befriended had been seized by slave catchers.

By the time Myers arrived at the Wrights' gristmill, he and his horse gasping for air, the dust bloom from the slave catchers' convoy down the road was barely visible. He clambered awkwardly from his saddle, nearly tumbling to the ground, and rushed into the mill building.

Aaron Wright and his son, John, were in the office, talking with two customers, when Myers burst in. Panting, Myers quickly related what had happened and, pointing to the road, told them that if they hurried, they might still be able to catch the men before they reached the Pennsylvania border.

Aaron Wright seized his shocked son by the shoulders. "Go after them," Aaron said, the anxiety in his voice palpable. "I'll find the sheriff and follow thee. Go now." He pushed John toward the door. "Quickly! And keep them in thy sight."

Grim faced, John Wright nodded and sprinted out of the office. He grabbed the nearest saddled horse, which actually belonged to one of the customers in the office, swung himself into the saddle, tugged at the reins, and galloped off down the road.

At first, Wright feared that he had lost them. But after a few minutes of hard riding, he could see a faint wisp of road dust in the distance. His heart pounding, he dug his heels into the horse's flanks to spur him on, hopeful that his father and the sheriff were close behind him. He was not sure what he could actually do if he caught up to the riders without the sheriff—there were many of them, all apparently well armed—but as he envisioned the faces of Kitty and her children, knowing how terrified they must be, he was determined that he would not give up the chase.

Charging through the hamlet of Fairplay, Wright began to worry. His horse—a farm animal, not a racer—was beginning to falter, its stride uneven, its strength sapped. But what distressed him most was that he—and the slave catchers—were now just minutes away from the Maryland border and the protection afforded by the fact that Maryland was a slave state, one that did not recognize Pennsylvania's antislavery laws. Once they crossed the border, there was nothing that he, or even the sheriff, would be able to do to rescue Kitty and her family. He flailed the reins and ferociously kicked the horse's flanks yet again, hoping for at least one more burst of speed.

When he rounded a curve, his heart sank as he spied the racing caravan of riders and wagon up ahead. They had crossed into Maryland. One of the riders had peeled away from the group and was now facing in his direction. Puzzled as to why one rider would have stopped, he charged on. Suddenly, he saw a puff of smoke, which was followed by the buzzing sound—*pffft!*—of a musket ball whizzing by his head. He pulled back hard on the reins, and the horse skidded to an abrupt halt, nearly toppling over.

Wright stared angrily at the rider, exasperated and pained at the realization that the chase had ended and the slave catchers had won. The rider waved his hat haughtily, jerked his horse's head around, and galloped after the others. As the man had turned to ride away, Wright thought he heard the sound of laughter. He pounded his saddle in frustrated fury, and tears began to stream down his dust-encrusted face.

CHAPTER 47

THE JANGLING OF CHAINS JOLTED KITTY OUT OF A FITFUL, ACHING sleep. Twisting her body carefully, she tried futilely to find some remotely comfortable position as she lay stretched out on the dirt floor. Heavy steel shackles circled both of her ankles, attached by a length of chain to each other and by another length of chain to a bolt hammered into the wall of the shed.

As she raised her head slightly and searched for the children, a stabbing pain, like a sudden bolt of lightning, shot through her shoulder. She gasped, paralyzed for a moment, and waited for the throbbing surge to pass.

Although she knew that she and the children were captives, held in chains in Sam Maddox's shed, her memory of how they had arrived there was blurred. She recalled vividly, of course, the attack at Amon Jones's farm and her struggle with Maddox. But after he punched her in the head, her recollections were scanty. Since she had lapsed in and out of consciousness during the days of the wagon ride back to Virginia, she could only vaguely recall the journey. What she did clearly remember, however, was the sensation of her body frequently slamming painfully on the floor of the bouncing, shuddering wagon, her head and jaw aching, her eye swollen shut, and her shoulder feeling as if it were on fire each time it struck the unforgiving wooden planks. She had a faint recollection of the children, who were tied securely to each other but whose hands were loose, trying to lift her bound body and force water and bits of food down her throat. But she had no memory of arriving back in Virginia or of being cuffed and chained in the shed.

As the pain subsided, Kitty struggled again to raise her head a few inches off the hard floor. This time it was her head and jaw that screamed in pain. She winced as she squinted with her one good eye and scanned the cramped, cluttered space, then sighed in relief when she spotted the children fast asleep just feet from her. Their little slumbering bodies were bound together by a long length of rope coiled around their waists and wrapped securely around a post, while their feet were also shackled and chained together.

Furious, Kitty kicked out with her legs for perhaps the hundredth time, desperately trying to somehow loosen the chains that tethered her to Sam Maddox's wall. The shackles did more than just bind her; they were a terrifying foreshadowing of her plunge—and that of her children—into the depths of a permanent captivity if she could not somehow free them all. Weak and woozy from her injuries and the lack of food and water, she fell back to the floor. Just before she felt herself fading back into a dark and dizzying oblivion, she silently cursed Sam Maddox as tears of frustration formed in her eyes, vowing to herself that somehow she would kill him if she ever got the chance.

At that moment, Sam Maddox was lounging in the parlor of the Witherses' mansion, slouched in a stuffed wing chair, his booted feet perched on an embroidered footstool, a glass of tea in his hand. Katie Withers sat across from him, balanced demurely on the edge of a straight-backed cane chair, captivatingly attired in her best afternoon receiving dress, her hair swirled into a bun atop her head, a cameo brooch adorning her slender neck.

"So," Katie asked in a soft, seductive, syrupy drawl, "when will you be leavin'?"

"Plannin' on leavin' day after tomorrow," Maddox said. "Need to get the wagon fixed first. Cracked an axle. Bringin' it to the wheelwright later this afternoon."

"Are you takin' all the niggras with you?"

Maddox nodded. "The woman should fetch a good price. Little girls, too. Already been kitchen trained. Don't know 'bout the little brat. Just have to see what I can get for him."

"How long will you be gone this time?" Katie asked, injecting just a touch of sorrow and longing into the question.

Maddox smiled. "Not too long, I s'pose. Take 'bout a week to get to Charleston. Then, depends on when the next auction's scheduled. Shouldn't be too long, though."

"Why not just sell 'em here?" Katie asked, pouting a bit. "Auction's next week right in Washington, at the courthouse. That way you wouldn't have to be away again for so long."

"Get a much better price down there," Maddox said, sipping his tea. "Can make more sellin' 'em there 'cause the agents'll then ship 'em either farther south or to the islands, where they'll double their money." He shrugged. "So it's worth it for me to travel to South Carolina. Even if it means missin' you for a while," he added with his most engaging smile.

Just then, Fanny entered the room, carrying a small stack of books. She stopped short, surprised to find Maddox and Katie there.

"My apologies," Fanny said coolly. "Didn't know you were here visitin', Sam."

"He just got back and stopped in to say hello," said Katie pleasantly.

"Have you been travelin'?" Fanny asked.

Maddox nodded but said nothing.

"He was gone, chasin' after some runaway slaves," Katie chimed in. "Finally tracked 'em down and brought 'em back," she added with a touch of pride.

Now curious and concerned, Fanny softened her tone and offered Maddox a slight smile. "That so?" she said. "Whose slaves?"

"Mine," Maddox answered.

Fanny frowned. "Thought you just had the one old man workin' on your place. And hadn't heard anything about you havin' any runaways."

Maddox shrugged. "Inherited some from my uncle when he died," he said. "Some of 'em—a woman and some children—ran off a few weeks ago. Took a while to track 'em down, but finally found 'em up north, in Pennsylvania."

Fanny struggled to contain her alarm. Clearly, Maddox did not know—or suspect—that Fanny had anything to do with the escaped slaves. She decided to play along with him to find out as many details as possible before she contacted Mary.

"How'd they get all the way up there?" Fanny asked innocently.

"Had some help. Damn Quakers! Think they can be buttin' into our business," Maddox said, his tone tinged with irritation. "Anyway," he added after a brief pause, the anger washing away as quickly as it had appeared, "found 'em in the end and got 'em back."

"All of them?" asked Fanny.

"Yep." Maddox nodded.

"Any problems? Damage to the slaves?" Fanny asked.

"Nope," Maddox said. "Well, had to teach the woman a bit of a lesson, but not so much that it'll cost me anything when I sell her," he added.

"You plan on sellin' them off? All of them?" asked Fanny. "After all the effort to get 'em back?"

"Yep," said Sam Maddox.

"He's headin' to Charleston day after tomorrow to sell 'em," Katie added. "Get a much better price for 'em down there."

Fanny nodded knowingly. "Makes sense," she said. "Charleston auctions serve a much bigger market than around here. Prices should be a good deal higher."

Maddox shook his head as he took another sip of his tea. "That's what I'm countin' on," he said.

"Will you sell them as a family? Keep them together?" Fanny asked, straining to keep her voice conversational.

"Don't much care," answered Maddox. "Together, separate—makes no damn difference to me. Whichever gets me more money."

"We've always tried to keep families together here," said Fanny. "Keeps everybody happier, so they work better," she added.

Maddox just shrugged. "Don't really care," he repeated. "Not as if they're some kinda real people who got feelings like us. Just a bunch of niggras, after all. Once I sell 'em, don't care what happens to 'em."

"But," began Fanny, "it's a mother and her children. Wouldn't you want—"

"Why do you care?" interrupted Katie. "None of our business what Sam does with his property," she added defensively.

Fanny took a deep breath to compose herself and suppress her irritation. "Quite right. None of our business at all," Fanny agreed as she forced a tight smile.

Katie nodded, shot a flirtatious look at Maddox, who was still slouching in his chair, and turned back toward Fanny. "We're just about to have some sweet cakes. Will you join us?" she asked half-heartedly.

"Thank you for the kind invitation, but I need to attend to some matters," Fanny answered.

"Suit yourself," said Katie, clearly relieved that Fanny would not be staying any longer.

"Well, then," said Fanny coolly, now anxious to get away from them. "I'll leave you two alone." She inclined her head toward Maddox. "Safe travels, Sam. Hope your trip goes well."

"Thank you, Fanny," Maddox said. "Pleasure seeing you, as always," he added with an unctuous smile.

Fanny slipped from the room, then closed the parlor doors behind her. She stood in the hallway for a moment, thinking. Then she hurried down the center hall and out through the kitchen in the rear and walked rapidly in the direction of the slave quarters.

CHAPTER 48

"**M**ISS FANNY SAY YOU NEED TO COME RIGHT AWAY," THE YOUNG black man said earnestly. "She say it's a 'mergency.'"

The slave stood in the doorway of Mary's farmhouse, panting from exertion after his cross-country ride on the back of the mule that now waited patiently, pawing the ground, a few feet behind him.

"Miss Fanny say you need to come," he repeated, his eyes wide and his lithe teenage body held ramrod straight. It was obvious that he felt the great responsibility of his job as messenger.

As soon as Sam Maddox had ridden away from the Withers plantation, Fanny had dispatched the trusted young slave to find Mary and bring her immediately to Fanny's home. She had instructed him not to leave Mary until she had agreed to accompany him to the house.

"Is Fanny ill?" Mary asked anxiously.

"No, ma'am. Miss Fanny fine," he answered. "But she awful upset." He shook his head. "She say you need to come," he insisted for the third time.

Mary was puzzled, but she knew that Fanny would not summon her in this way unless it was important.

"You go right on back and tell Miss Fanny I'm on my way," Mary said. "I'll get my wagon and be right behind you."

The young boy nodded vigorously, relieved that he had done his job successfully. He quickly turned and sprinted to his mule, jumped on, and coaxed the animal into a reluctant trot across a field, in the direction of the Withers plantation. Mary ran into the house, grabbed a coat and her medical bag—just in case—and hurried toward the barn.

When Mary drove up the long driveway, Fanny was outside waiting for her, pacing back and forth across the veranda. She rushed to the wagon as Mary climbed down, then took her by the hand and guided her away from the front of the house.

"Something terrible has happened," Fanny exclaimed breathlessly, glancing furtively around to be sure that they could not be overheard.

"What's wrong?" asked Mary.

"Sam found Kitty," Fanny said.

"What?" exclaimed Mary. "How?"

"Don't know for sure," Fanny answered. "All I know is that he's got her and the children. And he's planning on selling them all."

Mary shook her head, stunned by the news.

"But . . . I don't understand," Mary said, struggling to comprehend what Fanny was telling her. "When I left her in Pennsylvania, she was fine. She was living with a family that was taking care of her. Nobody knew who she was—or where she was from. I even signed emancipation papers for her and the children. How could he . . . ?" Her voice trailed off, as she was overtaken by despair.

Fanny reached out and placed her arm around her friend to console her. Mary looked into Fanny's eyes.

"How do you know about this?" she asked.

"Sam was here. This morning," Fanny answered. "Came to visit Katie. When I walked in on them, he was telling her all about it. I pretended to be impressed—and he surely doesn't know that I was involved at all—and he told me his plans."

"He's going to sell them?" Mary repeated, incredulous at the news.

Fanny shook her head. "But not round here," Fanny said. "Plans on taking them down to Charleston and selling them there. Said he'd get a much better price for them down there—that they'd probably be taken farther south and sold again."

Mary's hands went to her face, her eyes wide with dread at the notion of Kitty and the children being sold off to the dreaded Deep South plantations.

"Where are they now? When is he plannin' on leavin' for Charleston? How—" Mary asked, questions pouring out at a rapid-fire pace.

"Wait! Just wait a second," Fanny interrupted evenly. "Just calm down so we can figure this all out."

Mary took a deep breath and let it out slowly, then nodded. "Where are they now?" Mary asked, fighting to regain her composure.

"Not sure, but I think they're at Sam's," Fanny said.

"And when's he plannin' on headin' to Charleston?" asked Mary.

"Day after tomorrow," said Fanny. "Had to get his wagon fixed first. Busted an axle. Was taking it to be fixed this afternoon."

Mary's head jerked up. "This afternoon?"

Fanny nodded her head.

"So he'll be gone from his place for a while?" Mary asked.

"Think so," said Fanny, shooting her a suspicious look. "Why?"

Mary's jaw tightened, and her eyes narrowed. "Because I'm going to go get them," Mary answered.

"What?" cried Fanny.

"I'm going to go get them," Mary said determinedly. "Get them away from him. Before it's too late."

"And do what with them?" asked Fanny. "Don't you think if they go missing that Sam'll know right away that you took them? And come looking for you?"

"Don't care what he knows," Mary said. "Just know that I can't let him take them."

"Even if you do find them," said an exasperated Fanny, "what will you do? Where will you hide them? And then what?"

Mary was quiet for a moment, pondering what to do next. "Not sure yet. Maybe we head back to Pennsylvania. Maybe somewhere else." She looked at Fanny, the fear in her eyes now replaced by anger and determination. "All I know is I have to get them away from him." She paused. "And I'll do whatever it takes!"

"What about taking Sam to court? Get a judge to step in and stop him," said Fanny.

Mary shook her head. "Not enough time. They'd be gone by the time we got to a judge. None scheduled to be round here for a couple weeks. And no guarantee that a judge would agree with me and stop him," Mary said, shaking her head. "No. Got to go get 'em. And right away," she added resolutely.

Both women were silent, facing each other like statues in a museum, both lost in their own thoughts.

Finally, Fanny spoke.

"Are you sure?" she asked quietly.

Mary simply nodded.

"Well, then," Fanny said, "we'll need a plan."

Mary cocked her head, unsure what Fanny was suggesting. "What do you mean?" Mary asked.

"I mean just what I said," Fanny answered. "We need a plan."

"Listen to me, Fanny," Mary said, taking her friend's hands in hers. "This is different. What you did to help us before—giving us the horse and carriage to take us away, helping us with our plans—nobody knew about that. Still don't. But this . . . this is different. If we do this—you and me—people will know. They'll know that you were a part of it. That you helped slaves escape." Mary shook her head sadly. "This could ruin you. I can't let you do this."

Fanny gazed hard at her. "Don't remember asking for your permission," Fanny said sternly but not unkindly. "In case you haven't noticed it before, I tend to follow my own drummer. Never really much cared what other folks thought. Not much sense in starting now."

"But—" Mary began.

"But nothing," Fanny interrupted. "Here's how I see it. Sam Maddox is an evil man. Never liked him, never will, and you know that. And he's planning on doing a terrible thing to Kitty and her children. My daddy—and his daddy before him—always taught me that you need to be kind as possible to your slaves. Try to make them feel like they're part of the family. And that meant never splitting up *their* family." She paused and took a deep breath. "He's an evil man," she repeated. "And someone should stop him. I'm not sure how, but I am sure it's got to be done. And I know you could probably do it on your own," she said with a wry grin, "but what fun would that be for me?"

Mary stood staring at her friend. Finally, she reached out and hugged her.

"Guess there's not much chance of talkin' you out of this?" Mary asked.

"About a donkey's chance in a thoroughbred race," Fanny answered decisively.

"Well, then," Mary said, "guess we need to get a move on."

"I'll have the carriage brought around right away. Sooner we get there, better the chance that we can free them before Sam gets back."

"Then what?" said Mary.

"Figure that out later," said Fanny. "Let's go get 'em first."

CHAPTER 49

*T*HE TWO WOMEN RACED THE SETTING SUN TOWARD SAM MADDOX'S farm. They were traveling in the same carriage that had carried Kitty to freedom in Pennsylvania, and they were now hopeful of carrying her to safety once again.

After careening up the drive to the small, derelict farmhouse, Mary reined the horse in as they pulled up to the front porch. Maddox was nowhere to be seen, nor was his wagon. Mary and Fanny climbed down and looked cautiously about as they approached the front door. They opened the door and peered warily inside. There was no sign that anyone was home.

Retracing their steps, they moved quickly to the barn. The barn door was wide open. Again, they peeked inside but saw nothing. No horse. No wagon. And no Kitty.

Both women stepped away from the barn, their eyes frantically searching the property, fearful that they might be too late and that Sam Maddox may have already left with Kitty and the children. Fanny spotted the corner of a swaybacked wooden shed peeking out from the side of the barn. She nudged Mary and inclined her head in the direction of the shed. As they got closer, they could see that the door was closed with a length of lumber wedged up against it at an angle, to prevent it from being pushed open from the inside.

Mary kicked at the piece of wood, dislodging it, and Fanny tugged at the door. It screeched open on rusty hinges, disclosing a storage area containing a scattered assortment of tools, farm equipment, and boxes. As their eyes adjusted to the darkness, a shaft of dust-filled light revealed what first looked like large bundles stacked near the rear wall. They stepped inside, picked their way carefully through the rubble, and then stopped abruptly. One of the bundles moved.

Rushing to the rear of the shed, they realized that the bundles were actually Kitty and the three children. As she bent down to them, Mary gasped.

They were all lying on the earthen floor, with iron cuffs around their ankles and lengths of chain shackling them to each other and anchored to the wall. The children raised their heads weakly, their eyes staring blankly. Kitty did not look up, didn't move at all. Mary lifted Kitty's head off the floor. She gasped again, this time more from horror than surprise.

Kitty's face was battered, a spiderweb of scabbed cuts and scratches on both cheeks, one eye swollen shut, an ugly purple bruise surrounding it. She was wrapped in a moth-eaten, threadbare coat that barely covered a ripped, filthy sleeping gown. Mary shook her gently, fearful that she might be dead.

Slowly, groggily, Kitty opened her one good eye a crack and peered uncomprehendingly at the two women. Mary spoke to her softly.

"Kitty! We're here. We're going to get you out of here. Kitty?"

Mary turned to Fanny. "Help me get her up," she said to Fanny.

Fanny bent down and grasped Kitty by the shoulders. She and Mary carefully lifted and propped Kitty up in a sitting position.

"I'll get some water," said Fanny, and then she hurried out of the shed and headed toward the well in front of the barn.

"Kitty," Mary said to her again. "Can you hear me? Are you all right?"

Slowly, Kitty's good eye seemed to come into focus, and recognition set in. She cocked her head to one side so she could see better. "Mistress," Kitty said, her voice a raspy whisper. "Please . . . get us . . . away from here."

Mary shook her head. "We will," she answered, her fingertips softly brushing Kitty's damaged face.

"Sam . . . ?" Kitty muttered through swollen lips.

"Not here," said Mary. "In town, fixin' up his wagon. We'll get you away from here now . . . while he's gone."

Kitty nodded weakly. "The children?" she asked.

Mary twisted her head toward the children and was glad to see that all three of them were now awake and sitting up. Although little Arthur still seemed somewhat dazed, the two girls recognized her and were tugging on their chains, reaching out to her.

"Mistress Mary," said Eliza Jane in a barely audible squeak. "You take us home now?"

"Yes. Yes," Mary said, smiling kindly at them while trying to keep from bursting into tears. "I'll take you home now."

Mary turned back toward Kitty. "The children are fine," she told her.

Fanny burst back into the shed, carrying a bucket of water and a ladle. She stooped down to Kitty first, scooped a ladleful of water, and pressed it to Kitty's lips.

Kitty shook her head. "Children first," she rasped.

"We'll take care of the children," Fanny said. "But need to get you on your feet first. So, here . . . Take this," Fanny said, then tilted the ladle so the water began to dribble into Kitty's mouth.

Kitty tilted her head back and opened her cracked lips as the water trickled down her throat. She coughed, spilling some of the water, then drank some more. Then she inclined her head toward the children.

"Now them," she said, her voice a bit stronger.

Fanny took the bucket, knelt in front of the children, and allowed each one to gulp from the ladle.

"How'd you find us?" Kitty asked, straightening herself up.

"Tell you later," Mary answered. "Right now, we got to get y'all away from here. Quick as we can. Before Sam gets back."

Kitty bobbed her head, her strength and hope restored by the presence of Mary and Fanny. Then she looked down at her shackles and chains. "What about these?" she said, grabbing the chains and shaking them.

Mary bent down and examined the shackles. There was no padlock; rather a locking pin had been driven into a hole in each cuff, locking the two halves of the steel circle together around each of her ankles. Looking at the children, Mary could see that they were shackled in the same fashion.

Scrambling to her feet, Mary looked around frantically for something she could use to knock the locking pins out of their slots. When she saw nothing that might work, she ran out of the shed and into the barn. There, on a workbench along a wall, she spied a wooden mallet. She grabbed it and raced back to the shed.

"Help me with this," she called to Fanny, breathless from her run and the fear that Sam might return any minute. "Hold this steady," she said, grabbing the shackle on one of Kitty's ankles and twisting it around so the locking pin was exposed. Kitty grimaced from the pain of the steel grating against her raw, scraped leg but said nothing.

Mary gritted her teeth, gripped the shackle and swung the mallet. It struck with a ringing noise. The chains shook, but the locking pin did not move.

"Need to prop something underneath," Mary said, almost to herself. Glancing around, she saw a small, square block of wood, grabbed it, and wedged it tightly under the shackle for stability.

"Should help," she mumbled as she swung again.

This time, the force of the blow jolted the pin, nudging it partially out of the hole. Two more strikes and the pin popped out. Mary stripped the first shackle away and then quickly placed the block of wood under Kitty's other shackle and began hammering. After three blows, the pin dropped to the floor and the second steel circle snapped open.

Mary moved swiftly to the children and began hammering away at their shackles as Fanny helped Kitty to her feet. One by one, all the remaining shackles were unfastened, and the children were also freed and able to stand.

"Can y'all walk?" Mary asked anxiously.

The children all nodded. So did Kitty.

"Then we need to leave right away," Mary said. "Fanny, you take the children. I've got Kitty."

Fanny ushered the three children from the shed, while Mary placed an arm around Kitty, who was a bit wobbly. Within minutes, the women had loaded Kitty and the children into the rear of the carriage. As Mary climbed up to join Fanny on the driver's seat, Kitty grabbed her arm.

"Where we goin'?" she asked, a look of consternation on her face.

"Back to Fanny's," said Mary.

"Safe there?" asked Kitty uncertainly.

"Should be," said Mary. "For now, anyway."

Kitty shot her a crooked smile and inclined her head toward the carriage. "Thought I'd seen the last of this here wagon," she said.

"One more ride," answered Mary, smiling as she reached out and gently touched Kitty's damaged face. "Just one more ride."

CHAPTER 50

*N*IGHTFALL HAD COME QUICKLY. THE UNLIKELY GROUP OF CLANDES-tine travelers—a widowed farmwife, a rich plantation owner, and an escaped slave with her children—was thankful for the cloud-strewn, moonless cover of darkness that allowed them to arrive at Fanny's home undetected.

Fanny supervised the bathing and feeding of the children, while Mary tended to Kitty, gently salving her wounds, providing her with hot food, and replacing her torn rags with clean clothes. Once the children had been put to bed in a dormer room on the third floor of the mansion, the three women sat together around a table in the large, ornately decorated dining room, before the embracing warmth of a dancing, crackling fire.

"What now?" asked Kitty, her hands wrapped around a steaming earthenware mug of tea.

Mary and Fanny exchanged uncertain glances.

"Not exactly sure," said Mary. "First thing we had to do was get you away from there. Sam was plannin' on takin' you and the children to Charleston to sell you off."

A look of horror flashed across Kitty's face. "Assumed he was bringin' us back here," Kitty said, "but thought he just wanted to keep us for himself." She shook her head. "Never thought he'd be sellin' us off . . . least not right away."

"Fortunately, Fanny heard him talkin' to Katie about his plans . . . ," Mary began.

"He was here?" Kitty said, alarmed.

Fanny nodded. "Came to visit with Katie," she said. "I overheard him talking about taking all of you down to the Carolinas for sale and realized that we had to do something quickly. So," she added, holding her open palms out and shrugging, "we got you away from him. At least for now."

"What about Miss Katie?" Kitty asked. "She know we're here?"

"I suspect she will soon," said Fanny. "Think she's upstairs in her room right now . . ."

As if on cue from a stage manager, Katie stormed into the dining room.

"Do you care to explain this?" she exclaimed, her face flushed with fury, as she pointed at Kitty.

Fanny stood and stepped directly in front of Katie, stopping her in her tracks. "You seem to be under some illusion that I somehow owe you an explanation for what I choose to do," Fanny said sternly, her eyes flashing.

Katie took a step backward, her indignation momentarily blocked by her older sister's hostile stance. "This is my home, too," she spluttered angrily, "and you have no right sheltering *her*—a runaway slave—here without my permission."

"First of all," Fanny said coldly, "I don't need your permission for anything. Second, she's not a runaway slave. She's a free woman who was kidnapped and beaten by your *friend*." She spit out the last word derisively. "And I—we—don't intend to let him get away with such ungentlemanly conduct. So," she added as she took a threatening step closer to Katie, "if you're not happy offering the hospitality of our home to her, feel free to go someplace else while she's here as my guest."

The women glared angrily at each other for a long minute before Katie turned and stormed indignantly out of the room. Fanny returned to the table, sat down, took a deep breath, and exhaled slowly.

"Well," Fanny began, "I guess we can assume that Sam will know soon—if he doesn't know already—that y'all are here."

"Should we run?" asked Kitty. "Get as far away as we can before he gets here?"

Mary shook her head. "Don't think we'd get very far. Probably on his way here right now," Mary said.

Fanny was silent, contemplating the situation. Finally, she shook her head. "Don't think running would work. Not now." She paused and then looked at the two women. "But I think I've got an idea. What if we send for the sheriff? Tell him what happened, how you took Kitty and the children to Pennsylvania and freed them. How Sam then kidnapped them and brought them back here. Tell the sheriff we want Sam kept away from them. At least until a judge comes to town."

Mary nodded slowly. "Might work. At least for the time being," Mary mused. She turned toward Kitty, who had remained silent. "What do you think?"

Kitty straightened, a fleeting grimace a reminder of her injuries, and looked directly at Mary and then Fanny. "I want you to summon the sheriff," she said adamantly. "And when he gets here, I want to press charges against Sam."

"What?" said Fanny. "I don't understand."

"I want to press charges against him," Kitty repeated. "For what he did to me and my children. He kidnapped us and beat us, chained us up like animals. Want him to be held responsible."

Mary and Fanny exchanged confused glances. Finally, Fanny spoke.

"But, Kitty," she said gently, "you can't bring charges against Sam. The law doesn't allow it—"

"Why?" Kitty interrupted. "Because I'm a slave? Because I'm someone's property? And not a person?" she said, barely controlling her fury. "Well, I'm not a slave! I'm free! Set free by Mistress Mary in Pennsylvania and had the papers to prove it. He kidnapped and beat a free woman! No different than if it was either of you he kidnapped and beat."

"But I don't recall it ever being done before . . . ," began Fanny.

"Don't care about before," insisted Kitty. She swiveled to face Mary. "You told me I was free. The Pennsylvania court told me I was free. And then Sam comes bustin' into my room, beats me, and ties me up like I was some kind of criminal." She paused and looked carefully at Mary. "So, was I free or not?"

"Yes," said Mary, without hesitation. "Yes, you were free. But now we're back in Virginia. . . ."

"Makes no difference," asserted Kitty. "Was free in Pennsylvania, and that's where he kidnapped us. And," she added, "you would have freed us here in Virginia, anyway, if we didn't have to run from him."

"All true," agreed Mary. "But what Fanny's saying is right. Don't remember any slave trying to press charges against a white man, much less winning in court."

"Don't matter," answered Kitty firmly. "None of that matters. Because this isn't about a slave going against a white man. I . . . am . . . free! This is about a free woman going against a white man. And as a free person, a court has to listen to me."

Kitty sat back in her chair, her jaw set, her mind made up.

The silence in the room stretched out for a few minutes, marked only by the rhythmic ticking of a large grandfather clock standing guard in a corner of the room. Finally, Kitty spoke again, her voice calmer.

"Just tell me this," she said, shifting her gaze carefully from Mary to Fanny. "What would y'all do if Sam attacked you the way he attacked me? Would you let him get away with it?"

Fanny sighed deeply. "Now that you put it that way, no," she said. "I'd never let him get away with that."

"Probably just go and shoot him myself," said Mary, "if he ever put his hands on me."

Kitty shook her head defiantly. "Thought so," she said. "Well, I'm not goin' to just sit back and let him do that to me, either."

"Well, then," said Mary, "I think we've decided what we do next. At least, Kitty and I've decided." She looked at Fanny. "This here's not your fight anymore. You've already done more than a friend should be asked to do."

Fanny shook her head. "This is still my fight," she said. "My daddy told me that sometimes the only battle worth fighting is one where everyone else thinks you're wrong. Well, we're on the right side of this battle, and I don't much care what anyone else thinks."

Fanny picked up a small handbell from the table and rang it several times. Within seconds, the young slave who had been sent to summon Mary rushed into the room.

"Yes'm?" the boy said.

"I need you to please go find the sheriff. As quickly as you can. Tell him that I need him here right away. And," she added, "tell him there might be trouble."

CHAPTER 51

THE HAMMERING ON THE FRONT DOOR ECHOED THROUGH THE HOUSE like a series of thunderclaps. The three women, who had been dozing on couches in the living room, sat bolt upright. Fanny glanced at the clock and saw that it was after midnight. She was distressed that the sheriff had not yet arrived.

Mary scrambled to her feet, picked her way stealthily to a front window, and peered out from behind a heavy brocaded curtain. She caught her breath and turned toward Kitty and Fanny, a look of alarm on her face.

It was not the sheriff standing at the door. It was Sam Maddox, along with two other men, whom she did not recognize in the darkness. All three were carrying rifles. Maddox slammed his fist on the door yet again, the striking even more ferocious this time.

"Sam!" mouthed Mary.

Fanny nodded, stood, straightened her clothes, and walked to the door. Before opening it, she turned and looked to Kitty.

"Run to the third-floor room with the children," Fanny whispered. "Don't leave that room, no matter what happens. And keep the children quiet."

Kitty shook her head in acknowledgment and rushed out of the living room and toward the back stairs leading to the upper floors. Fanny shot Mary a worried glance.

"Stay inside," she whispered.

Mary nodded.

Fanny slid the large brass locking bolt back, swung the door open, stepped outside, and pulled the door closed behind her. As she walked onto the veranda, Sam Maddox retreated two paces, still flanked by the two men. Fanny glared at them.

"I'm not sure why you men think you can come—uninvited— to my home in the middle of the night, carrying weapons, and make a ruckus on my front porch," Fanny said harshly. "But you are most surely mistaken. I'd thank you to leave—now!" she ordered.

Maddox took a small step forward, while the two men accompanying him, now clearly uncertain, shifted backward toward the edge of the veranda.

"You got somethin' here belongs to me," Maddox said almost casually. "And I'm here to retrieve 'em."

"There's nothing—and no one—here that belongs to you," Fanny said. "Now please leave," she added firmly.

"What makes you think you can just up and take somethin' belongs to me? And from my own property? Just ride up to my home, break into my shed, and steal 'em from me?" Maddox said, glowering at her, his voice now as hard and threatening as the edge of a knife blade. "You think because you own all this"—he gestured toward the house and the surrounding property with a sweep of his arm—"you got some right to do what you want? That you're better'n everyone? That you're some kinda royalty who can tell everyone else what to do?"

Fanny returned his angry glare. "And what makes *you* think that you can just ride up north, break into someone's home, kidnap a woman and her children—a free woman—beat her, and then chain her up like she's some mangy dog?" Fanny said, straining to control her fury. "And then you think you can show up here, like this, and demand that I turn them all back over to you? Well, if you think that, then you're damn sure stupider than I thought you were—and I always thought you were pretty damn stupid to start with."

"Nice speech," Maddox sneered. " 'Specially from someone's got dozens of slaves workin' for her round here. Don't see you freein' none a your darkies. So what gives you the right to tell me what to do with mine?"

"She's not yours," Fanny said, seething. "And you'll never get your evil hands on her again—not if I can help it. Now," she said, raising her voice, "get off my property!"

Fanny and Maddox stared at each other for a long minute. The two men standing behind Maddox shuffled their feet, unsure what they should do.

"I ain't leavin' till I got what I came for," Sam Maddox said menacingly.

At that moment, the big front door swung open and Mary stepped outside. She carried two shotguns, one in each hand. Raising the barrel of one, she pointed it directly at Maddox, while she quickly handed the other to Fanny, who immediately grasped it and aimed it in the general direction of the other two men.

"Fanny *asked* you to leave," Mary said calmly. "Now I'm *tellin'* you to leave."

Maddox took a step backward, looking from one woman to the other. "You gonna shoot us?" he asked, his voice cracking slightly, the arrogance giving way to a trace of uncertainty. "Right here, on your porch?"

"Way I see it," said Mary, "here we are, two women, all alone and unprotected in this house, when a bunch of strangers show up in the middle of the night, trying to get into the house. Scared the hell outta us. So we're just tryin' to protect ourselves from who knows what and shot the intruders." She flashed Maddox a hard grin. "Nobody's gonna have much of a problem with that. Folks'll probably be talkin' 'bout how brave we were."

One of the men shifted slightly and began to raise the barrel of his rifle. Fanny immediately pointed her shotgun at him and cocked the hammer. He stopped moving and stood still as a statue.

"On the other hand," continued Mary, "if you shoot us . . . well, you'll have an awful difficult time explaining what y'all were doin' here in the middle of the night, threatenin' two poor, unpro- tected women in one of their own homes. My bet is they'd probably hang you by dawn." She paused and looked at each of the men. "So . . . what's it gonna be?"

"You're bluffin'," Maddox said. "You ain't gonna shoot us."

Mary smiled at Maddox, as if she was actually enjoying herself. "I'd shoot you down right now and wouldn't lose a lick of sleep over it," she said.

There was dead silence as neither Mary nor Sam Maddox moved. Then Fanny, her gun still trained on the two men, spoke.

"You two boys willing to bet your lives that we're bluffing?" she asked sweetly. "Seems like an awful lot to wager on a fight that isn't even yours." She shrugged. "Doesn't seem like such a great bet to me . . . but it's up to you, I guess," she added, swinging the barrel ominously back and forth between them.

"We ain't leavin'," Maddox said grimly.

"Sam," one of the men mumbled, "maybe we ought to talk about this. . . ."

"I said, we ain't leavin'," Maddox repeated.

Mary slowly used her thumb to pull back the hammer of her gun, the menacing clicking of the steel as it locked into place reverberating in the stillness of the dark night.

Suddenly, the pounding of hoofbeats could be heard storming up the long driveway, interrupting the standoff. As they all turned toward the noise, the sheriff, accompanied by three deputies, burst into sight.

CHAPTER 52

"WHOA, THERE! GUNS DOWN!" SHERIFF WILLIAM WALDEN YELLED, jumping from his horse and grabbing his own rifle from its scabbard. "Don't know what's goin' on here," he said, trying to keep his voice calm, "but do know that we ain't needin' all these guns drawn."

He took two cautious steps toward the veranda as the three deputies leaped from their horses and, following the sheriff's lead, drew their rifles and fanned out around him. Not wanting to get caught in any cross fire, he stopped at the bottom of the stairs. Looking up, he brushed his index finger to the brim of his hat and nodded toward Mary and Fanny.

"Miss Withers. Mistress Maddox. Sorry I got delayed. Got here soon's I could," he said courteously.

After turning toward Sam Maddox, he shot him a questioning look. "Sam," the sheriff said, a hard edge creeping into his voice, "you wanna tell me why you're standin' here on Miss Withers's porch—in the middle of the night—pointin' guns at her and Mistress Maddox?"

"Ain't what it looks like, Sheriff," Maddox answered quickly.

"Damn well better not be what it looks like," said the sheriff. " 'Cause I ain't happy at all with what it's lookin' like to me."

Maddox began to respond when Fanny interrupted.

"Sheriff," she said forcefully, "these men showed up uninvited, in the dark of night, carrying guns and scaring the living daylights out of us. And they've refused to leave my property. Kindly direct them to leave—or arrest them."

"Sam—and you men, too—put them guns down. Now!" the sheriff ordered.

"But, Sheriff," Maddox began angrily.

"Guns down! Now!" the sheriff repeated, raising his own barrel and leveling it directly at Maddox. "Ain't gonna ask again!"

Slowly, Maddox and the other men lowered the barrels of their rifles.

"Put 'em on the ground," the sheriff barked.

Reluctantly, the men leaned down and placed their weapons on the ground.

"Aw right, now," the sheriff said in a calmer voice. "What's this all about?" He looked deferentially to Fanny first.

"Mr. Maddox," Fanny began, deliberately refusing to lower her shotgun, "and a gang of cutthroats kidnapped and beat Miss Kitty, a former slave who had been freed by Mrs. Maddox," she said, gesturing toward Mary. "He brought her back here, chained her up, and is planning on taking her south, with her children, to sell them. Mrs. Maddox and I found her chained on his farm, cut her loose, and brought her here, and we plan on returning her to her legal freedom in Pennsylvania."

"That right, Mistress Maddox?" the sheriff asked.

"Yes, Sheriff," Mary answered. "That's all true. She belonged to me after my husband's passing, and I took her to Pennsylvania, where I set her free. Got the papers to prove it."

"Ain't true at all," Maddox exploded. "My uncle's will give me a right to them slaves. Never gave her," he continued, pointing at Mary, "any right to free 'em. Just took back what belongs to me, nothin' more. An' they got no right sneakin' onto my land and stealin' my niggras!"

The sheriff seemed perplexed. He turned back toward Fanny and Mary.

"Mistress Maddox," he said respectfully, "the will give Sam, here, any rights to yer husband's estate?"

"No, sir, Sheriff," Mary said vehemently. "That's an outlandish lie. He's just makin' that all up 'cause he's flat broke and tryin' to grab anythin' he can get his hands on to raise money. My property, left to me by my Samuel, to do with what I please."

"Ain't so," Maddox yelled. "My lawyer told me the will gives me rights to them. Plain as day!"

The sheriff was quiet for a moment, pondering his dilemma. Finally, he spoke. "Where's this Kitty and her children now?" he asked.

"Inside my home, under my protection," Fanny said. "Where I intend to keep them," she added, shooting a harsh glance at Sam Maddox as she kept the shotgun pointed at his chest.

"Here's what we gonna do," the sheriff said. "First off, Sam, you and yer friends here gonna pack up yer guns and head on back home."

"But—" Maddox spluttered angrily.

"But nothin'," the sheriff interrupted sharply. "I'm tellin' you what yer doin'. This ain't no discussion. Pick up those guns and get outta here, fast. Before I decide to arrest you for armed trespassin'."

The sheriff then turned toward the women.

"Miss Withers, you give me yer word that you'll keep these folks—Kitty and her children—here with you tonight? Won't take 'em anywhere?"

Fanny nodded. "You have my word, Sheriff," she answered, puzzled.

"Aw right," said the sheriff, seemingly satisfied. "They all stay here with you tonight. Tomorrow I want y'all to bring them to me in Washington."

"Why?" asked Mary.

"Gonna need a judge to sort this all out. Look at the will and decide who really owns the niggras. Meantime, gonna put 'em all in the county jail—for their own protection," he said, pointedly glaring at Sam Maddox. "Till the judge tells me what to do."

"But, Sheriff . . . ," began Fanny.

"Sorry, Miss Withers," the sheriff said. "Ain't that I don't believe you and Mistress Maddox. Up to me, be happy to let you take them niggras back up north. But I'm 'fraid this ain't the

kinda decision I'm s'posed to be makin'. Seems like we're all better off lettin' a judge decide."

"But the jail?" pleaded Mary. "That's no place for them."

"All be fine, Mistress Maddox," the sheriff said soothingly.
"Promise you they'll be taken good care of. I'll be sure to have the
jailer keep them in the debtors' rooms. Them're more like boardinghouse rooms than jail cells. Be comfortable there—and safe—
while we sort this all out."

The women looked at each other, unsure. After a moment,
Mary took a deep breath and nodded at the sheriff.

"I understand, Sheriff," Mary said. "And I appreciate your concern for their safety. We'll bring them to you tomorrow. And we'll
rely on your word that you will protect them."

"You can count on that, Mistress Maddox," the sheriff assured her.

"You can be sure that we will, Sheriff," Fanny added, her tone
making it clear that his job was on the line if he didn't protect
them.

"Well, I'll be goin', then," the sheriff said. "Sam, you men get a
move on. I'll be right behind you."

As Sam Maddox and his men stalked sullenly away, the sheriff
turned back to the women and tipped his hat.

"Good night, ladies. See you tomorrow."

"Good night, Sheriff. And thank you," Fanny said.

Both Fanny and Mary finally lowered the shotguns as the sheriff and his posse galloped off into the night.

"Thought I might have to shoot him," Mary sighed, drained by
the emotional stress of the confrontation.

"Kind of hoping you would," said Fanny, with a wry grin.

"Prob'ly should have," said Mary, with an answering grin.
"Might've been my only chance," she added regretfully.

"We should go talk to Kitty now. Let her know what's going to
happen," Fanny said.

Mary nodded. "Might be the best thing, after all. Least we know
she'll be safe and outta Sam's reach," Mary said. "We all need to get
some sleep now. Busy day tomorrow. And I'm thinkin' I'll be
needin' to talk to a lawyer while I'm in town."

"Zeph Turner?" asked Fanny.

"Think so," said Mary. "Talked to him a bit about the will before we left. I trust him. And I know Samuel liked him, too."

"Kitty's going to want to know how long she'll be staying at the jail," said Fanny.

"I know," Mary said, nodding thoughtfully. "Hoping that Zeph might have some answers and be able to figure out how soon we could get a judge involved."

The women stepped inside, carrying their shotguns, and closed the big door silently behind them.

CHAPTER 53

*T*HEY LEFT THE WITHERS PLANTATION AROUND NOON THE NEXT DAY, traveling in the family's large, richly ornamental six-passenger, two-horse carriage. When they arrived at the jail in Washington, a square, two-story red brick building located around the corner from the courthouse, several townspeople on the street stopped and gaped in near astonishment at the sight. The richest woman in the county emerged from her ornate coach, together with an entourage of Mary, Kitty, and the three children, and strode regally into the county jail, as if she was making an appearance at a high-society cotillion.

Inside, they were met by the jailer, Absalom Lillard, and his wife, Hannah. Lillard was a dour man, tall and rangy, with stringy gray hair down to his shoulders and a full beard framing a narrow, pinched face. His wife, however, was a complete contrast to her husband, as she was short and stout, with a kind face and a warm manner and a broad, welcoming smile.

"Miss Withers," Lillard said politely. "Been expecting you. Sheriff says these folks"—he gestured toward Kitty and the children—"gonna be stayin' with us for a while."

"Thank you, Mr. Lillard," Fanny said, bestowing a dazzling smile on the old man. "And you, also, Mistress Lillard. We are all very thankful to you for your hospitality." She gestured toward Kitty and the children. "This is Kitty and her children, Eliza Jane, Mary, and Arthur. And I'm sure you know Mistress Maddox."

Kitty offered a brief nod, while the children hovered close behind her, frightened by these new surroundings. Mary stepped forward.

"We all thank you," Mary said, smiling at the jailer and his wife. "Kitty and her children are . . ." She hesitated, searching for the right words, and then continued. "They are a part of my family since they were born. They are all free now, and I trust you will treat them as such," she added pointedly.

The jailer seemed uncertain about the status of his new residents—slaves until very recently—and how he should be dealing with them, but Hannah immediately put them all at ease, stepping forward and clasping Kitty's hands in hers.

"Y'all are very welcome here," she said sweetly. "Come, let me show you where y'all will be staying," she added, then gathered up Kitty and the children and steered them off in the direction of a narrow staircase in the corner.

"Been told by the sheriff to keep 'em all in the debtors' rooms upstairs, away from the jail cells down on this floor. Be safe up there. Rooms ain't too bad. And they're just above where we live, so we can look out for 'em," Lillard said. "Still ain't quite sure why they bein' here in the first place, though," he added, a puzzled and not very happy look on his face.

"It's a complicated story," offered Fanny, still ladling on the charm. "But you can be sure that the sheriff and all of us trust that they'll remain safe here with you and Mistress Lillard until their legal situation is resolved."

"Sheriff says keep 'em here, I'll keep 'em here." Lillard shrugged, still not convinced or appeased.

Upstairs, Hannah had ushered Kitty and the children into a modest-sized room with two beds, a washstand, a low bureau, and a single barred window that looked out at the courthouse next door.

"How long we stayin' here, Mama?" asked Eliza Jane softly as Mary and Arthur peered curiously out of the window.

"Not sure," answered Kitty, stroking her daughter's hair soothingly. "But we'll be safe here. And Mistress Mary and Miss Fanny will still be lookin' after us."

"We're happy to have y'all stayin' here with us," said Hannah, trying her best to make Kitty and the children feel comfortable. "A little later," she said to the children, "we'll all go outside so we can play a bit before dinner. Would you like that?"

The children looked at each other, puzzled, and then turned to Kitty. It had been so long since they had been able to actually play outside that they were unsure how to respond to this invitation. Kitty nodded at them and smiled reassuringly.

"That would be very nice, Mistress Lillard," Kitty said. "The children would like that."

"Well, then," said Hannah cheerfully, "let's get y'all settled in."

Kitty slipped back down the staircase into the main room, where Mary and Fanny were still talking to Lillard.

Mary looked questioningly at Kitty.

"The room is very nice," Kitty said. "Thank you, sir," she added, turning to Lillard. "My children and I appreciate your hospitality."

Lillard grumbled something about having to go check on a prisoner and inclined his head toward Mary and Fanny. "Good day, ladies," he said.

"Again, our thanks," said Fanny.

"Happy to oblige," Lillard said, offering a slight bow of his head.

As he turned to head off toward the cell wing of the building, Kitty followed him. "Mr. Lillard," she said. "Might you help me with one request?"

The jailer stopped and faced her, his head cocked to one side, and one eyebrow raised. "What now?" he asked.

"When you see the sheriff, could you tell him I must talk to him?" Kitty asked respectfully. "It's important," she added.

The jailer stared hard at her for a moment, nodded slightly, and then turned and walked away.

"What was that all about?" asked Mary.

"Have to talk to the sheriff," said Kitty.

"About what?" asked Mary.

"About pressin' charges against Sam Maddox," said Kitty grimly.

CHAPTER 54

"AIN'T NEVER BEEN DONE BEFORE," EXCLAIMED SHERIFF WILLIAM Walden. "Been sheriff here nigh on ten years now and ain't never heard of such a thing. Slaves just can't up and charge a white man with assault and kidnapping. It just ain't done round here. Ain't done anywhere! Law won't allow it!"

The sheriff was a broad man with a large potbelly and hands the size of ham hocks. His moon-shaped face was creased with doubt as he sat behind a small wooden table in the tidy closet-sized office of Jailer Absalom Lillard. Kitty sat in the chair in front of him, her hands folded in her lap.

"I understand, Sheriff," she said quietly. "But I'm not a slave. I'm a free woman."

The sheriff shook his head vigorously. "But you were a slave. And Sam says you're still a slave—his slave," he argued.

"He's lying," Kitty said firmly. "Mistress Mary showed you the papers. She freed me once we got to Pennsylvania. Since I was free, can't possibly be legal for Sam to go to Pennsylvania and bring me back here. And beat me and chain me up."

"But this is Virginia, not Pennsylvania. And I ain't seen nothin' says you're free here," he countered.

She paused and looked at him thoughtfully. "Would you let him get away with that if I was a white woman?"

"But you ain't," he answered, clearly frustrated.

"No, I'm not. But I am free," she said. "Those papers from Mistress Mary prove that's true. So I'm entitled to the same protections as any other free woman."

The sheriff leaned back in his chair and balanced his bulk on the back two legs, his hands now folded over his abundant belly. He stared up at the ceiling for a long moment, as if he was seeking some divine guidance. Finally, he leaned forward and spread his massive hands across the table.

"Listen here," he said firmly but not unkindly. "Don't like Sam Maddox. Never have. He's a mean son of a bitch. Up to me, I'd throw his ass in jail in a heartbeat." He paused. "But this ain't about me. Ain't just about you, neither. About much more. It's about who we are and how we live. It's about all them troublemakers up north tryin' to tell us what we should be doin' with our slaves."

"But, Sheriff—" began Kitty.

"No, just listen up," the sheriff said, cutting her off. "Not that I ain't sympathetic about what he done to you. I am. Don't take kindly to beatin' anyone—even slaves. But the law's the law, and my job's to enforce it." He shook his head sadly. "Just don't see any way that I can be signin' a complaint against him. Not if I want to keep my job," he added. "Sorry, but that's the way it's gotta be."

The silence enveloped the room like a heavy cloak. Neither Kitty nor the sheriff spoke for several moments. Kitty was staring out of the window at the courthouse, while the sheriff shifted uncomfortably in his creaking chair. Finally, Kitty sat up straight, placed her hands on the wooden table, nodded thoughtfully, and spoke, her words precise and steady.

"I understand. But I will not let what he did to us go unpunished. I'm no longer someone's property. Folks can't just do whatever they want to me. I'm free, and I have rights now, too." She took a deep breath and then continued. "*I* will sign the complaint against him."

The sheriff looked at her, perplexed.

"Not askin' *you* to sign the complaint. *I'll* do it," she said. "Folks allowed to sign complaints against someone, right?"

The sheriff hesitated and then answered uncertainly. "Well, yes . . . but usually for lesser types of charges, like trespassin' or stealin' animals. But this is different," he said.

"Why?" said Kitty. "Just because you're the one usually signs a complaint don't mean that nobody else can. Right?"

The sheriff thought for a long moment. "Guess it don't," he finally said.

"And that way, nobody's sayin' you're not doin' your job right or breakin' any laws," Kitty added.

"But still gonna be a question whether you're a slave or not, 'cause slaves can't sign complaints. Can't even testify in court," the sheriff said.

"Well, then," Kitty said confidently, "guess the judge'll have to make that decision, won't he?"

"Guess so," the sheriff said. "Outta my hands that way."

"We're settled, then," Kitty said and then paused a beat before continuing in a solemn voice. "Sheriff, I would like to sign a complaint against Sam Maddox for kidnapping and assault."

The sheriff shook his head gravely and unfolded his big body from the chair. "Let's get Jailer Lillard to take you on over to the court clerk's office. You can tell him what you want to say and then sign the complaint yourself," he said.

An hour later, Kitty and Absalom Lillard were sitting across from the court clerk, a bald, rodent-like man with wire-rimmed glasses that constantly twitched on the end of his nose. Although clearly troubled by what he was asked to do and resentful of being ordered to assist a Negro, he nevertheless reluctantly followed the sheriff's instructions, noted the details of Kitty's claims, and prepared an official complaint for her signature.

As the clerk passed the document across the table to Kitty, he raised his nose in the air as if he were encountering a noxious odor, and addressed her in a condescending tone. "I will read this to you, and you can then make your mark at the bottom, signifying that you understand," he said.

"No need," said Kitty, mirroring his attitude with a haughty tone of her own. "I can read and write," she said, and then she picked up the document and read it out loud, just to prove her point. She then signed it.

> *The undersigned plaintiff, Kitty, a Negro woman who professes to be free, hereby petitions for the benefit of herself and her children, Eliza Jane, Mary, and Arthur, against Samuel Maddox, a resident of Rappahannock County, claiming that the said Samuel Maddox did, with force and arms, beat, wound, hurt, and injure the said plaintiff and imprisoned her against her will. Wherefore, the said plaintiff sayeth that she is injured and hath sustained damages in the amount of $1000.00, and therefore she sues.*
>
> *Signed,*
> *Kitty*

"That is correct," sniffed the clerk after Kitty handed him the document. "I will have the complaint delivered to the court. The circuit judge will arrange for the complaint to be served on the defendant and will then set a schedule for the trial. That's all," he said, waving his hand dismissively.

"Thank you," Kitty said formally.

As she and the jailer rose, Lillard leaned toward the clerk and glared at him for a moment. The clerk recoiled, surprised at the jailer's apparent annoyance.

"*Miss* Kitty will be residing with us until this matter is resolved," Lillard said. "You shall contact me if you need anything from her. Understand?"

The clerk nodded his head vigorously, uncertain how he had offended the jailer but anxious to try to placate him. "Yes, sir," the clerk answered. "Certainly, sir. I will be sure that is noted."

"Little rat bastard," Lillard mumbled as he and Kitty left the clerk's office. "Beg pardon, ma'am," he said to Kitty. "Apologies for my language. Thinks he runs this here county. Gets my anger up every time I got to deal with him."

"No apology necessary. My thoughts exactly. Except my language might've been a bit stronger," Kitty said, chuckling.

As they walked past the courthouse toward the jail, Kitty noticed a covered wagon making its way down the street in their direction. The wagon braked to a halt, and two men carrying bullwhips jumped from the front and threw back the tarpaulin, revealing a dozen black men chained together in the wagon bed.

Kitty, alarmed, shot the jailer a questioning look.

"Slave market day today," Lillard said. "Been doin' more of 'em lately. Folks're havin' trouble makin' ends meet, so they been sellin' off slaves for the cash."

Kitty shook her head, confused. "They sell the slaves here? At the courthouse?" she asked.

"Yep," Lillard said, shrugging. "Been drawin' pretty good size crowds. Bunch of slave traders from down south been comin' up here, lookin' for good deals."

Kitty could not draw her gaze away from the manacled black men, who were shuffling along in leg irons as the white men pushed and prodded them toward the front steps of the elegant redbrick courthouse. Still staring at the slaves as she entered the yard of the jail building, she did not notice that her three children were outside playing with Mistress Lillard. Eliza Jane approached her cautiously as Mary and Arthur romped with the Lillards' dog.

"Mama? What they doin' with those men over there?" she asked quietly, nodding in the direction of the slaves lining up on the courthouse steps.

"Slave market," Kitty whispered. "Owners are sellin' 'em off. Down south."

Eliza Jane stepped closer and clasped Kitty's hand. "They gonna sell us off, too?" she asked.

"No, baby," Kitty answered softly. "I won't ever let that happen. And we got Mistress Mary on our side. And now Miss Fanny, too." She pulled her daughter close to her and kissed the top of her head. "Won't ever let that happen," she repeated. "We'll be free again soon. I promise."

CHAPTER 55

"*R*EPRESENT A SLAVE?" ASKED ZEPHANIA TURNER INCREDULOUSLY. "Bringing charges against a white man? And asking the court to be set free? Why would I ever want to do that?"

Mary and Fanny were sitting in armchairs, facing Turner across the desk in his office. The lawyer was dressed as always in a suit jacket and waistcoat, with an elegant blue silk cravat knotted stylishly around his neck, held in place by a pearl stickpin. He was leaning back in his chair, his arms folded across his chest, shaking his head in bewilderment over the suggestion.

"Because she's not a slave. She's free—I set her free," answered Mary. "We just have to prove it in court."

"I don't disagree with you on that point," Turner said. "I've told you—and Sam—that I believe the will gave you the right to free her and her children. But there is a significant difference between advising *you*"—he paused and then leaned forward, placing his hands on his desktop, his voice rising—"and actually representing a *slave* in court. You have to understand how difficult that would be. What would people think? What would they say?"

The room was silent for a long moment, and then Mary spoke.

"I would hope they'd say that you did the right thing," she said calmly. "That you did what lawyers are supposed to do. You helped to right a wrong."

"We understand this will be difficult," added Fanny solicitously. "It will be difficult for us, too. But understand something. We're not looking to become abolitionists here. Lord knows that's not what I want. I'm tired of all those know-it-all Northerners condemning me to hell for how we live. All you have to do is look at my plantation and how many slaves we have to know that." She shook her head. "And I'm sure there are folks who'll call me a hypocrite for supporting Kitty. But this is different."

"What we're arguing," Mary chimed in, "is that Kitty is *free*. And whether she's black or white, no one should be allowed to treat a *free* person the way Sam Maddox treated her. That's all we're saying."

"But we need you to help us say it," Mary pleaded. "We need you to be her voice in court. It's the right thing to do, morally and legally, Mr. Turner. I'm hopeful you can see that. And we are begging you to help us."

Turner leaned back in his chair again and let out a sigh. He gazed across the room, his eyes narrowed and nearly closed, contemplating the request and how he should respond. His father was a prosperous landowner, but he had chosen to follow the path of the law rather than that of his family business. But would his father, who had encouraged his choice of the law, and his family and friends understand if he now chose to defend a slave in court, especially a slave seeking her freedom?

"I've never owned my own slaves," he said. "There was always something about it that made me feel somewhat uncomfortable. Not really sure why," he added, almost as if he was musing out loud rather than talking to the two women. "I remember once puzzling over how Thomas Jefferson—whom I've always revered—could author such soaring rhetoric as 'We hold these truths to be self-evident, that all men are created equal' and nevertheless still be a slaveholder. I found it to be an interesting intellectual paradox, but really nothing more." He shook his head. "Can't say I've thought about it much since—"

"When you decided to pursue the law," Mary said, interrupting his reflections, "you must have hoped that somehow you'd be following a higher calling. That someday you might be able to do something—something more than just closing a land title or resolving a business dispute, something that would allow you to change someone's life. To change it for the better so that at the end of the day, you could say that someone was better off because of what you had done to help them. We don't get too many of those chances in our lives." She paused and looked at him intently. "But this could be your chance."

The lawyer remained silent, his hands steepled prayer-like in front of his face. Finally, he looked at Fanny. "You truly believe this is the right thing to do?" he asked.

Fanny nodded her head.

"And you're not worried about how everyone—your family and friends—will react?" he asked.

"Truthfully?" she said, with a wry smile. "A little. Well, maybe more than a little. I suppose my sister, Katie, will never talk to me again. Although I don't necessarily view that as such a terrible loss. And I suppose there'll be other folks who may not be so quick to invite me to their parties anymore. Or even speak to me again. But sometimes you have to do what you believe is the right thing, regardless of the cost. And," she added, looking at Mary, "I know that my true friends will understand."

Again, there was a lengthy silence, as Turner was clearly grappling mightily with his decision.

"One last thing," Fanny said. "If you choose to take her case— and I truly hope you do—it will be an act of good conscience on your part. But it will not be an act of charity. I would insist that I pay you for your services." She smiled sweetly. "And you would, of course, also receive our deepest gratitude."

Turner returned Fanny's smile but remained silent.

"Would you at least talk with her first?" Mary implored. "Before you decide."

"Perhaps that might be helpful," he agreed.

"Thank you," said Mary. "She's being held at the jail, in the debtors' rooms. Could you come with us now to see her?"

Turner thought a minute, looked up at the large clock in the corner, and then nodded. "I'm meeting with a client later in the day, but I have some time right now," he said.

"Thank you," added Fanny as they all rose from their chairs.

* * *

A few minutes later, Turner, along with Mary and Fanny, was seated in the cramped office of the jail when Kitty entered. Turner stood and offered her a slight bow.

"My name is Zephania Turner. I am an attorney," he said formally as he gestured to an empty chair. "Please be seated."

Kitty sat and shot a questioning look at both Mary and Fanny.

"We've asked Mr. Turner to come speak with you, and he's been kind enough to agree," said Mary.

"Mr. Turner is a fine lawyer," said Fanny. "And he is a friend," she added, turning a beguiling smile on the lawyer, who offered a shy half smile in return.

"Thank you for your time, Mr. Turner," Kitty said politely. "But I should tell you right up front, I have no money to pay you, so . . ."

The lawyer waved his hand dismissively. "No need to talk about that right now. I simply wanted to meet with you and discuss your case," he said.

Kitty looked at Mary and Fanny once again, and each offered a nod of encouragement. She turned back to Turner. "Thank you," Kitty repeated.

"Now," Turner began, "Miss Withers and Mistress Maddox have told me the essence of the story, but I'd like to hear it again, this time from you. So please tell me everything that has happened since you and Mistress Maddox began your journey from here to Pennsylvania."

Thirty minutes later, Kitty completed her telling of the saga. Turner had listened carefully, his face expressionless, prompting her occasionally with specific questions. He was silent for a short time, apparently contemplating the details and implications of the tale. Then he spoke directly to Kitty.

"It's a frightening story," he said, shaking his head in both wonder and admiration. "You've shown great courage," he noted. "As have Mistress Maddox and Miss Withers. You are fortunate to have them as friends and supporters."

"I am mindful of that," Kitty answered, with a nod and a grateful smile to the two women.

"Let me discuss with you—with all of you—the difficulties I envision if you go forward with this case," he said.

"Pardon me, Mr. Turner," Kitty said firmly, yet still politely. "But I do intend to go forward, no matter the difficulties."

"I understand," said Turner. "But please indulge me for a moment so that I am certain that you completely understand the legal complexities—as you go forward." He took a deep breath and then continued. "There appears to be no question that you have been assaulted by Sam Maddox and held against your will. But here is the problem. Under the laws of the Commonwealth of Virginia, slaves are considered property, not persons, and as such, they do not have any recognizable rights in a court of law. Not only do they have no rights, but they are also not even allowed to actually give testimony in a courtroom."

"But," interjected Kitty, "I'm not a slave. . . ."

Turner held up his hand to silence her. "I appreciate that. And I will get to that issue in a moment, I assure you," he said courteously. "So, I believe the threshold question a judge will have to decide is your standing to proceed with these charges against Sam."

"What does that mean?" asked Kitty.

"It means that if the judge determines that you were, in fact, free at the time, you would be able to proceed with the case and your claims against Sam," Turner explained.

"But I have the papers I signed freeing her and the children," Mary said.

Turner waved his hand again. "I realize that," he said patiently. "Please let me finish, and then we can discuss that." He turned back to Kitty. "However," he continued, "if the judge determines that Master Maddox's will did not actually give Mistress Maddox the title to his slaves and thus the right to free you—as Sam will argue—then you will be deemed a slave in the eyes of the law and will have no standing to sue. Indeed, you will not be allowed to testify at all. Your claims would be dismissed. Do you understand?"

"I do," Kitty answered. "But, Mr. Turner, I need you to understand something from me. I am free," she said defiantly. "Don't matter to me what Sam or some judge or anybody else thinks. I know I am free. Although God didn't see fit to have me born free, Mistress Mary saw fit to rectify that. For me and my children. And I plan on standin' up in that courtroom—with your help or without it—and provin' to the world that I'm free. And then I'll trust in God to bring me justice."

No one spoke for a full minute, as Turner, after listening to Kitty, shifted in his chair, his head inclined to one side, and gazed thoughtfully out the window toward the redbrick courthouse. The silent minute seemed to last forever. Finally, he turned back to Kitty.

"Miss Kitty," he said respectfully, "you have persevered through a great deal on your journey. I am deeply impressed by your fortitude. And you've been fortunate to have good friends accompanying you and guiding you along the way." He paused a moment, looked at Mary and Fanny. Then his gaze went back to Kitty as he continued. "I cannot predict exactly what a court will do with your case. But I would consider it a privilege to act as your attorney in this matter."

CHAPTER 56

*T*HE SPECTACLE AND CEREMONY OF CIRCUIT COURT DAY ARRIVED SEVeral weeks later. It was a crisp, clear Virginia summer day, and the pleasant weather acted like a magnet, drawing large and festive crowds to the usually drowsy hamlet of Washington. Those with business before the court mingled with the merely curious on the lawns surrounding the courthouse, waiting patiently for the imposing double doors to swing open and the curtain to rise on the theater of justice. The chorus of sounds—the low murmuring of nervous litigants; the self-important proclamations of the few lawyers roaming the grounds, seeking business; the hawking of wares by vendors in the street—all combined to create the anthem that accompanied this regularly scheduled and highly anticipated day of dispensing fairness and wisdom.

There seemed to be a particularly strong undercurrent of expectation coursing through the crowd. The first court day of each session always brought flocks of petitioners, defendants, and observers to town, but the numbers of visitors and the aura of energy encircling the stately columned red brick building far exceeded those of a traditional first day. That was because today was the day that the court would begin hearing the case of *Kitty v. Samuel Maddox.*

The story of the slave woman suing a white man for damages, claiming that he had assaulted and kidnapped her, had captured the interest of many—and the ire of some—in Rappahannock

County and beyond. Sam Maddox was well known—though not necessarily well liked—throughout the county, and Mary Maddox and her late husband, Samuel, had been respected residents for decades. This clash of family versus family, enhanced by the central presence of the unknown and reputedly beautiful young slave woman, had given rise to classic dramatic theater, now set to play out within the walls of a courtroom.

Many were milling about, driven by simple inquisitiveness and anxious to find seats inside to witness the spectacle; others were present, fueled by anger over the prospect of a slave asserting legal rights to redress some perceived wrong perpetrated by a white man, hopeful of witnessing the crushing of the slave's arrogance by the legal system and a reaffirmation of their way of life and social code.

At precisely ten o'clock, the doors swung open and the deputy clerk stepped outside to herald the start of the session in the words first utilized more than a century earlier in the courthouses of colonial Virginia.

"Oyez, Oyez, Oyez. All manner of persons that have anything to do at this court, draw near and give your attendance. All who have complaint to enter or suit to prosecute, let them come forth and be heard."

The members of the crowd pushed and cajoled their way through the doors, down the short hallway, and past the arched entrance that led to the courtroom. Within seconds, every seat in the double rows of benches was inhabited, and those who were not quick enough found themselves standing along the walls of the room or exiled up one of two curving, creaking back stairways to the small second-floor gallery, which looked down over the courtroom.

It was not a particularly large courtroom, nor was it especially ornate. But the layout and the gracious decor conveyed both the majesty of the law and the solemnity of what occurred inside those wainscoted and painted walls. A waist-high wooden balustrade cleaved the room nearly in half. In the rear section sat the wooden benches set aside for interested members of the public. The front section was dominated by the judge's bench, an impressive raised, hand-carved wooden structure that stood sentinel over the entire chamber and announced clearly that its occupant was the ruler of this domain.

Directly in front of the bench sat twelve cane chairs where jurors would reside for certain more substantial cases. To the left of the judge's bench was a solid rectangular table where the court clerk worked, shepherding the array of case files that were scheduled for that day. Two small tables sat in the front section, reserved for the litigants and the occasional attorney.

The buzzing and muttering inside the chamber came to an abrupt halt when a door behind the bench opened and a court attendant stepped out from within.

"Silence!" the attendant commanded in a deep, thunderous tone. "All rise! The Circuit Superior Court of Law and Chancery for the County of Rappahannock is hereby in session! The Honorable Richard Field presiding!"

The attendant stepped aside and allowed the judge to enter the room. After quickly taking his seat behind the bench, the judge took a moment to carefully arrange a collection of files and heavy leather-bound law books displayed on his desktop. He then looked up and, with a slight imperious wave of his hand, indicated that all should be seated.

Judge Richard Field was a slender, wiry man in his forties, with a wispy receding hairline, a narrow face with sharp features, and deep-set, intelligent eyes. The scion of a prosperous family, he had, in a way, been born to the bench: both his father and his grandfather had sat as judges at some time in their careers, following Virginia's long, well-entrenched tradition of handing down judgeships within the generations of a family. Studious, charming, and stern when necessary, he had a well-earned reputation as a precise, demanding, and fair jurist.

Once all had been seated, he adjusted a pair of wire-rimmed glasses on the edge of his nose and peered out at the crowded room.

"On behalf of Rappahannock County, I welcome you to this first day of the court session," he announced somberly. "There is a great deal to be accomplished, so I will expect your complete cooperation. In a moment, the clerk"—he gestured toward the man perched at the table below and to the left of the bench—"shall call the role of cases scheduled for this morning. We will endeavor to resolve these matters as fairly and as expeditiously as possible." He paused briefly. "This afternoon I shall commence a jury trial. The sheriff has summoned a number of freeholders, from whom we will select a panel to sit in judgment of the case. I suspect, seeing how many citizens are present today, that you are aware of this particular case and that many of you are present to witness these proceedings. I will admonish you now, as I will again later, that this is a court of law and I will expect all who have gathered here to act accordingly."

The judge took a moment to gaze pointedly out at the crowd, then adjusted his glasses and continued. "So, then, if I have made myself perfectly clear, we will proceed with the morning's docket. Would the clerk please call the calendar?"

CHAPTER 57

*I*T WAS SHORTLY AFTER ONE O'CLOCK IN THE AFTERNOON WHEN THE circuit court reconvened. The morning docket—consisting mostly of claims for unpaid debts and land disputes—had been disposed of swiftly. Even many of the litigants had been anxious to resolve their cases quickly so they might be free to attend the afternoon trial. The chamber was packed, with many spectators having refused to leave during the lunch recess for fear of never regaining their seats.

Moments before court was scheduled to resume, Kitty entered the courtroom, led by Zephania Turner and flanked by Mary and Fanny. She was dressed in a blue and yellow calico dress that reached nearly to the floor, with long sleeves, a high neck, and a cinched waist. Her long hair had been plaited and bound in a knot behind her head. Both Mary and Fanny were dressed in their best church clothes, dark and sober, with few frills.

As Kitty walked down the center of the two rows of benches, she felt like she was running a gauntlet, flanked on both sides by nemeses, most of whom were merely curious or mildly unfriendly, while some others were openly hostile and eager to see her fail, thus preserving the balance of the strict echelons of their way of life. There was a smattering of hisses from the throng as she marched up the aisle, her head held high and her gaze straight ahead, refusing to acknowledge the acrimony as she entered the well of the court. *I am free*, she thought, summoning strength from the words. Then she repeated them to herself like a mantra. *I am free. I have as much right to be in this courtroom as anyone else.*

Sam Maddox and his lawyer, Moffet Strother, were already seated at one of the tables. Maddox, looking relaxed, was dressed in a gray wool formal coat, with a lighter gray cravat tied around the neck of his white shirt. He was smiling broadly and gesturing pleasantly in the direction of several supporters seated in the front row.

Moffet Strother, despite his obvious attempt to look professional in a new jacket and waistcoat, nevertheless appeared as rumpled and disheveled as if he had just been awakened from a night of sleeping in a barn.

Strother ignored Kitty as she passed by the table, but Maddox made a pronounced show of standing and bowing slightly in her direction, while offering an amiable smile and a polite nod of the head to Mary and Fanny. Turner ushered Kitty to her seat at the counsel table, while Mary and Fanny took seats directly behind her.

A moment later, the door to the judge's chamber opened, and the court attendant appeared and announced in a commanding voice that the court was once again in session and all should rise. Judge Field stepped out from the anteroom and took his seat behind the bench.

The judge took a moment to survey the courtroom, using the silence and the strength of his magisterial glare to reinforce the notion that he was completely in charge. Satisfied, he gestured for all to be seated. He then nodded toward the two lawyers.

"Gentlemen," the judge said, "are we prepared to proceed with the trial of this matter?"

Turner, dressed impeccably, gracefully rose from his seat, while Strother scrambled from his, struggling to free his bulk from the chair and nearly knocking his file from the tabletop. Turner spoke first.

"We are, indeed, prepared to proceed on behalf of the plaintiff," he responded formally, directing a slight bow to the bench.

"Your Honor," Strother said, "we are also prepared to proceed on behalf of Mr. Maddox."

"Very well," said Judge Field. "We shall summon the prospective jurors."

The judge inclined his head toward Sheriff Walden, who was sitting alongside the court clerk. The sheriff stood immediately and marched briskly down the aisle toward a small room in the hall just outside the courtroom. He returned a moment later, leading a group of twenty men, all looking uncertain and uncomfortable. As the sheriff led them into the well of the court, Judge Field spoke.

"Gentlemen, I would ask that the first twelve of you take a seat in the jury area," he said, gesturing with his hand toward the twelve seats in front of the bench. "I would request that the remainder of you sit in the available seats that we have set up nearby," he added, pointing to a row of chairs in the front section of the courtroom, right behind the counsel tables.

Kitty gazed curiously at the twelve potential jurors sitting in the jury area. The men—all white—were of various ages: four young men were in their twenties, six seemed middle aged, and two men, by virtue of their difficulty walking and their stooped and frail physiques, appeared to be quite old. The younger men were dressed in work clothes, while the older men had apparently dressed for the event and were in their best go-to-church-meeting attire. All seemed ill at ease, their anxious gazes dancing frenetically from the judge to Kitty and Maddox and their lawyers, then to those spectators gathered on the benches, and finally back to Judge Field.

"Gentlemen," the judge said to them once they had settled into their seats, "you have been summoned, as freeholders of this county, to possibly sit as jurors in this matter. As I believe Sheriff Walden indicated to you when he delivered your summons, it is expected that this trial may take two days to complete, and we would require your presence for that time. Now," he continued, sounding like a courteous professor lecturing to a class, "I want to take a moment to thank you for taking the time from your lives to fulfill your duty as citizens and join us here today. Our great Constitution guarantees all of us a trial by jury—a jury of our peers—

and that is only possible when citizens like yourselves are willing to embrace your civic responsibility. So, thank you once again."

Although some of the men in the jury area glanced briefly in Kitty's direction, none of them actually made eye contact with her. *Well,* thought Kitty ironically, *the Constitution might talk about a jury of your peers, but I'm right sure these men don't look like any peers of mine.*

The judge paused briefly, glanced around the courtroom once again to ensure that all were paying attention, and then continued. "Now, in a moment we will begin the process of selecting the jury that will hear this case—only twelve of you will be asked to serve—but before we begin, I want to offer a few additional thoughts about your presence here," he said. "I realize that this case, by its unusual nature, has garnered a significant amount of interest, but I want you to be assured that this case will be handled no differently from any other. My charge as a judge—the oath I have taken—is to guarantee that justice is done in this courtroom, and that fairness is extended equally to the poor and the rich." He shifted his gaze from the prospective jurors to the gathered spectators. "And I fully intend to uphold that charge. And," he added firmly, "I shall not tolerate any outbursts or expressions of emotion or opinion from anyone in this courtroom. I hope I have made myself perfectly clear."

A number of the spectators shifted uneasily in their seats, but no one spoke.

"Well, then," the judge continued, "before we begin to select the jurors, I want to advise you of the nature of the complaint in the case."

The judge nodded in the direction of the court clerk, who immediately picked up a document and handed it up to the bench. After grasping the paper, the judge began to read from it.

"The plaintiff, Kitty, a Negro woman who claims to be free, makes complaint against the defendant, Samuel Maddox, that she was illegally assaulted and harmed by the said defendant, and that she, together with her three children—Eliza Jane, Mary, and Arthur—were kidnapped and illegally held in captivity by said defendant, and she therefore sues for such injuries and claims damages in the amount of one thousand dollars."

Judge Field slowly and deliberately placed the document down on the bench and looked toward the potential jurors. "Now that you are advised of the nature of this case, it is incumbent upon me to pose a number of questions to you to determine your suitability to act as jurors in this matter. I will admonish you that it is necessary for you to be completely truthful in your responses to me. Now, let us proceed."

CHAPTER 58

*I*T HAD TAKEN NEARLY AN HOUR FOR THE JURY TO BE SELECTED. THREE prospective jurors were dismissed by the judge when they expressed—quite forcefully—their opinions that a Negro, free or not, should never have the right to sue a white person. One juror was excused when he claimed that his back ailed him so much that he was unable to sit for any extended period of time. One of the elderly jury candidates was excused because he could barely hear. And a final prospective juror was excused when he proclaimed that Sam Maddox—who, in his words, is "that scoundrel Sam Maddox"—owed him money. That assertion generated a chorus of laughter in the courtroom and a roguish smile and a genial wave from Maddox.

Eventually, the judge decided, with the acquiescence of the two lawyers, on a jury panel of twelve men. The members were mostly farmers, with the exception of one carpenter and one tradesman. And nine of the twelve were slave owners, ranging from as few as a single slave owned to as many as fifteen. After swearing an oath "to do justice," the jurors took their seats.

Judge Field cleared his throat and looked austerely first at the twelve jurors and then at the spectators. "We are now ready to proceed. I will remind all of you once again that you are to remain silent throughout these proceedings. If you are not capable of that, I will have you escorted from the courtroom by the sheriff." He turned toward the lawyers. "Now," he said, "Counselors, I would invite you to provide your opening statements."

Zephania Turner rose from his seat, bowed slightly to the judge, tugged on his waistcoat, and turned toward the jury.

"Gentlemen," Turner began solemnly, "a moment ago you each placed your hand on a Bible and swore to do justice in this matter. And that is precisely what we shall be asking of you. Justice," he repeated, drawing the word out slowly, as he scanned the panel, making eye contact with each juror. "It's an interesting concept. Because true justice—the kind that I seek on behalf of Miss Kitty—has no concern for a person's financial status. It has no concern for a person's ancestry."

Turner paused dramatically for a beat and then continued. "And it has no concern for a person's skin color. Justice—true justice—is, indeed, blind to all these things. If you look at the statue of Lady Justice right there on Judge Field's bench," he said, pointing to a cast silver statue that was perched to the left of the judge, "y'all will notice that as she holds the balancing scales of justice in her one hand and a law book in the other, her eyes are covered by a blindfold. She does not need to see who stands before her in order to render a fair decision, because justice is, indeed, blind."

He paused again for a moment, appearing to be deep in thought. "Despite the attention that this case has received," he continued, "this is not a terribly complicated issue for you to resolve. In fact, it's quite simple. For most of her life, Miss Kitty was a slave. She belonged to Samuel and Mary Maddox, whom many of you are acquainted with. When Samuel passed, his will very clearly left all his possessions and property to his wife, Mary. You will hear from Mary that, on his deathbed, this good and God-fearing man had a last request. He asked that Miss Kitty and her children should be set free. And Mary honored that request, as any good Christian would."

Turner stepped back and pointed a finger at Sam Maddox. "But Sam Maddox insisted on attempting to dishonor his uncle's last wish, making a baseless claim to the ownership of Kitty and the children, and threatening to sell them immediately"—he arched an eyebrow sinisterly—"to satisfy his extensive debts. So Mary was forced, in order to honor her pledge to her dying husband, to flee from Sam's treacherous clutches. She and Kitty and the children engaged in a perilous journey to Pennsylvania, where she signed a deed of manumission, freeing them, as she had promised."

Turner took a deep, theatrical breath. "But this man," he said, pointing again to Sam Maddox, "would not let his dead uncle's spirit rest easily. He engaged a band of armed criminal ruffians, pursued Mary and Kitty into Pennsylvania and, in the dead of night, engaged in a cowardly deed, forcing his way into the home of another and inflicting a terrible beating upon this young woman." He pointed now to Kitty. "And then he forcibly transported her and her children—all of whom were now legally free persons—to Virginia, where he kept them bound and chained under inhuman conditions."

The lawyer shook his head sadly, his face a mask of disdain. "When we have completed the testimony in this case, I will have the opportunity to speak to you again. Until that time, I will implore you to remember the court's charge to you—to do justice. Justice that is not reserved just for white folks. But justice that we as a nation, and as a commonwealth, have guaranteed to all our free citizens, regardless of their color." He took a few seconds to scan the faces of each of the jurors. "Thank you, gentlemen," he concluded soberly.

Kitty offered Turner a slight smile and nodded thankfully as he walked back to the counsel table. It was the first time that she had heard her story told publicly, and she was impressed by Turner's performance. She had watched the jurors carefully, looking for some sign of sympathy or understanding, but all twelve had remained stoic, devoid of any response or any gestures that might have revealed their reactions to Turner's entreaties.

As Turner took his seat, Strother rose and walked toward the jurors. The comparison between the two lawyers was stark. If Turner, in all his personal elegance and sartorial finery, was a show horse, then Strother, in his wrinkled, ill-fitting garb and shambling presence, was something akin to a plow horse. But it was instantly apparent that mere looks could be deceiving. He quite clearly knew his audience and began to play to them immediately.

"Gentlemen," he began, shaking his head in bewilderment, "y'all are probably wonderin' what in the world we all are doin' here. I know I am. Why are we takin' up the precious time of this here court to let a slave, a slave, for goodness' sakes," he said, his voice rising as he contemptuously spit out the word *slave*, "accuse a white man of some such nonsense that you just heard about from Mr. Turner. Let me tell you what y'all need to know and what y'all will hear in this trial."

He turned and jabbed his finger accusingly toward Kitty, who met his glare with a calm, confident look, her hands folded before her on the table. "She's a slave. Always has been and still is. Mistress Maddox—and I mean no disrespect to her and the memory of her deceased husband—but Mistress Maddox did not have any legal right to steal her away under cover of darkness. No legal right to spirit her away to some other jurisdiction." He paused for a second. "Someplace that has no respect for us and our way of life," he added disdainfully. "The last will and testament of Samuel Maddox gave his nephew—whom he loved like a son—the title to those slaves. So Sam Maddox simply did what any law-abiding citizen would do. What each of you would do. He attempted to recover his property that was stolen—yes, stolen!—from him. You cannot, and should not, hold a man somehow responsible in a court of law for attempting to recover property that belonged to him in the first place."

Strother directed a pointed gaze at each of the twelve jurors. "And you most certainly can't allow a white man to be subjected to the spurious claims of a slave," he said angrily. "No, you most certainly cannot!" Strother turned and strode back to his seat.

"Gentlemen, thank you," Judge Field said gravely from the bench. "Mr. Turner, I'd ask you to please call your first witness."

CHAPTER 59

"THE PLAINTIFF WOULD ASK THE CLERK TO PLEASE CALL MISTRESS Mary Maddox to the stand," said Turner, standing and nodding toward Mary.

The clerk, seated next to the bench, stood and gestured toward Mary. "Mistress Maddox," he said, "would you please approach the witness chair?"

Mary rose from her seat in the row behind Kitty and strode resolutely between the counsel tables, staring straight ahead and refusing to acknowledge Sam Maddox, to the single chair that sat on a slightly raised platform located in front of both the judge's bench and the jurors.

"Mistress Maddox, you have been called as a witness by the plaintiff in this matter," the clerk intoned officially. "Do you offer your oath, in the name of God, that the evidence you will produce shall be honest and truthful?"

"Yes, I do," answered Mary.

"Please be seated," the clerk ordered.

Judge Field inclined his head politely toward Mary and then nodded his assent to proceed to Turner.

"Mistress Maddox," Zephania Turner began, "are you familiar with my client, Miss Kitty?"

"Yes, I am," answered Mary confidently, sitting ramrod straight, her hands folded in her lap, her demeanor belying her true emotions. Never before in her life had she been asked to speak in public, and the size of the crowd—with all eyes focused intently on her—together with the stakes involved, had her terrified. But she knew she would have to rein in her fear and soldier on for Kitty's sake.

"How long have you known her?"

"Since she was born, more than twenty-five years ago."

"And please tell us the circumstances of your relationship to her when she was born."

"She was born to one of our slaves on our farm."

"So then," Turner said, "she became, by law, one of your slaves?"

"Yes, sir, that is correct," Mary responded.

"Now, Mistress Maddox, with my deepest apologies, I'd like to ask you about the passing of your husband, Samuel Maddox."

"Certainly," Mary said.

"First of all, how long had you and Samuel been married?"

"We've been . . ." Mary paused briefly and then corrected herself. "We had been married for thirty years . . . before he passed on."

"Did you and Samuel bring any children into the world during that time?"

"No, sir."

"Please forgive me for being somewhat indelicate, but had you attempted to bear children?"

"Yes," Mary said, her voice dropping, "but, unfortunately, it was not in God's plans."

Turner inclined his head empathetically. "So, then, when Samuel passed, you would have been his only direct heir, is that correct?"

"Yes, sir," answered Mary.

Turner walked to the clerk's table, picked up a document from the tabletop, and handed it to Mary.

"Mistress Maddox," he said, "I am presenting to you a document, entitled 'Last Will and Testament of Samuel Maddox,' that has previously been submitted to this court. Do you, in fact, recognize this document?"

"Yes, sir."

"Is this the will of your late husband?"

"Yes, sir, it is."

"And are you named as the executrix of his estate in the will?"

"Yes, sir."

"Was this will, in fact, duly proven and admitted to record in the County Court of Rappahannock County?"

"Yes, sir, it was."

"Did the provisions of your husband's will require you to post any security in order to act as the executrix?"

"No, sir, it specifically did not."

"So then, after Samuel's death, did you assume your duties as the executrix of his estate?"

"Yes, sir, I did."

Turner took the document from Mary, returned it to the clerk, and turned to the judge.

"Your Honor," he said, "the plaintiff would request that this document—the last will and testament of the said Samuel Maddox—which has previously been submitted to the court, be entered into the record as proof of the terms and conditions stated within."

Judge Field looked to Moffet Strother, who nodded his consent.

"I have previously reviewed the clerk's file concerning the estate of Samuel Maddox and determined that this is a true copy of his will. There being no objection heard, this document shall be entered into the court record," the judge said. "Are there any other documents regarding the estate that will be offered to the court for its consideration?"

"None from the plaintiff," said Turner.

"And none on behalf of the defendant," added Strother.

"In that event, you may continue, Mr. Turner," said the judge, seeming slightly perplexed.

"Thank you, Your Honor," said Turner. "Now, Mistress Maddox, would you please describe to us the relationship between your late husband and his nephew, Sam?"

For the first time since she had entered the courtroom, Mary turned toward Maddox and glared at him for a brief moment before turning back to Turner and answering the question.

"By the time Samuel passed away, he had little use for his nephew," she answered, one eyebrow arched and her voice hard.

"Had their relationship always been that way?" asked Turner.

"No," said Mary, shaking her head. "When Sam was a young boy, Samuel spent a great deal of time with him, hoping to give him the guidance he was not getting from his own father—who was Samuel's brother. But as Sam got older—and it became clear that he was not following Samuel's advice about becoming an honest and trustworthy man—Samuel despaired of him and his future and eventually distanced himself from Sam."

"Did Samuel ever talk to you about leaving any part of his estate to Sam?"

"No, sir. By then, Samuel wouldn't have trusted Sam to muck out the outhouse, much less handle any of his estate," Mary said derisively.

There was a brief spurt of snickers and chuckles at her comment, which was immediately silenced by an icy glare from Judge Field.

"So, then," Turner asked, his brow furrowed in puzzlement, "if Sam were to claim that Samuel had promised him, shortly before his death, that he planned to leave him part of the estate, would that be true?"

Mary first shot a look of disdain at Sam Maddox and then turned toward the jurors. "That would be an absolute lie," she declared. "The entire estate—land and property—was left to me, and me alone."

"Now, Mistress Maddox," said Turner, "I would like to shift our conversation to the journey you embarked on—with Miss Kitty and her children—to Pennsylvania. Would you kindly explain to the court and jury what the purpose of this journey was?"

"I had decided to free Kitty and the children. But then I heard that Sam intended to challenge my right to free them in court. He was deeply in debt and desperate for money and hoped to sell them off to slave traders from down south."

"Would you have allowed that?"

"Absolutely not!"

"Why not?"

Mary paused a moment and then continued. "Because Samuel had asked me on his deathbed to free them. And I fully intended to follow his wishes," she said softly.

"But I suspect the jurors may be puzzled by one question," Turner said thoughtfully. "If you were so confident in the terms of the will, why did you not go to court and establish, once and for all in the eyes of the law of the commonwealth, that Sam was not entitled to any portion of the estate?"

"Because," Mary began, looking directly at the jurors once again, "I trusted the law—but I did not trust Sam Maddox. I feared, knowing him and his moral failings as I do, that he would simply steal Kitty and the children away and sell them before the law had spoken. And by then, it would have been too late. And I could not run the risk of that happening."

Turner paused theatrically, nodding his head knowingly. "I would ask now that you describe to the court and these jurors the details of your journey to Pennsylvania," Turner said.

Thirty minutes later, Mary concluded the saga. The jurors had listened carefully but had shown no emotion at all during her recitation. Many in the audience, however, had been on the edge of their seats, as if attending a dramatic reading of a gripping adventure novel.

"An astonishing feat of courage—by both you and Miss Kitty," Turner said admiringly when Mary had finished. "After you had arrived in Pennsylvania, were you eventually able to arrange for housing for Miss Kitty and her children?"

"Yes, sir," said Mary. "Arrangements were made by a Quaker group who had aided us on the trip for Kitty and her children to lodge with the family of a free black man named Amon Jones. In return for their lodging, they would provide domestic services to Mr. Jones and his family."

"And did they, in fact, take up residence with Amon Jones?"

"Yes, sir, they did."

"Were they residing there when you left to return to Virginia?"

"Yes, sir."

"And did they appear to be safe there?"

"I thought so. I had executed a deed of manumission at the county court, declaring that they were now free, so I believed they would have no difficulties creating a new life there." Mary paused. "I believed that they were safe when I left. Unfortunately, I was wrong."

At this time, Turner delivered a sheaf of documents to the clerk, who handed it up to the judge.

"If it please the court," Turner said, "I have delivered to the court clerk a copy of the deed of manumission that was executed by Mistress Maddox and accepted by the Adams County Court. In addition, I have provided a certified copy, signed by the Secretary of the Commonwealth of Pennsylvania, of a statute, passed in the year of Our Lord seventeen eighty-eight, making it a crime against the peace of the commonwealth for any person to seize and carry away any free person of color for the purpose of enslaving them. I would request that these documents be made part of the record in this case."

Judge Field took a few minutes to review the documents and then returned them to the clerk.

"The documents will be recorded as evidence in this matter. You may continue your examination, Mr. Turner."

"Thank you, Your Honor. Now, Mistress Maddox, when and how did you discover that you had been wrong and that Kitty and the children were not safe?" asked Turner.

Mary then related how Fanny had disclosed that Sam Maddox had seized Kitty and the children and brought them back to Virginia, where they were being held captive at his farm.

"And did you and Miss Withers then decide to take some action to aid them?"

"Yes," Mary said. "We traveled to Sam's farm, where we found them chained in a shed." She paused and glared at Maddox, whose face revealed no expression. "Kitty had been beaten brutally by Sam, her face bloody and bruised and one eye swollen shut. She was barely conscious when we arrived. We freed them all from the chains and brought them back to Fanny's home."

"Was there then a confrontation with Sam?" asked Turner.

"There was. He arrived late at night with several other men. They were all armed, and Sam threatened us unless we returned Kitty to him."

"Let me be certain that the court and the jurors understand," said Turner. "An armed group of men, led by Sam Maddox, came to the Withers home late at night and threatened two unarmed women? Is that correct?"

"Yes. Except for the fact that after being threatened by the men, we—Fanny and I—grabbed shotguns to defend ourselves. Fortunately, it was at that precise time that Sheriff Walden appeared. He ordered them off the property and determined that he would take custody of Kitty and the children until the matter was resolved."

Turner took a moment to review his notes and then continued. "Finally, then, Mistress Maddox, do you have any doubt in your mind that the will of your late husband empowered you to make whatever disposition you chose of his property, including the right to free Kitty, as he had requested with his dying breath?"

"No, sir. I have no doubt at all."

"And is there any doubt that you had actually freed them all, according to the laws of the Commonwealth of Pennsylvania, once you had arrived there?"

"No, sir, there is not. And the deed of manumission that I executed proves it," Mary said decisively.

Turner bowed to Mary and then turned to the judge. "Thank you, Your Honor. I have completed my examination of this witness."

"Thank you, Mr. Turner," the judge said. He then turned to Moffet Strother. "The witness is now available to you, sir, for your examination, should you please."

CHAPTER 60

MOFFET STROTHER STOOD, TUGGED ON HIS ILL-FITTING JACKET, which heroically resisted the effort to smooth out the waves of wrinkles, and offered a slight bow to the judge.

"With the court's permission," Strother said.

Judge Field gave a brief nod of his head in assent. Strother stepped a few feet closer to the witness chair and Mary.

"Mistress Maddox," he began, his tone calm and solicitous, "I would ask your indulgence as I have just a few questions for you."

"Certainly," Mary responded. She squared her shoulders, steeling herself for the expected verbal onslaught. As she attempted to maintain her false air of confidence, the flickering of her fingers betrayed the fact that now that she was no longer in the protective grasp of Zephania Turner, her sense of self-assuredness was swiftly melting away.

"Initially, I am curious about something you mentioned a few moments ago. You told this court that you enlisted the aid of a number of so-called 'Quakers' in your escape to Pennsylvania. Is that correct?" Strother asked.

"It is correct that a number of Quakers assisted us on our journey. But it is not correct that we were 'escaping,'" Mary said.

Strother waved his hand dismissively. "You may call it whatever you please. My point is that you enlisted the aid of members of what has been referred to as an Underground Railroad—these

Quakers—whose purpose is to blatantly violate our laws by providing aid and comfort to our escaping slaves. Is that correct?"

"Well, Mr. Strother," Mary said adamantly, "I would suggest that
it is you who may call it whatever you please. I would simply call it
what it was—good Christian people aiding other good Christian
people on a difficult journey, as we were being pursued illegally
by a band of lawless ruffians. Nothing more sinister than that."

"Well, Mistress Maddox," Strother said, trying to regain control
of the questioning, "we will leave that for the jury to decide."

Mary inclined her head in agreement.

"Now, if I may proceed to another issue, you've told this court
that you intended to free the slave woman," Strother said, gesturing with his hand toward Kitty, "because it is what your late husband requested. Is that correct?"

"Yes, sir."

"Would it be fair to say that your late husband, Samuel, was a
man of strong opinions?"

"I believe that would be fair."

"And would it also be fair to say that he was very precise in his
business dealings?"

"Yes, I believe so."

"And that the late Mr. Maddox had no reservation about let-
ting his opinions be known?"

"Yes, sir.

"And that, in both his business and personal dealings, he expected his directives to be followed?"

"I would say that is generally true."

Strother walked to the clerk's table. "With the court's permission," he said to the judge, "I would like to show the witness the
will of her late husband, which has been previously entered into
the record."

"You may," said the judge.

Strother took the will from the clerk and handed it to Mary.

"Mistress Maddox," Strother said as he walked away from her
and faced the jurors, "I'd ask you to please point out to the court
and these jurors precisely where in the will your husband directed
you to free any of his slaves."

Without looking at the will, Mary responded. "He made no mention of that wish in the will," she said.

"He did not?" asked Strother, an exaggerated look of surprise on his face. "This man, who you have agreed was exceptionally precise and specific in all his business dealings, would somehow neglect to include something as important as his intention to free valuable slaves?"

"It is correct that he did not include those words."

"Did he share this intention with any other person other than you?"

Mary shook her head. "Not that I am aware."

"So then, is it fair to say that other than your recitation of this deathbed scene, there is no proof whatsoever that your late husband actually wished to free any slave?"

"I beg your pardon, sir," Mary said angrily, "but there is, indeed, proof. The proof is my word!"

"With all due respect, Mistress Maddox," Strother said, shaking his head in disbelief, "you must see how difficult it is for these jurors to believe that your husband—with apologies, a man of fairly limited means—would willingly part with extremely valuable property, such as these slaves, for no good reason at all. You must see that!"

Mary was silent for a long moment. When she spoke next, her voice was barely audible. "There was a very good reason."

"And what reason was that?" Strother asked doubtfully.

"Kitty was Samuel's daughter," she said softly.

"I beg your pardon," Strother said, puzzled. "I don't think I heard you."

Mary sat up, straightened her shoulders, and looked directly at the jurors. "I said that Samuel was Kitty's father," she said boldly.

There was an audible gasp in the courtroom. The twelve men in the jury seats looked at Mary in astonishment. Moffet Strother appeared so disconcerted by Mary's statement that he was speechless.

At the defense table, Kitty closed her eyes for a moment. When she opened them, she looked first to the jurors—none of whom returned her glance—and then back to Mary. She had hoped, for

Mary's sake, that this—an admission in open court, before friends and neighbors, of Samuel's infidelity with a slave woman, a fact perhaps suspected but never spoken—would somehow not be necessary. But after the shock of hearing the words said aloud in the sanctity of a courtroom, she felt strangely relieved, almost jubilant. Although she knew that it certainly must have pained Mary to confirm this fact so publicly, the disclosure released a feeling of satisfaction deep within Kitty, a satisfaction that now all would know exactly who she was and where she had come from. A satisfaction that this part of her life was no longer shrouded in secrecy. And with that satisfaction came a renewed sense of purpose, a flaring of her resolve that challenging Sam Maddox in this courtroom had been the right thing for her to do. And with it also came a surging new wave of gratitude for Mary and her willingness to completely uproot her life in order to ensure Kitty's freedom.

Mary took a deep breath and continued. "Samuel fathered Kitty with one of our female slaves. After the birth, her mother was sold. Samuel always treated Kitty differently from the other slaves because of that . . . relationship. So it was not surprising to me that his dying wish was to set her and her children free." Mary turned away from the jurors and back to Strother. "That may shock you, Mr. Strother, and it may shock others in this courtroom, as well. But it happens to be the truth. And that is why I fully intend to follow Samuel's last wish."

Strother, stunned by this turn of events—and the resoluteness of Mary's admission—struggled to regain his demeanor. "So," he stammered, "you are telling this court, upon your oath, that your late husband sired this"—he turned and pointed to Kitty—"this slave? And that is why he allegedly desired to free her?"

"That is correct, Mr. Strother," Mary said calmly. "That is, in fact, my testimony."

Moffet Strother, still flustered by Mary's revelation, walked over to his counsel table and made a point of shuffling through his notes before he looked up at the judge. "Your Honor, I would extend my thanks to this witness. I have no additional questions at this time," he said.

"The witness is then excused, with the thanks of the court. You may step down, Mistress Maddox," Judge Field said.

As Mary stood and walked to her seat, there was a wave of muttering throughout the chamber.

The judge rapped the bench sharply with his gavel. "We shall be in recess for a brief period." He looked to Zephania Turner. "Please be prepared to call your next witness when we return, Mr. Turner."

Chapter 61

ONCE THE JUDGE HAD LEFT THE BENCH, KITTY, MARY, AND FANNY, led by Zephania Turner, began to weave their way through the crowded courtroom, heading toward the hallway. As Mary passed among the spectators, it was as if Moses was parting the Red Sea. Many of the men and women stepped aside respectfully. Some purposely turned their backs on her, while words such as "ungrateful," "trash," and "traitor" were muttered loud enough for her to hear.

Outside the courtroom, Turner ushered the group into a small sitting room and closed the door behind them. He turned immediately to Mary.

"That was a courageous thing to do," he said kindly.

Fanny shook her head in agreement, while Kitty grasped Mary's hands.

"You should not have said that . . . not in public," Kitty said gently. "Some out there will never forgive you for that."

Mary offered a resigned shrug. "It's not as if there weren't rumors about it," she said. "Sure some people been talkin' about it for years. So now the truth's out there. Just as well." She paused and took a deep breath, then exhaled slowly. "Like to throttle that no-account Strother, though," she added.

Fanny smiled. "Well, that certainly shut him up. Had no idea what to do after you said that out loud. Just stumbled around and finally sat down."

"But now you have to live with everybody knowin' for sure about Master Samuel and me," said Kitty, still holding on to Mary's hands.

"I just decided that it was the right thing to do. And the right time to do it. I can live with it now," said Mary. "Kind of glad it's finally public. Don't need to pretend anymore."

"Well, it should certainly help our case," said Turner. "Answers a big question the jurors would have been asking themselves."

There was a knock on the door, and Sheriff Walden leaned into the room. "The judge's about to take the bench. Need y'all to come back inside," he said.

As they resumed their positions in the courtroom, the clerk announced that court was back in session. The judge entered from the door behind the bench and took his seat.

"Mr. Turner, if you please," the judge said to Turner.

"May I request that the clerk call to the witness stand Mr. Charley Myers?" said Turner.

After being summoned by the clerk, Myers was placed under oath and took his seat. Turner stood and strolled casually to the witness chair.

"Mr. Myers, may I ask that you tell us where you currently reside?" asked Turner amiably.

"Near Bendersville, in Adams County," Myers said nervously, his fingers fidgeting and his eyes darting around the courtroom.

"And is that in the Commonwealth of Pennsylvania?"

"Yes. I'm sorry. In Pennsylvania."

"Would you tell the court how it is that you, as a resident of Pennsylvania, have come all this way to testify here today?" said Turner.

"Well," Myers began, shifting his gaze constantly from the judge to the jurors and then back to Turner, "after I received a letter from you tellin' me there was to be a trial, I volunteered to travel here to give my testimony."

"That's a very long journey for you, Mr. Myers. Why would you volunteer to make such a trip? Are you being paid by anyone to be here?"

"No, sir."

"Then I ask you, sir, why?"

Myers looked toward Kitty and nodded. "Don't like what those fellers did to her. And was sorry I couldn't stop it," he said quietly. "So I thought the next best thing I could do is give my testimony and let the law provide the justice."

"We certainly appreciate your concern for justice and your willingness to undergo this journey. I promise you that I shall be brief so that you may return to your home as soon as possible."

"Appreciate that," said Myers.

"Am I correct that you own and operate a roadhouse tavern in the vicinity of Bear Mountain in Adams County?"

"Yes, sir."

"And did you, sometime in the early morning of July twenty-fourth of last year, have occasion to be awakened by a group of men?"

"Yes, sir, I was."

"Do you recognize anyone from that group in the courtroom today?"

"Yes, sir, I do."

"Could I ask you to identify that person for us?"

Myers shifted in his chair and pointed directly at Sam Maddox. "That man there. He was with 'em that night," Myers said. "Seemed like he was the boss."

"Could you describe this encounter to the court and the jurors, please?"

Myers related the events of that night, starting with being awakened by the pounding on his door and concluding with the return of the men to reclaim their horses.

"Now, then, Mr. Myers," said Turner, "where was the defendant, Sam Maddox, when you first saw him that night?"

"He was on a horse, along with two other mounted men, and the man who'd been poundin' on my door. And there was another feller in the wagon."

"Now, sir, when you saw these men a few hours later, was there anyone else accompanying them?"

"Yes, sir."

"Can you tell the court who else was with them?"

"This woman right here," Myers said, pointing at Kitty.

"Where was she?" asked Turner.

"In the back of the wagon. All tied up."

"Did you actually see her in the back of the wagon?"

"Yes, sir, I did. Could tell that someone was back there, so I walked over by the wagon and peeked in. Saw her all tied up like a trussed pig. Believe the children were all tied up, too."

Turner paused a moment for dramatic effect and then continued. "Could you describe for us, Mr. Myers, her condition when you saw her?"

Myers shot an angry glare at Sam Maddox before he answered, his jaw muscles clenching. "She was all beat up," he said heatedly. "Blood all over her. Face all swollen up. Don't think she was conscious. Looked like they just threw her in the back of the wagon and left her there. And the children," he added quietly, "they was all cryin'."

"Please tell us what happened then," said Turner.

"They was all in a big hurry, so after waterin' the horses, they just took off down the road like a bat outta hell."

"What then did you do?"

"Knew somethin' was seriously wrong, so I jumped on my horse and followed 'em till I got to the Wright place. They was the ones who had brought her"—again he pointed to Kitty—"by my place a few weeks before. I told them what was goin' on. Then young John Wright, he grabbed a horse and took off after 'em."

"Had you ever seen any of those men before?" asked Turner.

"No, sir," Myers answered, shaking his head.

"Ever seen any of them since?" asked Turner.

"Not till today, when I saw him right here in the courtroom," Myers said, pointing to Sam Maddox.

"We thank you, Mr. Myers, for your willingness to journey here and for your testimony." Turner turned to the judge. "Your Honor, I have completed my examination of this witness."

"Thank you, Mr. Turner," said Judge Field. "Mr. Strother, do you have any questions of this witness?"

"With the court's permission, I will be brief," said Strother, rising from his chair. "Mr. Myers, do you recall asking one of the men, when they first arrived, what their purpose was in traveling there that night?"

"Yes, sir. I was more than a bit curious, given how late it was and the fact they was in such a rush."

"And that man told you, did he not, that they were seeking to locate a woman and children who belonged to Mr. Maddox? Is that not correct?"

"Yes, sir, somethin' like that. Believe he said they was lookin' to find the man's 'woman,' who'd run away."

"So they did not attempt to disguise in any way their purpose that night, did they?" Strother said, sounding quite pleased with the witness's response.

"No, sir, can't say they did," said Myers.

"Quite so," said Strother. "Thank you, Your Honor. My examination of this witness is complete."

"Mr. Myers, you are dismissed from this court, with our thanks to you, sir. Safe travels home," said Judge Field.

As Myers left the courtroom, he touched Kitty lightly on the shoulder and offered her a small smile. She nodded her thanks in return.

CHAPTER 62

"**M**R. TURNER, YOUR NEXT WITNESS, IF YOU PLEASE," SAID THE judge.

"Your Honor, I'd ask the clerk to please call Mr. John Wright to the witness stand," said Turner.

The young Quaker was summoned by the clerk, proffered his oath, and took his seat. He appeared to be even more ill at ease than Charley Myers had been, shifting nervously in his chair.

"Mr. Wright," Turner began, "can you tell us if you are also a resident of Adams County, in the Commonwealth of Pennsylvania?"

"That is correct," the witness said.

"Did you travel from your home with our previous witness, Mr. Myers, to testify here today?"

"Yes, sir, I did."

"Would you tell the court and this jury why you have chosen to travel such a significant distance to provide your testimony?"

John Wright looked at the jurors and then turned to gaze briefly at Kitty. He took a deep breath and exhaled slowly. "When we learned in a letter from thee that there was to be a trial and that Miss Kitty intended to hold that man responsible for his in-humane conduct," he said, inclining his head briefly toward Sam Maddox, "I felt that God would expect me to assist. And so, I am here."

"Now, Mr. Wright, you are a Quaker, are you not?" asked Turner.

"Yes, I am."

"May I ask you to explain your beliefs as a Quaker?"

John Wright inclined his head politely. "It is quite simple," he said. "We believe that every person is loved and guided by God and that there is something of God in everyone. So that what is in me is also in thee."

"And are you, as a Quaker, guided by the words of the Bible?"

"We certainly respect the words of the Bible, and we believe it to be one of many sources of wisdom. But we invite the Word of God to be written in our hearts, rather than as words on paper, and so we have no particular written creed. We believe that if we are sincerely open to the Divine Will, we will be guided by a wisdom that is more compelling than our own superficial thoughts and feelings."

"And can you tell us, as a Quaker, what your position is on the question of slavery?"

The witness moved about uneasily in his chair, glancing worriedly first out at the audience and then at the judge before he began to respond. "I fear that my answer may be deemed an insult to many of thee gathered here today," he said hesitantly.

"I understand," said Turner. "Nevertheless, I would request that you provide an answer to the question without regard to the feelings or emotions of those present."

"Well, then, I would say to thee that many of us believe that slavery is an abomination. That it is a refutation of the Word of God and of God's will that all men are free beings, who are the repositories of God's Word and His wisdom."

"You say 'many' of us believe," said Turner. "Is that what *you* believe?"

"Yes, sir, it is," said Wright solemnly.

"And have you acted on these beliefs?"

"Yes, sir, I have."

"In what fashion?"

"I—along with members of my family—have provided aid and

assistance to slaves who have sought to escape their bondage and find freedom elsewhere," Wright said proudly.

"Is it in this fashion that you first came in contact with Miss Kitty?"

"Yes, sir."

"Would you please relate those circumstances to the court and jury?" asked Turner.

Wright related the story of how he had met Kitty and Mary and the children, and how they had all been hidden at his family's home. He then detailed how he and his father had delivered them to the home of Amon Jones, a free black man, who was to provide them shelter in return for their labor until they were ready to set out on their own. Finally, prompted by questions from Turner, he described learning that Kitty had been abducted and his subsequent futile pursuit of the slave catchers and the wagon containing Kitty and the children.

"You have our thanks, Mr. Wright," Turner said, "for your efforts that day and for traveling all this way to provide your testimony today. Your Honor, my examination is complete," Turner added to Judge Field.

"Mr. Strother, do you require the opportunity to question this witness?" asked the judge.

"With the court's permission, again very briefly," said Strother as he approached the witness chair.

"Mr. Wright, I am curious. Do you detest all of us here who are slave owners?" Strother said caustically.

"No, sir," the witness said earnestly. "I try never to allow hatred to enter my heart. I may disagree with those who choose to own slaves, but I pray for their souls rather than hate them."

Strother shrugged dubiously. "But even if you profess not to hate all of us down here," Strother said, with a pointed glance at the jurors, "I am correct, am I not, that you would do anything in your power to assist any of our slaves in escaping from us? Even if the law quite clearly states that these slaves are, indeed, our property?"

Wright was silent for an awkward moment before he answered. "Thee are correct," he said softly. "I do not hate thee. But I would do anything within my power—short of engaging in acts of violence—to help save these enslaved souls."

Strother shook his head disdainfully and turned his back on John Wright. "I have completed my examination, Your Honor."

CHAPTER 63

*A*FTER JOHN WRIGHT HAD BEEN EXCUSED FROM THE COURTROOM, Turner stood and addressed the judge.

"Your Honor, with the court's permission, I would call the plaintiff, Miss Kitty, to offer her testimony."

Strother leaped to his feet, as if jolted by a bolt of lightning.

"Your Honor, I must offer my objection to this outlandish attempt to circumvent the law," he said indignantly. "My learned colleague surely knows that in the Commonwealth of Virginia the rule is—and always has been—that slaves have no right to testify in a court of law."

Judge Field raised his hand to silence Strother and looked to Turner. "Mr. Turner, is Mr. Strother not correct in his recitation of the controlling law in the commonwealth—that slaves cannot be allowed to testify and can have no voice in a matter such as this?" the judge asked.

"He would, indeed, be correct, Your Honor . . . ," Turner answered and then paused a beat. "He would be correct if Miss Kitty was, in fact, a slave. But she is not. We have submitted both the testimony of Mistress Maddox and the deed of manumission from Pennsylvania to prove that. As a free person—regardless of her prior status—she has the same right as every other citizen to offer testimony and have her voice be heard." He turned toward Strother. "And my colleague, learned or otherwise," he added archly, "must certainly realize that."

"But, Your Honor . . . ," Strother stammered angrily.

Judge Field raised his hand again to silence both of the bicker-
ing lawyers. "Mr. Turner," he said, "I understand your position.
But are we not here precisely to resolve that question? Must we—
this jury and the court—not first resolve the issue of whether she
is, in fact and in law, free before we can proceed to even contem-
plate her claims against the defendant? Because if the determination is that she is not free, at least not according to the precepts of
Virginia law, then you must agree that she has no right to offer
testimony and that her claims against Mr. Maddox must accordingly fail. On the other hand, if she is deemed to be free, then
these complaints can move forward. Is that not a correct statement of the applicable law?"

"That would most certainly be true if the fact of her freedom
was, indeed, an issue. But I would contend that we have delivered
proof beyond any measure that she is, both in fact and in law,
free," Turner said. "And if the court were to uphold Mr. Strother's
objection, Your Honor would be creating an insurmountable
paradox. Miss Kitty would not be allowed to testify until there was
a verdict rendered. However, once that verdict is rendered—and
if it is in her favor and she is deemed to be free—it would be too
late for her to testify since the case would be concluded. So she
would then be denied the rights of a free person to offer testimony in support of her claims. A distasteful and troubling paradox, indeed!" exclaimed Turner angrily.

Kitty leaned forward, her hands placed palms down on the
counsel table, and rocked slightly as she listened intently to the
arguments, confusion etched across her face. She had spent
hours with Zephania Turner preparing for her testimony. He had
painstakingly guided her through the questions he would ask her
and how she should phrase her answers. They had even re-
hearsed the scornful and hostile cross-examination she could expect from Strother. She had felt completely confident and had
been anxiously looking forward to taking the witness stand. But
now, suddenly, her testimony had been thrown into turmoil. Her
head swiveled as she shifted her gaze from Turner to Strother and

now to Judge Field. The look of calm confidence in her eyes had been replaced by a mask of bewilderment. *What is happening?* she thought frantically. *Why are they arguing about me testifying? How could they not allow me to tell my story?*

Judge Field remained thoughtfully quiet for a few long minutes, leaning back in his chair, his fingers steepled before his face. The only sound in the courtroom was the soft, anxious murmuring of those seated in the audience who now clearly understood what a pivotal moment this had become in the trial. Finally, the judge shifted forward and began to speak decisively to Turner.

"I do fully understand your position and your dilemma, Mr. Turner," he said. "And I am not without sympathy for your legal conundrum. But I nevertheless find myself bound by the strictures of the law. Until there is a binding determination that the plaintiff is, in fact, free, she cannot be allowed to offer any testimony in a court of law. And the unfortunate circumstance for you is that such a determination will not—and cannot—take place until this jury has reached its conclusions concerning the facts in dispute in this matter. And perhaps the paramount fact in dispute is whether the plaintiff is free or remains a slave. It may be, as you proclaim, a distressing paradox, but it is nonetheless what the law dictates. Therefore, I will uphold Mr. Strother's objection and rule that the plaintiff may not offer testimony in this matter. You have been allowed to offer the testimony of other relevant witnesses, and that will have to suffice."

The soft murmuring in the courtroom gave way to a smattering of cheers and applause. Judge Field slammed his gavel on the bench and glared out at those gathered in the chamber.

"Silence!" he exclaimed. "I will have silence in this court, or you will be forcibly removed!"

When the noise swiftly died down, the judge turned again to Turner.

"So, then, Mr. Turner, do you have any other witnesses to present?" the judge asked.

"No, Your Honor," Turner replied, the bitter disappointment obvious in his tone. He then slumped into his seat.

"In that case—" the judge began, but he was interrupted by a sudden movement.

Kitty had risen from her seat and now stood erect, her head held high. She began to speak, surprising all in the courtroom.

"Your Honor," she said, her voice soft but defiant, "with due respect to you, I must tell you that the law is wrong. I do have a voice. I have a name. I have a family. I have a God-given soul. And whether the law or anyone else in this courtroom agrees or not, *I know that I am free!*"

And then she sat down.

CHAPTER 64

KITTY'S SHOCKING SPEECH CAST A HEAVY, FOREBODING SILENCE OVER the entire courtroom. No one dared to speak as all eyes focused on Judge Field, awaiting his reaction to this stunning challenge to his authority. The judge was still as a marble statue, his face an impenetrable mask, his stony gaze fixed on Kitty. She returned his stare, her eyes tranquil rather than angry, her demeanor calm, her head still held high. Finally, after a barely perceptible nod, Judge Field turned away from Kitty toward the jurors.

"Gentlemen, I hereby instruct you that you shall give no consideration whatsoever to the comments just offered by the plaintiff," the judge said. "Only testimony that has been provided by a witness under oath, and been subject to cross-examination by the adversary, may be considered by you in your deliberations. Do you understand?"

Each of the jurors inclined his head, indicating that they did, in fact, understand the judge's instructions.

"Mr. Turner," the judge said sternly, shifting his gaze to the lawyer, "I will ask you to instruct your client, in no uncertain terms, that she shall not speak again in this courtroom, unless it is to respond to a question from me."

"Yes, Your Honor," Turner answered contritely.

"Mr. Turner, do you then rest your case on behalf of the plaintiff?" the judge asked.

"Yes, Your Honor," Turner said, rising from his seat. "We have completed our presentation."

"Mr. Strother, do you intend to call any witnesses to testify on behalf of the defendant?" the judge asked.

"Yes, Your Honor. If it please the court, I would request that the clerk call the defendant himself, Mr. Sam Maddox, to provide testimony," Strother said somewhat officiously.

Maddox rose from his position at the counsel table and strode confidently to the witness chair. After being sworn in by the clerk, he sat, crossed his legs indolently, nodded in the direction of the jurors, and turned back expectantly toward Strother.

"Mr. Maddox," Strother began, "you are the defendant in this matter, are you not?"

"I am," said Maddox.

"You have been a resident of Rappahannock County your entire life, is that correct?"

"That is correct."

"Am I also correct that the late Samuel Maddox was your uncle?"

"Yes, he was."

"Could you describe your relationship with your uncle, before his passing, to the court and the jury?"

Maddox twisted in his chair so that he was now facing the jurors, flashed an engaging smile, and began to speak. "My uncle Samuel and I had been quite close all my life. More of a father-son relationship, I would say, than one of an uncle and nephew. And that continued until his untimely death."

"Had you ever discussed with him his expectations concerning his estate upon his death?"

"Many times," said Maddox. "He made it clear to me that he was concerned that Aunt Mary would not be capable of doin' all that would be necessary to continue to run the farm. So he said that it was his intention to leave me in a position to join in making whatever decisions needed to be made. He was actually quite insistent about that."

"Is it, then, your understanding that the terms and conditions of his will reflect that concern and provide for your role in managing the estate, along with your aunt Mary?"

"Yes, that is, indeed, my understanding."

"And did you fully intend to engage in that role?"

"Yes, I did." He paused and shot a glance at Mary. "At least until my Aunt Mary made it clear that, despite my uncle's wishes, she did not intend to allow me to participate."

"Did you quarrel with her about that?"

"Yes, sir, I'm sorry to say we did."

"About what in particular?"

"Mostly about the slaves."

"Why did you quarrel about the slaves?"

"Well," said Maddox, now looking directly at the jurors, "she just didn't know how to manage 'em right."

"Can you provide the court and the jury with an example?" asked Strother.

"Sure. Perfect example's how she handled that one"—he pointed to Kitty—"runnin' away. Fortunately, the sheriff here caught her and brung her back. Now we all know the law says you gotta whip a runaway. And you gotta do it in public. To send a message to the rest of 'em so no one else gets the idea to run. But she refused to whip her. Didn't do nothin' about it. So, what kinda message does that send?"

A few of the jurors nodded in agreement.

"So, then," Maddox continued, "I knew the farm was havin' money troubles, so we needed to sell off some of the slaves. Made sense to get rid of this one"—he gestured toward Kitty—"since there was no doubt she was a troublemaker. But again, Aunt Mary refused, claimin' she was in charge and would make all the decisions."

"What did you decide to do about this problem?"

"I talked to you, and we agreed that we needed to take the whole thing to court. Get a judge to force her to follow Uncle Samuel's wishes." He offered a frustrated shrug. "But after you served the court papers on her, she up an' ran. Took the slave woman and her children an' ran off to Pennsylvania."

"What did you do after your aunt absconded with your slaves?"

"Chased after 'em. Same as anyone woulda done if someone stole your property."

"Did you eventually find them?"

Maddox nodded. "Took some doin', but we finally tracked her down. They was hidin' out on a farm on Bear Mountain in Pennsylvania."

"You said 'we' finally found them. Were you being assisted by someone?"

"Yep. Hired a group of slave catchers who knew what they were doin' and where we should be lookin'."

"Would you now describe to the court and the jury what happened when you finally tracked down your slaves?" Strother asked.

Again, Maddox shifted in his seat to face the jurors. "We got to the farm late at night. They was all sleepin'. The owner—a black man—came out an' told us where they were. We went inside, gathered 'em all up, put 'em in a wagon, an' hightailed it back to Virginia, where they all belonged."

"Can you tell us what happened when you returned?"

"My aunt and Miss Fanny Withers decided that they'd take the law into their own hands," he answered, anger creeping into his voice. "They rode to my place and stole them slaves right out from under me. Took 'em back to the Withers place. That's where I found 'em all."

"What happened then?" asked Strother.

"Sheriff showed up, and he decided to take the slaves back to the jail for safekeepin' until we all figured it out. Then, next thing I know, I'm bein' sued by her—by a slave," he said, pointing again at Kitty. "Y'all believe that?" he added, looking at the jurors. "White man being sued by a slave—"

"Mr. Maddox," Judge Field interrupted forcefully. "Please refrain from offering comments and your opinions to the jury, and limit yourself solely to answering the questions posed to you by your counsel. Do you understand?"

Maddox glared at the judge for an instant before he responded. "Yes, sir," he answered sullenly.

"Mr. Strother, please continue," said the judge.

"Just a few final questions," said Strother. "Since you returned with your slaves, has your aunt allowed you to participate in the running of the farm, as your uncle wished?"

"No, sir."

"Have you been allowed to dispose of your property—those slaves—to raise funds for the operation of the farm?"

"No, sir, I have not." He shot another hard look at Kitty. "They been livin' in the county jail since the sheriff took 'em. Sheriff said he'd release 'em to me pendin' the trial if I posted a thousand-dollar bond to insure that I'd not sell 'em and I'd keep 'em here till then. But I ain't got that kinda money lyin' round. So, that's where they been."

"And, finally, is it your belief, based upon your understanding of the law, that you were entirely within your rights to travel to Pennsylvania and retrieve your stolen slaves?"

"Yes, sir, I was," Maddox answered adamantly.

"Thank you, Mr. Maddox." Strother turned to the judge. "Your Honor, I have completed my examination of my client."

Judge Field nodded to Strother and turned to Zephania Turner. "Mr. Turner, you may commence your examination of the witness," he said.

CHAPTER 65

*A*N EXPECTANT HUSH SETTLED OVER THE COURTROOM AS TURNER rose from his chair and paced a moment in front of the jurors, a pensive, somewhat puzzled look on his face. Maddox crossed and then recrossed his legs haughtily as he fixed the lawyer with an arrogant glare.

"Mr. Maddox," Turner began, "I must admit to being puzzled by much of your testimony, and I'm hopeful that you can help me to understand your position concerning these allegations against you."

"Glad to oblige," Maddox replied smugly.

"The will—which was proved and admitted here in the county—is the only document that reflects your Uncle Samuel's wishes, is it not?"

"I believe so."

"And other than your own interpretation of the language in the will, no one has ever declared that the terms of the will provide anything other than that Mistress Maddox—and Mistress Maddox alone—shall be entitled to all rights to the entire estate. Is that not correct?"

"Well, my lawyer thinks it says I got rights, too."

"Ah," Turner said. "I see. So you and the lawyer you're paying to represent you agree with your interpretation. Anyone else?"

"Well, you looked at it . . . ," Maddox blurted out testily but then caught himself and stopped.

"Well, then," Turner said with a half smile, "as long as you've brought it up, is it not correct that you came to me to review the terms of the will, and once I assured you that the language clearly provided for Mistress Maddox only to inherit the estate, you stormed out quite angrily?"

"Don't remember the details," Maddox muttered sullenly.

"So, based upon nothing more than your own opinion, and that of Mr. Strother, you decided that it would be legally allowable for you to pursue Mistress Maddox and Miss Kitty into the Commonwealth of Pennsylvania?"

"That's right," Maddox sneered. "And you should know that the law gives me permission to chase after my slaves, seize them, and bring them back—wherever they run to."

"What law would that be, Mr. Maddox?"

"The Fugitive Slave Act," answered Maddox self-assuredly.

"And do you claim to know the provisions of that law?"

"I do."

"And do you further claim that the provisions of that law allow you to do what you did in this instance—travel to Pennsylvania, seize persons who claim to be free, physically assault them, and forcibly return them to Virginia?"

"I do," Maddox insisted.

Zephania Turner returned to his table, picked up a document, and handed it to the court clerk.

"Your Honor," he said, "anticipating that the defendant might make such a preposterous claim, I have delivered herewith to the court clerk a copy of the Fugitive Slave Act, legislation enacted by the Congress of the United States in seventeen ninety-three. I would request that the court enter this document into the court record to serve as evidence in this matter."

The court clerk handed the sheaf of papers up to the judge. After briefly reviewing the document, the judge handed it back.

"The document is, in fact, a valid copy of the Fugitive Slave Act of seventeen ninety-three—and I might note that I am quite fa-

miliar with its terms—and it shall be entered into the record,"
said Judge Field. "You may continue with your examination of the
witness, Mr. Turner."

"My thanks to the court," Turner said with a slight bow. "Now,
then, Mr. Maddox, would it surprise you, given your self-professed
knowledge of this statute, if I told you that you are completely
wrong—that the law does not allow you to seize someone who
claims to be free and essentially kidnap them?"

"Always heard that you could," Maddox said. "Anyway, don't
make no difference how I get 'em back if it's my property."

"Makes no difference how you get them back?" Turner exclaimed incredulously. "Makes no difference what the law demands? Is that what you're saying to this court?"

Maddox flashed a questioning look toward Strother, seeking
some help out of this predicament, but his lawyer averted his
eyes, focusing on papers he was shuffling on his table.

"Mr. Maddox? Is that what you are saying?" Turner repeated.

"All I'm sayin' is I did what any white man would do. I went
lookin' to get back my property. Property that'd been stolen from
me!" Maddox declared angrily.

Turner grabbed a copy of the statute from his table and bran-
dished it in the air.

"This law—which you *claim* you relied upon—says quite clearly
that a person may pursue a slave into another jurisdiction, but
that if that slave claims to be free, that slave *must* be taken before
a court before they can be removed from that jurisdiction, and
that the *court* will determine if the slave can be removed." Turner
paused. "Did you take Miss Kitty before a court for a determination of her claim, as the law requires, before you beat her, tied her
up, and kidnapped her?" Turner demanded, his voice now soaring in anger.

Maddox did not answer but simply glared at Turner.

"Mr. Maddox, did you somehow not understand my question?"
asked Turner.

"Didn't need no court to tell me what I already knew," Maddox growled. "She belongs to me, and I can damn well do whatever I like with her."

Turner took two steps toward Maddox. "So, you are telling this court that you are somehow above the law? That Sam Maddox can do whatever he pleases, regardless of what the law says?"

"I'm tellin' you that she was mine and was stolen from me, so I had every right to go get her and bring her back," Maddox insisted heatedly.

"And did that give you the right to brutally beat this defenseless woman?" Turner said, his voice dropping low and dripping with contempt. "To punch her repeatedly? To tie her up and throw her in a wagon? To chain her inside a shed and let her suffer, with no aid for her horrible injuries you had inflicted?"

"Get this straight, Turner," Maddox said, spitting out each word. "That ain't no woman." He pointed at Kitty, who squared her shoulders and seemed to rise up in her chair as she met and held his glare. "That there's a slave—and my property. I own her. And I'm free to treat her any way I please. If I wanna beat her, I'll beat her. If I wanna chain her up, I'll chain her up. Only way to treat some of these niggras and make 'em understand who's boss. And if you don't like it, you can just move up north and join up with them lily-livered abolitionists."

There was a heavy mantle of tense silence in the courtroom. No one uttered a sound as the two men glowered at each other. Finally, Turner spoke.

"You, sir, are no gentleman," Turner said quietly.

"Never pretended to be one," Maddox answered.

"Your Honor," Turner said, turning his back on Maddox, "I have no more use for this witness," he said scornfully.

"Mr. Maddox, you are excused as a witness and may step down," Judge Field said stiffly. "Mr. Strother, do you intend to call any further witnesses?"

"No, sir," said Strother, scrambling to his feet. "With the court's permission, the defense would rest its case."

"Gentlemen," Judge Field said, turning toward the jurors, "that will complete the presentation of evidence in this matter. Given the lateness of the hour, we will recess until tomorrow morning, when the lawyers will present their closing arguments. Following that, you will begin your deliberations toward a verdict." He rapped his gavel once on the bench. "Court is adjourned until tomorrow morning."

CHAPTER 66

*T*HE FOLLOWING MORNING, THE CROWD BEGAN TO ASSEMBLE OUTSIDE the courthouse even before the shimmering blood-orange summer sun peeked above the horizon. The hopeful spectators, fascinated by the unfolding of this unlikely drama, staked out their territory early in front of the broad double doors, their numbers larger than the first day of the trial, drawn like ants to a picnic by word of the explosive courtroom confrontations of the previous day.

Lingering silently on the periphery of the gathering was a handful of free black men and women, curious to witness the rare spectacle of bloodless combat between one of their own and the powerful and deeply entrenched traditions of Piedmont Virginia society.

When the doors were flung open, the crowd surged forward and, like flowing water seeping into an open crevice, filled every available space inside the building. The black spectators, knowing that they would not be allowed to sit in the downstairs chamber, immediately climbed to the upstairs gallery, where they found seats. However, they rose and submissively relinquished their spots soon after, when several white men, finding no available space in the first-floor courtroom, climbed the stairs to the gallery, looking for a place to view the proceedings. Despite having arrived there first, the blacks were exiled to the farthest recesses of the gallery.

Inside the courtroom, the combatants were settled in their places, awaiting the next clash—the closing arguments—which

would be launched in just minutes. Zephania Turner sat calmly at
the counsel table, conversing earnestly with Kitty as he sought to
quiet her nerves. Across the room, Moffet Strother was a study in
contrast, squirming in his chair, shuffling through notes, steadfastly avoiding any conversation with Sam Maddox, who had shed
his veneer of anger from the previous day and was now smiling
and nodding at supporters in the audience. Meanwhile, the jurors, some of whom seemed to be basking in their accidental and
temporary celebrity, were seated in the jury area, anxious to resume the trial.

The door behind the bench swung open, and Judge Field entered, accompanied by the clerk and his announcement that
court was once again in session. After taking a moment to carefully arrange his books and files, the judge looked up and began
to speak.

"We are at that stage in this matter where the attorneys shall
present their closing arguments to the jury." He shifted his focus
to the audience. "I shall once again remind those members of the
public who are attending this trial that I will tolerate no outbursts
or expressions of support. If you are unable to comply with this
order, I shall have you removed immediately. I hope that I have
made myself perfectly clear." He then turned to the lawyers. "Mr.
Strother, are you prepared to proceed?"

"I am, indeed, Your Honor. Thank you," Strother said as he
stood and faced the jurors. "Gentlemen of the jury, I would like to
begin by thanking you for the time you have devoted to this case.
And I know that my client—and your neighbor—Mr. Maddox,
thanks you also." He paused and took a deep and theatrical
breath. "When I spoke to you at the start of this trial, I suggested
that you might be wondering why there was any necessity for a
trial at all. That you might be asking yourself why you had been
summoned to sit in judgment of a neighbor—indeed, of one of
you—who has been accused of the assault and kidnapping of a
slave. Not of a citizen, mind you, but of a *slave!* A slave who has no
rights, a slave whose very existence depends entirely on us—and
yet a slave who dares to enter this hallowed hall of justice, seeking

punishment against one of us. If it was not so very offensive to our social order, it might almost be comical.

"But it is not comical. Indeed, it is real—and it should be frightening to all of us. Let me take just a moment, for just a moment is all it deserves, to dispose of the laughable legal claim that is made to attempt to justify this farce. This slave claims that Mistress Maddox—who is a longtime neighbor but is sadly misguided in this instance—was granted the power to free her by the late Samuel Maddox's will. And she further claims that the late Samuel Maddox wished her to be freed, offering a slander on his name by claiming, with no proof whatsoever, that she was sired by that good departed soul. And, based upon this act of slandering the good name of a man who is no longer here to defend himself, she asks you to be complicit in this act of slander by agreeing that she is somehow now free." Strother paused, shaking his head in bewilderment.

"I would ask that you simply review the language of the will in question, and you will undoubtedly conclude that the late Samuel Maddox intended that his beloved nephew, Sam, should have a role in the administration of his estate. And that there is no evidence whatsoever of any intention to part with valuable property— to simply allow valuable slaves to walk away, with no recompense whatsoever. You will conclude that this is merely a farce, a baseless charade that is attempting a fraud on the justice system."

"But there is something more sinister at work here," he added ominously as he stepped closer to the jurors. "This is not just an attack on the law—this is an attack on the sanctity of our way of life," he proclaimed, his voice rising. "This is an attempt to disrupt and destroy our very social order. Slaves are slaves! They are not our equals, because God has chosen to make them less than our equals. God has chosen to place these inferior creatures in our care and control. Because that is the natural order of things. It is the order that God has provided, as we are taught in the Bible, and it is not within our charge to change that order. And Sam Maddox's conduct toward these slaves—his slaves, as he sought to recapture them after they had been stolen from him—

is most certainly justified by that natural order of things." Again, he paused, looking pointedly at each of the twelve men seated in the jury chairs.

"Gentlemen of the jury, your ancestors would roll over in their graves if you were to choose to punish a white man—one of you— based upon the unjustifiable claims of not another person, but of a *slave*. We would ask you—indeed, we would beg you—to reject this assault on our way of life, on God's established order, and on who we are as a people."

CHAPTER 67

A SOFT MURMUR OF APPROVAL RIPPLED THROUGH THE COURTROOM as Strother strolled back to his seat, a self-satisfied smile creasing his broad face. A rap of the gavel by Judge Field swiftly silenced it.

"Mr. Turner, are you prepared to proceed?" asked the judge.

"I am indeed prepared and, I should add, anxious to proceed, with Your Honor's permission," Turner said, inclining his head toward the bench. After rising majestically, resplendent in a powder-blue suit and a fawn-colored waistcoat, he strode confidently across the room and stopped in front of the jurors.

"It is a curious system of justice that we have created in this country," he began. "In creating this new nation a mere generation ago, we chose to reject much of what had been imposed upon us as colonists and, instead, created our own enlightened system. And the hallmark of that system—the element of which we are most proud, and appropriately so—is our reliance upon juries to dispense justice. We have made the decision that what is most fair is to ask jurors such as yourselves—our neighbors, who share our experiences, our aspirations, our frustrations—to determine what is right and what is wrong. To essentially act as the conscience, individually and collectively, of our community. It is a brilliant approach to the administration of justice, but one that can function only if we can, indeed, count on the fairness and impartiality of those chosen to resolve our conflicts," he mused softly. "And that is what we ask of you today."

"Make no mistake," he continued, "we are asking a great deal of you. We are asking you to do what is right, not what is merely expedient. We are asking you to make a decision that you might not be entirely comfortable with, that you might be criticized for by your neighbors—but one that is the correct decision, the fair decision, to make. We are asking you today to exhibit the courage that justice sometimes requires.

"Miss Kitty is free," he said in a firm and loud voice, gesturing toward her. "We have proved that to you beyond any doubt. It was Mistress Maddox's decision to free her, following the deathbed wishes of her late husband. She has bared her soul to you—to all of us here in this courtroom—in disclosing the reason for these wishes. It could not have been easy for her to reveal, so publicly, such a distressing and embarrassing fact as the infidelity of her husband. She should be admired for her courage in doing so.

"And I would suggest to you that a simple perusal of the terms of Samuel Maddox's will makes it abundantly clear to anyone that he had invested complete control of his estate—along with the ability to part with any assets she chose—to his wife. That, gentlemen, is beyond dispute, despite the illogical and unfounded meanderings of the defendant.

"Now, then, let me speak a moment about this same defendant," he continued, offering a disdainful glance at Sam Maddox. "About this man who would so brutally assault a defenseless woman—a free woman—and her young children and then seek your approval by claiming that not only was his conduct acceptable but that, in fact, each of you would have acted in the same fashion. That, gentlemen, should be an insult to each and every one of you. No society, and especially not our society, should allow the type of senseless brutality espoused by this defendant. He believes, as you heard from him yesterday and from his counsel today, that God has empowered him to inflict pain on others—not just on slaves but also on people who are free—if he so chooses, claiming somehow that such abominable conduct is God's will. That is not the will of our God, a God of compassion and concern for those who are less than us. Rather, such a statement is a slander on our God! And, make no mistake, this is not about the boundaries of discipline imposed upon a slave—this is about viciously assaulting a woman who is as free as any one of us in this courtroom!

"Our God," Turner continued sternly, "has entrusted us with the welfare of those in our care, the lesser among us. And that trust requires kindness and fairness—and sometimes firmness— but always a commitment to God's will. And it is most definitely *not* God's will to brutally assault, kidnap, and then cruelly imprison a *free woman* and her children, even if she is a woman of color."

Turner paused as he turned and gestured toward the seal of the Commonwealth of Virginia that was affixed to the wall behind the judge's bench. "Virginia," he continued, "this great state of ours, is the birthplace of Washington, of Jefferson, of Madison. It is the birthplace of great ideas and ideals. In many ways, it is the very birthplace of our democracy and our cherished freedoms. It is the place that we are proud to call our home. And here in Virginia, we are a land of laws—laws based on wisdom and fairness, and not based on the coarsest instincts of evil men."

Turner took a step closer to the jurors and looked carefully into the eyes of each one. When he began to speak again, his voice was low and solemn.

"Despite what many in the North may think of us, we are civilized men. And we must make it clear to those, near and far, who are watching what we do here in this courtroom today that as civilized men we cannot—and will not—countenance acts of violence against any *free* person, regardless of the color of their skin. You must act as the conscience of this community—of this commonwealth, of this very way of life that we have chosen—and declare for all to hear that we are not barbarians, that we are a civilized people, and that we will not allow such ungodly conduct to go unpunished."

Turner paused dramatically, gazing skyward, as if drawing inspiration from the heavens, and then continued in a quiet, deeply impassioned voice. "We are counting on your courage, on your willingness to stand up and proclaim that the principles of fairness and liberty, which had their birth right here in our colony and gave rise to the creation of this great nation, are alive and well. We are counting on you to tell this defendant—and everyone else who is watching—that justice exists for all free people in the Commonwealth of Virginia. I thank you, gentlemen."

CHAPTER 68

THE JURORS HAD BEEN DELIBERATING FOR NEARLY THREE HOURS WHEN they summoned the court clerk. Following the closing arguments, Judge Field had instructed them about the law relating to each of the charges leveled against Sam Maddox and had discussed with them their role as jurors. He had then directed them to begin their deliberations and had sent them—a parade of twelve perplexed, uncomfortable white men—off to the small private room situated in the back corner of the courtroom. For the past hour, loud and sometimes angry voices could be heard inside the room, the tenor of the sounds rising and falling like the rhythm of waves crashing on a beach.

When the court clerk exited the jury room a few minutes later, he was carrying a note written by the jury foreman. He scurried immediately into the judge's chambers. Minutes later he emerged, with orders to gather all the participants in the courtroom.

Kitty had been waiting in her room at the jail, playing with the children and attempting to focus on anything other than the trial. Meanwhile, Mary and Fanny had joined Zephania Turner in his office across the street, and all had been pacing restlessly as they awaited some word from the jury.

Once the lawyers and parties had resumed their places, and the anxious spectators had come streaming back and had scrambled again for every seat, Judge Field materialized on the bench.

"Gentlemen, I have received a communication from the jurors," he said somberly, addressing the lawyers and holding a piece of paper in the air. "It appears that they have been unable to reach agreement on a verdict and are seeking assistance from the court. In this letter, signed by the jury foreman, James O'Bannon, they outline their discussion of the contested facts of the case and then write as follows . . ." The judge read from the letter.

But whether or not upon the facts in evidence the decision should be for the plaintiff or for the defendant, the jury cannot say, and therefore they pray the advice of the court. If, upon consideration of the facts and law, it shall seem to the court that the case should be resolved in favor of the plaintiff, then the jury finds for the plaintiff, and in that case they assess damages of one cent. But if, upon consideration of the facts and law, it shall seem to the court that the resolution should be in favor of the defendant, then the jury finds for the defendant.

"According to the wishes of the jury, then," the judge said, "I will provide the *court's* opinion of the facts and the law in this matter, and that opinion will effectively serve as the verdict. Would either attorney be inclined to offer an objection to this procedure?"

Both attorneys nodded their heads in agreement.

"Thank you, gentlemen," the judge said. "In that case, I will ask all of you to remain in your places while I retire for just a brief period to review my notes and organize my thoughts. I will then resume the bench to offer my opinion forthwith."

Once the judge had retired to his chambers, there was an explosion of sound in the courtroom. A cacophony of whispers and louder exclamations reverberated throughout the chamber as all gathered there struggled to understand what was to happen next.

"What does this mean?" a puzzled Kitty asked Turner as Mary and Fanny joined them, circling the table.

"It means that the final decision will be made by the judge. So no one has been declared the winner yet . . . ," Turner began.

"I understand that part," Kitty said. "But what did they mean when they said that if I win, the damages would be only one cent?"

"That is the difficult part," admitted Turner. "They have decided that even if the case is decided in your favor . . . you should receive only one cent in damages."

"But how can that be?" asked Kitty, clearly confused and distressed. "If the court agrees that Sam did all those things—the beatings, the kidnapping—and that I was free at the time, how can the damages be only one cent?"

There was a painful silence.

Finally, Mary spoke. "Because, whether you're free or not, you're still not white," she said angrily.

Kitty looked from Mary back to Turner. "Is that right?" Kitty asked grimly.

"I'm afraid so," Turner said, shaking his head forlornly. "I suspect that at least some members of the jury were sympathetic to you, while others were surely opposed to allowing a slave—even a former slave—to win a court case against a white man. Even a man as distasteful as Sam Maddox. My guess is they struck some kind of a compromise—let the judge decide the matter but ensure that a message would still be sent in the event that he ruled in your favor. And that way, if you win, nobody will be able to criticize them, to suggest that they betrayed their own kind. A clever evasion, actually, but a message sent regardless of the outcome."

"And that message is that even if you are free, you still can't escape the color of your skin?" asked Kitty bitterly.

"I'm afraid so," said Turner.

CHAPTER 69

AN IMMEDIATE HUSH FELL OVER THE COURTROOM WHEN JUDGE Field returned to the bench just minutes later. The parties, spectators, and even the jurors, who had resumed their seats, now appeared nearly paralyzed by an overwhelming surge of tension and uncertainty.

"As a consequence of the request by this jury," the judge began, with a nod toward the jurors, all of whom returned his gesture, "I am prepared to render the court's opinion in this matter." He paused for a moment as he looked down at his notes, and then began to read. "The bequest contained in the will of Samuel Maddox in favor of his wife gave to her, and to her alone, a legal right to emancipate her slaves—"

His reading was interrupted by a groan from the audience and the sound of Sam Maddox slamming his fist furiously against the counsel table.

"The next person to offer a noise of any kind will find himself spending time in the county jail," the judge said angrily, his gaze sweeping the entire room and landing on Sam Maddox. "I urge you not to try the court's patience."

After a tense moment, he returned to the reading of his opinion. "Or to make any valid disposition which she might choose to make of the whole estate, real or personal. But in reference to the personal estate of the testator, including all slaves, Mistress Maddox did not actually acquire the legal right thereto until she, as the executrix, formally assented to, and accepted, her role and responsibility. In this case, for some unknown reason, that assent was never formally declared by her and entered as a part of the estate record. As a result, Mistress Maddox did not yet actually have the authority to dispose of any estate assets, including the slaves in question, when she took them out of Virginia and into Pennsylvania.

"The plaintiffs—Miss Kitty and her children—claim a right to freedom. However, in order to proceed in a court of law, they must first show a good subsisting legal title to freedom. If they cannot show that freedom at the outset, they have no legal capacity to sue another person in a court of law such as this.

"The plaintiffs claim their freedom based upon two arguments. The first is under a deed of emancipation executed by Mistress Maddox as the executrix of her late husband's will. However, as I have previously explained, Mistress Maddox, despite being named as the executrix, had not yet received the formal appointment to that position that would have allowed her to execute that document and effect their freedom. Therefore, the plaintiffs' claim to freedom cannot be recognized on this ground.

"They also claim their right to freedom under the laws of Pennsylvania, based upon the fact that they were settled there by Mistress Maddox after having left Virginia and thus were deemed free according to that state's laws. However, this court does not believe it is necessary for it to enquire into how the relation of master and slave might be affected by the laws of another state if such slaves were carried into another state whose law does not recognize that relationship. That is not necessary for this court, since, as explained previously, the removal of the plaintiffs to Pennsylvania by Mistress Maddox was, unbeknownst to her, an illegal act, since she did not yet possess the authority to do so. Accordingly, since the plaintiffs had not been legally transported within the borders of Pennsylvania, that state's laws would provide no recognizable basis for their claim to freedom.

"For these reasons, the court finds itself constrained to declare that the plaintiffs are not, in fact, free and thus have no standing to sue in this court. As a result, the verdict of this court must be in favor of the defendant."

CHAPTER 70

AS SOON AS THE JUDGE HAD CONCLUDED THE READING OF HIS VER-
dict, the courtroom erupted, mostly in jubilation. Sam Maddox
sprang to his feet, his fist thrust in the air in triumph, and within
seconds he was surrounded by friends and supporters, who were
shaking his hand and pummeling his back joyously, while others
shouted their pleasure over the verdict.

A handful of the spectators sat in stunned silence, while a very
few offered cries of protest. In the gallery, the tiny enclave of
blacks simply hung their heads. Inside the well of the courtroom,
Kitty sat completely still, hands folded on the table, her chin held
high, staring silently and stoically at the seal of the Commonwealth of Virginia hanging from the wall. Still seated behind her,
Mary had her hands covering her face in dismay, while Fanny
merely shook her head in shocked disbelief.

Judge Field, surprisingly, allowed the commotion to continue
for a few minutes before he began to gavel the court into silence.
It took several moments of powerful hammering on the bench
before order was restored.

"Please resume your seats. Court is still in session," the judge
commanded, striking his gavel once more. Finally, as the room
settled down, he continued. "There are two matters remaining
that I must dispose of before this court is adjourned," he announced with a stern glare. "And I expect that all of you will be-
have properly until I am finished."

Once again, he looked down at his notes, retrieved a single

sheet and placed it before him, then took a brief glance at it before resuming.

"As I have indicated in my opinion, Mistress Maddox, although clearly vested with the *sole* authority to dispose of her late husband's estate, had not completed the legal process necessary for her to function as the executrix of the will. As a consequence, she did not, at that time, possess the authority to emancipate her slaves. However, the court has concluded that her failure to complete the necessary legal process was a simple technicality—a mere inadvertence—on her part."

A puzzled murmuring began to ripple through the courtroom. The judge slammed his gavel once more, calling for silence.

"Therefore, the court will issue the following directions. Mr. Turner," the judge said, speaking directly to the lawyer, "I would ask that you prepare for her signature the necessary document to reflect Mistress Maddox's assent to function as the executrix. Since the will expressly provides that no bond shall be required of her to act as executrix, I will then direct that the court clerk accept and file that assent immediately." The judge paused and nodded at the clerk. "And by 'immediately,' I mean today."

The soft puzzled murmuring had now become more of a distinct humming as the spectators struggled to understand what was happening. Kitty had shifted her frozen gaze away from the official seal on the wall and was now staring at Judge Field, wondering also exactly what this surprising proclamation actually meant.

The judge's firm glare swept across the courtroom and lingered for just a moment on Sam Maddox before coming to rest on a perplexed Kitty. "The court will also direct," he continued, "that upon the execution and filing of the assent, Mistress Maddox, as the now official executrix of the will, shall, if she chooses"—he paused a beat as he shifted his gaze to Mary—"as I assume she will, be allowed to immediately execute a deed of manumission." He paused dramatically before resuming. "That deed shall be filed today with the court, thus freeing Miss Kitty and her children—effective today."

The courtroom was shrouded in a crushing, bewildered silence for a few seconds. Then, as a stunned comprehension set in, there was yet another eruption of sound, this time a reversal of the noise that had pulsed through this same chamber just minutes earlier. A chorus of boos and angry shouts ricocheted off the walls, while the collection of Kitty's supporters cried out in joy.

At the counsel table, Kitty folded her hands prayer-like in front of her face and closed her eyes, her face oddly serene, given the pandemonium surrounding her. Slowly, she raised her still folded hands to the sky. And then she began to cry, large, joyful tears, which somehow found an escape through her shuttered eyes and streamed jubilantly down her face.

Seated beside Kitty, Zephania Turner, his face creased in a satisfied smile, placed his arm gently around her in congratulations. Behind them, Mary and Fanny embraced as Mary whispered, "Thank you . . . for everything!" in Fanny's ear.

Across from Kitty and Turner, Sam Maddox sat immobile as his bafflement was replaced first by astonishment and then by a blinding rage. Shooting to his feet, with Strother tugging on his arm in a futile attempt to control him, he pointed his finger at the judge.

"You can't do that!" he screamed. "I won! You just said I won! And now you're settin' her free? That ain't right!"

Judge Field, who had remained on the bench, his face an emotionless mask, while the chorus of discordant cries had echoed throughout the courtroom, now slammed his gavel one more time. The room reluctantly quieted down, a harsh, resentful silence replacing the angry protest, as Maddox remained defiantly standing, his finger still boldly thrust out at the judge.

"Mr. Maddox," Judge Field began stonily, fixing an icy glare on Sam Maddox, "you are mistaken when you say this 'ain't right.' It is indeed right—because I have ruled that it is right. And I would caution you concerning your conduct. Unless, of course, you would prefer to be led out of this courtroom in handcuffs. Now, I'd strongly suggest that you be seated immediately."

Sam Maddox remained standing for one last, brief rebellious moment before he allowed Strother to tug him back into his seat.

"There is, then, one final matter to be attended to," the judge said as he continued to glare at Maddox. "Mr. Maddox, since the court has ruled in your favor, finding itself *constrained* to dismiss the claims against you for the reasons stated previously, it is now incumbent upon you, by court rule, since you had refused to post the bond to ensure the plaintiffs' presence at trial"— the judge engaged in a brief dramatic pause—"to attend to the costs incurred by the county due to that refusal. You are hereby ordered to reimburse the county for the costs of housing the plaintiffs in the county jail during the course of these proceedings."

There was a gasp of surprise throughout the courtroom as Maddox slammed both of his clenched fists on the table, barely suppressing his fury.

"I am informed by the jailer," the judge continued, ignoring the outburst in the court and Maddox's conduct, "that the total owed by you to the county is $138.45. I shall direct the sheriff to make arrangements with you for the prompt payment of that sum." He looked away from Maddox and scanned the courtroom magisterially. "If there are no other matters to be resolved, this court is now adjourned," the judge proclaimed, providing one last symbolic strike of his gavel.

As Judge Field gathered up the documents and law books from his bench, he glanced momentarily at Kitty. The barest hint of a smile crossed his face as he inclined his head briefly toward her. Then he turned, briskly left the bench, and disappeared into his chambers.

EPILOGUE

*T*HE SOUNDS OF A NEGRO SPIRITUAL FLOATED THROUGH THE TREES, the words uplifting, the melody deep and rich, the voices rejoicing in the evocative hopes and dreams of a better time and place. Kitty sat on a stump in the center of the slave cabins on the Maddox farm, surrounded by her children, Ol' Joshua, Young Joshua, and the other slaves. It was a cool, bright Sunday morning, and the slaves had congregated, as they almost always did, for their weekly spiritual gathering. Their cathedral was the yard, with its glorious canopy of foliage, just now starting to reveal hints of the colorful changes of the approaching autumn; Ol' Joshua was their pastoral leader, a position bestowed throughout the generations upon the oldest and wisest among the enslaved community.

Four days had passed since the trial, and much had happened. As soon as court had adjourned, Zephania Turner had raced across the street to his office and swiftly prepared the necessary documents. Once he had obtained Mary's signatures—and the signatures of Fanny and himself as witnesses—he sprinted back to the courthouse and delivered the papers to the court clerk. By sundown, Kitty and her children were free.

The first night of her freedom, sitting in Mary's front room, Kitty had grudgingly decided that she would leave Virginia and return to Pennsylvania, a decision dictated in part by the fact that Virginia, although it allowed for the emancipation of slaves, required that freed slaves permanently leave the state within six months of their emancipation. Mary had reluctantly agreed, expressing her concern that Kitty would never be safe in Virginia as long as Sam Maddox was still around.

The plan was for Kitty and the children to depart on Sunday. This time, they would be traveling on foot, an arduous journey that could take many weeks. Charley Myers and John Wright, who had remained in Washington until the conclusion of the trial, had offered to alert those friends along the Underground Railroad route, on their journey back home, that Kitty and the children would be traveling through again soon and would once more need their help.

Now, as the last notes of the mournful anthem faded away on this Sunday morning, Kitty reached across and clasped Ol' Joshua's hand. They had shared their tearful good-byes earlier, agreeing that it would be easier for her and the children if they left during the gathering. Ol' Joshua merely nodded his head, the kind smile spreading across his wizened face betrayed by the deep sadness in his eyes. Kitty scooped up the children and quietly slipped away toward the farmhouse.

Mary was waiting by the front porch. Several bags were sitting on the steps, along with a large basket of food and drink.

"I wanted you to know something . . . before you left," Mary said.

Kitty looked at her quizzically.

"I've decided to free the rest of them . . . all the slaves," Mary said.

"Why?" asked a puzzled Kitty.

"Not really sure," Mary answered pensively. "Just seems like the right thing to do."

"But what'll happen to them? To Ol' Joshua?" Kitty asked.

"I'll help get 'em all situated. Sure they'll all be fine," said Mary.

"But Ol' Joshua . . . ," Kitty began.

Mary held up her hand. "I've already told him—" she began.

"He knows?" Kitty interrupted.

"Told him early this morning. I suggested that he be the one to tell you about it, but he insisted that I tell you," Mary said, shrugging.

"But then he'll have to leave Virginia, too. Where'll he go at his age?" Kitty protested.

"He and I got that settled," Mary assured her with a smile. "He wants to stay on here—and Lord knows I'll be happy to have him. Said he doesn't know any other home. But he asked that I sign his emancipation papers, anyway—but don't file them. Instead, give 'em to him to keep. Said it'll be enough for him just to know he's free if he wants to be."

Kitty tried to speak but found herself choked up.

"All right, then, time to get a move on," Mary announced to the waiting children, turning away from Kitty.

The children scrambled around her and latched onto her skirt. Mary bent down and hugged each one in turn, a long, lingering squeeze followed by a kiss on the forehead. Then she turned to Kitty.

"Don't expect we'll be seein' each other again—least not on this side of heaven," said Kitty.

"Don't expect so," agreed Mary. "Think I'm too old to ever again be makin' that trip we made. And it's not safe for you to come back here."

"But I want you to know," Kitty said, her eyes welling up with tears, "that when I get there—up to heaven—I'll come lookin' for you. I'll ask the Good Lord to point me in the direction of my other mama."

Mary now was the one who struggled to speak, her voice strangled by emotion. "I'll be waitin' for you," she finally said in a bare whisper.

They stood looking at each other for a long moment, tears now cascading freely down their faces. Then Kitty reached out and wrapped her arms around Mary. They held each other tightly, rocking gently, knowing that it was both the first time and the last time that they would ever embrace.

Finally, Mary released her grip and held Kitty at arm's length.

"Time for you to be movin' on," Mary said, her voice cracking. "Got a ways to go before the sun sets."

Kitty sniffled as she wiped the tears from her cheeks with the sleeve of her dress. "Should be interestin' to see what the journey looks like . . . this time in broad daylight," Kitty said wryly.

After shouldering her bags and settling the basket on her arm, Kitty gathered up the children and turned back one last time to Mary, offering her a wide, sad smile. Then they began to walk.

As Kitty and the children disappeared down the drive, the singing began anew—a hand-clapping, foot-stomping rendition of a different hymn—as the hopeful voices soared, once again, toward the heavens.

> *Great day!*
> *Great day, the righteous marching.*
> *Great day!*
> *God's going to build up Zion's walls.*
> *Great day!*
> *Chariot rode on the mountain top.*
> *My God spoke and the chariot stop.*
> *God's going to build up Zion's walls.*
> *Great day!*
> *This is the day of jubilee.*
> *The Lord has set his people free!*
> *Great day!*

AUTHOR'S NOTE

I first discovered Kitty and her story on a blustery winter afternoon outside an old courthouse in Virginia. In February of 2014, my wife and I were staying at the Inn at Little Washington, located in a village often referred to as "the first Washington," a village not much larger today than it was in 1749, when it was first surveyed by a young George Washington. Since I have spent so much of my professional life inside of courtrooms—first as a prosecutor and trial lawyer and later as a legal journalist—I often seek out interesting courthouses in my travels. And the village of Washington had just such a destination. I visited the 1830s-era courthouse in the center of town, an elegant redbrick, white-columned structure that still functions as the county court for Rappahannock County, and wandered through the building, spending most of my time in the small courtroom on the second floor.

After leaving the courthouse, I was strolling around the grounds when I encountered a plaque in front of the building. The caption on the plaque read KITTY PAYNE***FREEDOM LOST AND REGAINED. Curious, I read the text that described the scant contours of Kitty's story, including the fact that she was born into slavery in 1816; that her biological father was her master; that her mistress decided to free her following the master's death; that upon her emancipation, she and her children traveled with their mistress to Pennsylvania; that she was kidnapped by the master's nephew, who claimed ownership of Kitty and her children, and was forcibly returned to Virginia; and that "after complex court proceedings, she regained her freedom" in this courthouse.

I was both puzzled and intrigued by the story. Puzzled because as a student of our justice system and a visiting professor at Yale University, New York University, and the University of Virginia, where I have taught a seminar about famous trials, I had never heard of Kitty's case. And intrigued because the idea that a slave in the antebellum South of 1846—where slaves were deemed to be property and, as such, generally had no legal rights—had won her freedom in a Virginia courtroom seemed not only highly improbable but also nearly impossible.

This was the beginning of my quest to discover more about Kitty and her unlikely journey to freedom. The Rappahannock County Clerk's Office, to my surprise and delight, provided me with access to the actual handwritten court records of the 1846 trial, including the witness list, the jury's deliberation notes, and the judge's final decision. From there, I was directed to the Rappahannock Historical Society, where I was able to review an array of local newspaper articles and general information concerning the trial and the participants. Eventually, thanks to a suggestion from the Rappahannock Historical Society staff, I made my way to the Chester County (PA) Historical Society, where I discovered a virtual treasure trove of research material. A Pennsylvania historian, Dr. Albert Cook Myers, had devoted nearly a decade in the 1940s to researching Kitty's story, apparently with the intent of eventually writing a book. Although the book was never written, the boxes of material that he had gathered—including letters and personal recollections from the descendants of Kitty and other significant players in the saga, contemporary newspaper accounts, public records, and court documents—were donated to the Chester County Historical Society upon his death and provided extraordinary detail and depth for the story.

Yet, for all the biographical and chronological information that I was able to gather, the answers to certain compelling and fundamental questions remained elusive. Why would Kitty's mistress choose to free her? What was their relationship? What dangers did they encounter on their Underground Railroad flight to the perceived safety of the North? Why would the mistress continue to fight for Kitty's freedom after the kidnapping, placing her own social standing in deeper jeopardy? How did the mistress enlist the aid of the richest woman in the county, a slave-owning symbol of traditional Southern society, in their battle? Why would an established, pillar-of-the-community lawyer agree to represent a slave in her unprecedented legal challenge? And, most important, just who was this extraordinary woman named Kitty—a slave who had the courage to challenge the laws and traditions, both written and unwritten, of the time?

It was a storyteller's challenge. Here are the essential facts; now tell us how and why this happened. In order to accomplish this and to stitch the elements of the story together, it became necessary to imagine the characters' motivations and their conversations. But as I began to write the story, I found that they were not the thoughts and words of complete strangers. As with many relationships, at some point after immersing myself in the details of their lives, as scarce as they were, I came to feel that I somehow knew these characters. That I could sense what they might have been thinking and hear the words they might have spoken. At least, I hoped I did.

Although the resulting story is a work of fiction, the majority of the foundational facts are true. With just a few exceptions, all the characters described here actually existed, and their backgrounds, relationships, and roles in Kitty's narrative are generally accurate. Despite the fact that there is no record of the precise words spoken at Kitty's trial, the portrayal of the proceedings reflects the available court records and the manner in which a trial at that time would have been conducted. And although the judge's actual decision was cloaked in arcane elements of Virginia law of that era, the essence of the startling ruling depicted in the story is accurate and, at times, utilizes the judge's authentic language.

This novel ends with Kitty's departure from Virginia following her surprising courtroom triumph and with her return journey to Pennsylvania, where she hoped to forge a new and better life in freedom. But that was not, of course, the end of Kitty's actual story or the stories of those characters who populated her saga.

Mary Maddox remained close to Kitty and her children, and although the two women never saw each other again, they apparently corresponded occasionally. Several years after the death of her husband, Samuel, Mary married a Revolutionary War veteran named John Corder and lived on his farm in Rappahannock County until his death, at the age of ninety, in 1849. After that, she was lost to history, and there appears to be no record of where and when she died.

Fanny Withers continued to own and manage her plantation and real estate holdings. A few years after the trial, she married Washington A. Marlow, who died in 1856. They had no children. Fanny passed away in 1864.

Zephania Turner practiced law in Virginia for many decades following the trial. After the Civil War, he served for a number of years as the Speaker of the Virginia House of Delegates and as a member of the Board of Visitors at Virginia Military Institute. He never married and died in 1876.

Judge Richard Field remained on the bench, serving with distinction for years as a Virginia court judge. During the period leading up to the Civil War, he published a letter urging Virginians not to secede and to remain loyal to the Union. In a tragic irony, both of his sons lost their lives fighting for the Confederacy.

Sam Maddox, after negotiations with Mary Maddox, did eventually take over the ownership and operation of his uncle Samuel's farm. Although he and several other men, including Tom Finnegan, were indicted in Pennsylvania for the kidnapping of Kitty, he never retuned there to stand trial. Finnegan was the only member of the gang to be captured, tried, and convicted. He spent less than two years in prison for the crime. Maddox eventually married a woman named Margaret Tobin, and they had several children. In 1885, due to unpaid debts, he lost his uncle's farm in a foreclosure sale.

Sadly, the life Kitty found upon her return to Pennsylvania was not the kinder, gentler long life she sought and so richly deserved. After traveling by foot for nearly six months, aided once again by Quaker families and others along the Underground Railroad, she and her three children settled near Gettysburg, Pennsylvania. Kitty became a domestic worker, living in various homes with her youngest child, Arthur. Eliza Jane and Mary, despite being not yet ten years old, were sent to live and work in neighboring homes.

In 1847 Kitty—who had begun using the name Catharine—married a free black widower named Abraham Brian, who had four children from his previous marriage, and moved into his home in Gettysburg. According to recollections offered by her descendants, it was not a happy union. Brian apparently did not welcome Kitty's children into his home, so they were forced to remain apart from their mother, working and residing with local families.

On August 15, 1848, Kitty gave birth to a daughter—her fifth child—and named her Frances, after Fanny Withers, one of the two women who had championed her fight for freedom. Two years later, in 1850, Kitty gave birth to another child, who, sadly, did not survive.

Of Kitty's six children, four survived into adulthood. Eliza Jane worked and lived in Gettysburg for a number of years before moving to the Midwest. She survived the Battle of Gettysburg by hiding from Confederate soldiers—who were known to kidnap free blacks and send them back into slavery—in the home of her employer. Mary became a Quaker, married an African American man who had also escaped from slavery along the Underground Railroad, and eventually relocated to the Midwest, as well. Arthur enlisted in the 27th United States Colored Troops during the Civil War and fought at the Battle of the Crater, part of the siege of Petersburg in Virginia, in 1864. Little is known about the rest of Arthur's life, including where and when he died. Frances was raised by her father, Abraham Brian, on his farm in Gettysburg. The Brian family fled from their farm during the Battle of Gettysburg, also fearful of being captured and sent back into slavery by the Confederate troops. The farmhouse was severely damaged during the fighting but was not destroyed, and it remains today as part of the Gettysburg National Military Park. Frances married a former slave who had escaped from the Confederate army during the battle, and they also ultimately settled in the Midwest.

On August 12, 1850 (there is some question as to the precise date), just four years after the courageous struggle that resulted in her emancipation, Kitty passed away. She had lived thirty-eight difficult years on this earth, thirty-four of them as a slave and four years as a free woman. Kitty is buried next to her husband in a small plot located at Gettysburg National Cemetery. Her final resting place is marked by a simple weathered granite headstone that reads:

CATHARINE

WIFE OF ABRAHAM BRIAN

DIED AUG. 12, 1850

AGED 38 YEARS

It is an unremarkable epitaph for a woman who lived a remarkable life.

ACKNOWLEDGMENTS

I am enormously grateful, as always, to my wife, Dorothy Ann, for her support and guidance throughout this project. She was with me when we first discovered Kitty's story on the plaque in front of the Rappahannock County Courthouse in Virginia and was instantly as fascinated by this extraordinary woman's tale as I was. She read every word of each draft of the book, contributed to the story lines and plot points, and helped to imagine the conversations and motivations of these elusive and often mysterious characters. My children, Ashley and Colin, and their respective spouses, Pat and Susie, were a constant source of encouragement and inspiration during the research and writing of the novel. Susie was especially helpful, reading each draft, offering cogent suggestions, and acting as a sounding board for the development of the characters, and I'm thankful to her for her significant contributions.

The journey from the accidental discovery of an unknown event in a remote courthouse to the finished novel was aided by a number of people. The Rappahannock (VA) Circuit Court Clerk, Peggy Ralph, was the first to introduce me to the details of Kitty's adventure when she placed a file before me containing the yellowed, tattered handwritten court records of the 1846 case of *Kitty v. Samuel Maddox*. I am grateful to Peggy and her staff for their hospitality and assistance on each of my research visits. I am also thankful to Judy Tole and the staff of the Rappahannock Historical Society for providing me with access to their records and, particularly, for directing me to the Chester County (PA) Historical Society, where I discovered a wealth of detailed information. And I would also like to thank Peter Luke, a Virginia attorney and the unofficial historian of the Rappahannock County Courthouse, for taking the time to share his knowledge of the history and early details of this lovely historic building.

When I entered the Chester County Historical Society, the exceptionally helpful staff provided me with a vast collection of information and research, thanks to the years of painstaking and detailed investigation by the late Dr. Albert Cook Myers, a local historian who devoted a decade of his life in the 1940s to discovering all he could about Kitty's life. Each time I returned, I was treated to additional boxes of notes, letters, and newspaper clippings, all of which helped bring me closer to an understanding of Kitty and the characters in her life. Although Dr. Myers never wrote the book that he had so devotedly researched, my sincere hope is that he would have enjoyed and appreciated this telling of Kitty's tale.

I am also thankful to my dear friend Ellie Monahan, who was so very helpful in sorting through ideas and visualizing the story when it was in its infancy. And speaking of friends, Patrick O'Connell and his caring staff at the Inn at Little Washington took wonderful care of us during each of our research visits, not just nourishing and comforting us but also helping us to understand their little community of Washington today so that we might better understand the Washington and Rappahannock County of nearly two centuries ago.

Finally, I am forever indebted to my agent and friend, Paul Fedorko, for his guidance and constant support. And I also offer my heartfelt thanks to my editor, Selena James, for her instincts and suggestions, and for providing innumerable improvements, both large and small, to the novel. From the very first moment we talked, she understood and embraced Kitty and played an essential role in the telling of her remarkable odyssey.